THE AUGURIES

THE AUGURIES

F.G. Cottam

This first world edition published 2019
in Great Britain and the USA by
SEVERN HOUSE PUBLISHERS LTD of
Eardley House, 4 Uxbridge Street, London W8 7SY.
Trade paperback edition first published
in Great Britain and the USA 2019 by
SEVERN HOUSE PUBLISHERS LTD.

British Library Cataloguing in Publication Data
A CIP catalogue record for this title is available from the British Library.

ISBN-13: 978-0-7278-8869-3 (cased)
ISBN-13: 978-1-84751-994-8 (trade paper)
ISBN-13: 978-1-4483-0207-9 (e-book)

All Severn House titles are printed on acid-free paper.

Severn House Publishers support the Forest Stewardship Council™ [FSC™],
the leading international forest certification organisation.
All our titles that are printed on FSC certified paper carry the FSC logo.

MIX
Paper from
responsible sources
FSC   FSC® C013056
www.fsc.org

Typeset by Palimpsest Book Production Ltd.,
Falkirk, Stirlingshire, Scotland.
Printed and bound in Great Britain by
TJ International, Padstow, Cornwall.

For Gabriel and Avalon, the twin lights that brightly illuminate my path

ONE

The incense burner was properly named a thurible. The vessel from which the incense was spooned was called a boat. Fourteen-year-old Andrew Baxter had been an altar boy for six years and had handled the thurible since he was twelve. He was confident about the process. You swung it gently back and forth and the circular tablet of charcoal inside it glowed unseen with heat and the incense rose as scented smoke that, to the grieving congregation, standing or kneeling, gave the air in its vicinity a bleared, hazy look. They were in the pews on the far side of the coffin from where Andrew swung the thurible and observed their sorrow, thinking vaguely that something this morning wasn't quite right with the world. Something seemed somehow slightly out of balance.

It was Andrew's task to keep the thurible actively burning incense until the priest required it. When that moment came, Father Gould would take it from him and swing it over the coffin and recite the part of the liturgy blessing the dead person in the wooden box.

It was Andrew's personal conviction that any blessing was coming rather too late for this particular corpse – that of a man burned to death in a top-floor flat fire after he had been unable to escape down a blazing stairwell. This event had been the grisly conclusion to forty-eight years of life. Prayers seemed both late and unlikely, to Andrew's mind, to be very effective in improving matters.

But it wasn't this that bothered Andrew Baxter. He had served through a fair number of requiem masses. Generally, they involved a generous tip. On weekdays, they meant a welcome break from school. He was used to the mood that prevailed among the dead man's friends and relatives. He even knew the word for it. It was called stoicism. Sometimes the mourners weren't stoical. He'd seen that too, mostly when the subject of the requiem had been a child. There was a biblical phrase, wailing and gnashing of teeth.

He thought that about covered it at some of the more emotional funeral services he'd personally witnessed.

Sometimes, the coffin would be open. Undertakers went to great lengths to make some of the recently dead look lifelike. It was Andrew's opinion that they never succeeded in this. He'd quite often overheard mourners say that the occupants of open coffins looked like they were only sleeping. He didn't think this was ever true. Sleeping people twitched and breathed and sometimes snored or farted. The dead were just too still for sleep. Open coffins weren't wrong, they were just a bit unnerving and odd. Anyway, for reasons that were obvious, on this box the lid was screwed tightly shut.

The altar was both exotic and familiar to Andrew. It was the centre of a place of worship. The church had painted statues of saints and the Virgin Mary and Christ himself. The windows were pieces of religious art, stained-glass depictions of episodes from the scriptures, and against one wall a series of oil paintings described the brutal ordeal of torture and death by crucifixion politely known as the Stations of the Cross. There was a great deal of brass and gilt, and vases of fresh flowers put there by the retainers of the faith, middle-aged women Andrew's adolescent sensibility told him were married only to the Church. There was the tabernacle, in which were kept the chalice and the hosts. None of this was wrong. It was elaborate and even lavish, but he'd grown used to it all over time.

What was wrong, and also strange to him, was the incense, trickling upward into the air from the patterned holes cut into the metal of the object he swung by its delicate chain. Ordinarily it smelled sweetish in a gentle sort of way. Today, it didn't. Today it smelled harsh and sour and also, somehow, cold. And old. Very old. Andrew would have said ancient, even, like a smell from another time unwelcome in the modern world. Uninvited, a gate-crasher of a scent present only by some sort of weird trickery. Almost a stink.

The texture of the smoke – if smoke could be said to possess a texture – was wrong. Ordinarily it was pale and dry. Today it was dark and greasy and for the first time it was stinging his eyes in a way that he thought would undoubtedly make them bloodshot, if they weren't bloodshot already.

When the moment came for Andrew to hand the thurible to Father Gould, he thought he saw the hint of a frown on the old priest's face, as though something about the incense bothered him, too. He was relieved to be rid of the implement for a moment. He was even more relieved when the mass ended, and they trooped back to the sacristy and he was able to put it down, reeking now, the usual shine of the polished metal tarnished and filthy as it continued to smoulder.

At the graveside Andrew was happier to be in the fresh air, even in a cemetery. The priest was splashing holy water with his ceremonial brush and incanting more liturgy, the coffin at the bottom of an open grave, when he experienced his second dose of strangeness on that memorable day.

The sun was shining. Tiny droplets of holy water were rainbow-coloured, sparkling on the pale wood of the box. Father Gould's voice was soft and soothing as he recited words he must have been saying in ceremonies like this for fifty years or so when, with his sharp, fourteen-year-old ears, Andrew heard a scrabbling sound rise faintly from inside the coffin. He blinked, and the box tremored, but he knew that was just the consequence of his blinking and the sensation of shock thrilling through him. Just his imagination, working overtime, as his mum insisted it so often did.

He strained to hear the sound from the coffin's interior again. But there was nothing beyond the voice of the priest, the snuffled breathing of relatives struggling to hold their feelings in, the singing of birds happy about the sunshine. And then the first few ritual handfuls of earth spattering and thumping on the lid of the box before the mourners dispersed and the gravediggers got to work with their little caterpillar-tracked earth mover. The furtive lighting of cigarettes, tobacco smoke scenting the breeze as Father Gould's pious little troop made their ceremonial way among the bereft along the path that led to the main gate and the waiting procession of cars parked on the road outside.

Andrew changed out of his cassock and cotta back at the sacristy and went to get his bike from the bike stand where he'd locked it. Peter Jackson, who'd flanked him holding the boat on the altar, would now ride back with him the two miles to school.

'You're quiet,' Peter said, as they pushed their bikes out of the churchyard.

Andrew saw Peter then, almost as though for the first time. Peter, wearing a shirt with a soiled collar. Scuffed shoes. Tousled hair with white specks of dandruff in it. Trousers without a crease in them. Peter, who had a weird twin sister, whose parents had died when a lorry hit their car on the motorway and lived now with his granddad. Peter, who sometimes, in all honesty, nowadays smelled like he didn't bath or shower very often.

They'd been given a fiver each, the altar boys, for the service. Andrew said, 'Just wondering how to spend the loot.'

'Liar.'

Andrew sighed. He said, 'Thought I heard a noise. At the graveside.'

'Sort of noise?'

'Coming from the coffin.'

Peter laughed. 'He was well dead, mate. Proper barbecued, I heard.'

'I didn't dream it, Pete.'

'Maybe a rat. One that likes cooked food.'

'That's gross.'

'It's what happens, mate. Rats, worms. The crem's the better option. Hopefully not for a few years, though.'

'Ashes to ashes.'

'Like the old David Bowie song.'

'Exactly.'

But Andrew didn't believe it had been a rat. It had come from inside rather than from under the box and the coffin had been too substantial for even the most ferocious rodent to chew through the wood that quickly. He had only heard it faintly and only for a moment, but there was a word for the character of the sound he'd heard. And that word was 'frenzied'. He rode back to school next to Peter in silence and felt very subdued for the rest of the day. And that night he dreamed a burning man chased him through cobbled streets in a choking fog as a church bell clanged in a futile bid to summon the faithful to prayer.

When he woke, early the next morning, he thought he smelled incense again: wrong, acrid, old. He lay in his bed and dozed, waiting for the impossible scent to fade. Which, eventually, it did. Brushing his teeth, dressing, he thought that maybe he should have asked Peter about the oddness of the service of the

previous day. But he thought he would just have brushed the
question off and maybe even have laughed at him. You were
the imaginative type or you weren't, was the truth of it. And Peter
Jackson just wasn't.

TWO

'We know that the German alchemist Gunter Keller
came to London. We know from the records at the
inn where he resided that he stayed in Blackfriars.
He was here for just under three months. What he was doing here
isn't documented. The best documentation concerning Keller's life
surrounds the event that ended it. And that was his trial for heresy
in Hanover two years after his time in England. Like many people
of both sexes convicted of heresy in the period we're discussing,
he was burned alive.'

After making this statement Professor Juliet Harrington
paused with the phone against her ear. Her caller was a journalist
from the *Telegraph*. Periodically, she had to field calls like
this one. She supposed that the *Almanac of Forbidden Wisdom*
was like the Loch Ness Monster or the *Mary Celeste*: speculative
page-filler in a season when hard news was scarce. Her academic
credentials gave the titillation a scholarly sheen of respecta-
bility, but she needed to be careful. Discussions with the press
about dark magic did nothing at all for her reputation at the
university.

'What was Keller's specific crime?' the journalist asked.

'He inflicted a plague of the dead.'

'What does that mean?'

'We don't precisely know. We know the date of his arrest. We
know the castle at which he was incarcerated. The cell is still
intact. We know the trial dates and we know the name of the
presiding judge and where and when the sentence was carried out
after his conviction. We know that he died cursing his accusers,
defiant to the last. But the trial was heard in camera and if there's
a transcript, I've yet to see it.'

There was another silence. The inevitable question was coming, Juliet could sense it.

'Can we talk about the Almanac?'

'If we must.'

'Keller was one of its compilers.'

'Allegedly.'

'Is that what he was doing in London?'

Juliet closed her eyes. 'Your question presupposes that the Almanac exists.'

'You're the leading authority on that book.'

'I'm an authority on a period in which practitioners didn't differentiate much between science and magic. There's no hard proof that the Almanac ever existed, much less that it still survives today. The evidence is anecdotal. It could just be a conflation of myth and rumour.'

'Yet Gunter Keller was here for three months. And he wasn't here for the fishing. And the authorities back in Germany thought he was the real deal.'

'Two facts and an assumption,' Juliet said. 'It's hardly incontrovertible proof.'

'I'll ask you straight out. Do you believe the Almanac exists?'

'A cabal of black magicians, alchemists, soothsayers and practitioners of witchcraft gather in secret and pool their knowledge of the dark arts. Their aim is to compile all the most potent charms and curses in a single volume. I think the competing egos would make it unlikely. But stories that have persisted for centuries tend to have at least some basis in fact.'

'If the book was found, would the spells work?'

'Spells that work are either miracles or coincidences. I don't really much believe in either.'

'And that's a neat closing quote, for which I'm grateful.'

'Slow news day?'

'Professor Harrington, you've no idea.'

After this conversation concluded, Juliet pondered on what she hadn't shared with the man from the *Telegraph*.

Rumours flourished like mushrooms in loamy darkness. And the *Almanac of Forbidden Wisdom* had provoked a fair few. And they were colourful. It was the source of William Shakespeare's imaginative gift and Napoleon Bonaparte's mercurial rise to power.

The book had apparently passed through Rasputin's hands in pre-revolutionary Russia. It lay with a hoard of undiscovered Nazi loot in an abandoned mineshaft at the foot of the Alps. Its spells were the source of the almost incalculable wealth amassed in the twentieth century by the oil magnate Paul Getty.

Juliet believed none of this. But she thought it fair to assume that Gunter Keller had indeed been in London to help compile the Almanac. When he re-crossed the North Sea and returned to Hanover, he was able to buy a large house sited in substantial grounds. He'd apparently been handsomely paid for what he'd contributed in London.

This was what had soothed the competing egos of the men who had pooled their occult secrets. The Almanac hadn't been a spontaneous collaboration. The book had been commissioned, its contributors hand-picked by someone with deep pockets and a profound lust for power prepared to risk the block, the gallows or even the stake in pursuing this project.

Men, and women too. Juliet had examined the English land registry in the period of Keller's return to Hanover to see if anyone else had splashed out with a sudden windfall.

She discovered that someone had. The widow Mary Nye had possessed little visible means of support before buying a handsome four-storey house on Holborn. She'd also had a dubious reputation as someone gifted with second sight. Matters became graver for Mary eighteen months after her house purchase, when she was accused by a neighbour of witchcraft. After a short trial, she was hanged without ceremony at Tyburn, her body subsequently buried in unconsecrated ground.

It was far from proof, but Juliet now thought it likelier than not that the Almanac had indeed been created; a single copy, written in English or Latin in London, where it had been compiled. And where it still resided, forgotten on the neglected shelves of a reference library. Or perhaps a private library. Or maybe even a second-hand bookshop with a particularly careless proprietor.

Unless its custodian was a descendant owner aware of the book's mythic status and alleged potential for dark mischief.

There was a persistent story concerning the use of the Almanac. Its influence apparently came at a metaphysical cost. Its use provoked strange events, signals that someone was using it. These events even had a name. They were called 'The Auguries'. The problem was that no one knew precisely what the Auguries were. There were vague allusions to the dead becoming restless. Juliet thought there might be some way she could cross-reference that with Gunter Keller's 'plague of the dead'. But it was insubstantial stuff and she had to tread very carefully. She was fascinated by the notion that the *Almanac of Forbidden Wisdom* might actually be a real document she could read and study, hefting its weight, holding it between her hands, turning its time-stiffened pages, exposing its arcane secrecy.

Her problem was that her head of department didn't at all share her enthusiasm for this sort of subject matter. It was prurient nonsense, local colour, footnotes at best. The Almanac was a pub quiz trivia question, and no more than that.

Juliet knew that more than a century after Keller, Isaac Newton was still spending as much time on alchemy as he was on mathematical calculus. Theology was another of that great scientist's passions. But Juliet's boss liked his history measured in bills of lading and laundry lists. He took a coolly forensic approach. He preferred the demonstrably provable to the speculative. Mystery didn't move him; facts and statistics did.

She was a bit concerned about what might appear in the following day's *Telegraph*. She had blanket approval to talk to the press but also an ongoing responsibility to the reputation and standing of the college. She was expected to be not only serious, but credible.

She picked up her gym bag from where it reposed in the corner of her office and took her key from her pocket. Her conversation with the journalist had provoked a bit of nervous energy she thought half an hour on the treadmill would usefully dissipate. It only registered with her how dark the room was when she unzipped her bag to check the contents and had to switch on her desk light to see properly.

When she got outside, clusters of students and staff stood still in the gloom, collective necks craned, staring, all of them, at the sky. Juliet looked in the same direction and saw with surprise that the sun was eclipsed. Not fully, but partially, though she hadn't known an eclipse was expected.

'An unscheduled event,' a voice beside her said. It was Martin

Doyle, her boss – and, she sometimes thought, her nemesis – complete with his familiar cocktail of scents: tweed, pipe tobacco, too much Polo aftershave. He had small brown eyes and the swarthy pallor of a man who needs to shave twice a day.

'Astronomy doesn't do unscheduled,' she said.

Martin shrugged. His eyes had left hers. He was staring at the sun, which looked as though something had bruised it. 'Doesn't usually,' he said. 'But there's always an exception that proves the rule.'

THREE

Peter Jackson knew that he was nowhere near as clever as his twin sister. She'd been made part of their school's elite and prestigious Special Study Group. He'd have bet money she could take her A-Levels now at the age of only fourteen, and not just pass them but also attain excellent grades. She'd learned Italian just for fun and was now fluent in the language. She'd learned Latin after that because, she said, the similarity to Italian would make it fairly straightforward. Not Church Latin, she'd told her brother airily, but the language the Romans had spoken in the ancient world. Next, she'd said, was Classical Greek.

Dawn Jackson was the sort of high achiever who liked to tick off accomplishments. It was slightly irritating to Peter, who struggled a bit with the Spanish he was studying for an eventual GCSE exam. And her precocious cleverness didn't stop his sister being a bit weird.

He'd accused her more than once of being 'on the spectrum'. He didn't fully know what this meant, but there was a boy in his class their form teacher Mrs Mahoney described as 'on the spectrum'. This boy never made eye contact and stood in a slightly strange folded-up sort of way and liked to listen to recordings of trains through headphones attached to an old-fashioned iPod in the playground. He would rock with the rhythm of the steel wheels on the rails and pull faces. When the trains he was listening to whistled, he would whistle along with them.

In common with Peter's sister, this boy was exceptionally good at maths and had a gift too for music. His technical drawing was also just about perfect. Peter didn't think that Dawn had ever done any tech drawing but suspected that if she ever did, she'd be world class at that too. He didn't really think she was on any kind of spectrum. He just said it in the way siblings do to hurt one another's feelings and score a few cheap points. All the teachers made a fuss of her at school. It was his considered opinion that she got too easy a ride and needed a bit of pain in her life and if her own brother couldn't be depended upon to provide that, who could?

It was six o'clock in the evening and Peter was sitting at the kitchen table in his grandfather's house. He was constructing an Airfix kit, which, he thought, was as close as he ever got to a hobby. Most of his school friends were into computer games but he'd never really seen the attraction of those. He liked building models, the more complex and intricate the better. Painting them once they were put together could be a painstaking task, but he liked that too.

His current project was Nelson's flagship, HMS *Victory*. The masts were a challenge and the rigging an absolute bastard. And there was the smell of the glue. But the smell of the glue masked another far worse odour.

He looked across to the fish tank in which Freddy the terrapin swam in aimless, flapping circles. Freddy's swimming at all was a bit of a miracle, really. His clever sister had used the garden secateurs from Grandpa's shed to snip off Freddy's head a week earlier, two days after finding Grandpa dead in his bed and a day after finding and opening Grandpa's antique book and deciphering some of the claims made there. Headless, Freddy hadn't really appeared capable of swimming. Even of floating. But with the help of the book his sister had fixed Freddy . . . sort of.

Now, he could hear her coming down the stairs. She appeared at the kitchen door with the book held up at her chest between both hands. Like a shield, Peter thought. Or like a religious symbol. Powerful and sacred. She looked at the model he was building, the bright mind behind her bright green eyes quickly taking in its intricacies.

'Do you know what this is?'

'It's a First-rater from the late eighteenth or early nineteenth century. I'm guessing Nelson's flagship, the *Victory*.'

'You know everything.'

'That's an exaggeration.'

But not much of one, Peter thought. He said, 'Something weird happened today at that requiem mass I served at. Well, at the cemetery.'

'Go on.'

'Handy Andy thought he heard a noise coming from the coffin.'

'Andy Baxter?'

'Freaked him out.'

Dawn Jackson frowned. 'The Auguries,' she said.

'The what?'

'There's a warning about them in here.' She put the book down carefully on to the table. It was big and thick with no title on the cover and bound in cracked hide that had the look to Peter of elderly human skin. His sister had told him this stuff was called vellum. 'It's like fallout, or a sort of contagion,' she said. 'It's a phenomenon they called "the unrestful dead".'

'Jesus.'

'It happened because you were there and because of what I did with Freddy and because you've been around the book.'

'That's scary, Dawn.'

'It would only have been for a couple of seconds. Handy Andy must be more alert than he looks.'

There was a plop from the fish tank, where their headless pet had tried to clamber out and had fallen back into the water.

Dawn had discovered the book in the attic. The attic had been strictly out of bounds during their grandfather's lifetime. You accessed it through a locked trap-door but Dawn had found both the key and a step-ladder in the shed. She'd gone up there and discovered what amounted to treasure.

There was a row of medals pinned to a board covered in red velvet. There was a fully loaded Luger pistol. A foot-tall marble statue Dawn said was a nymph. Four small oil paintings, all landscapes. A metal champagne bucket filled to the brim with antique gold coins. There was a ceremonial sword. And a solitary book.

Dawn had since looked the medals up. There were six of them in total: two awarded for gallantry and four campaign medals.

Dawn did the maths and reasoned that they must have been given originally to Grandpa's dad, their own great-grandfather, who had apparently served in Italy, Germany and the Far East.

'Great-gramps was partial to a bit of looting,' she said, leafing through a library reference book about medals given to serving soldiers in the British Army in the Second World War. 'If they'd caught him, they'd have court-martialled and shot him.'

'Blimey.'

Dawn wasn't interested in the weaponry or the art. She seemed completely indifferent too to the bucket full of bling. But the book fascinated her from the moment she opened it. Maybe from before that, from the moment she first laid eyes on it. She studied its pages for hours. And then she performed her party trick with their terrapin.

Sitting in front of his ship model, with the book on the table next to it, Peter said, 'Magic seems to have consequences.'

'Everything has consequences, Pete. Everything worthwhile does, anyway.'

The book was written in Latin. Dawn had said more than once that this seemed to her like fate. She hadn't deciphered all of it. Some of it was dense and obscure. Some of it seemed deliberately ambiguous. There were passages written in a code she said she'd have to crack. But Dawn was good at that sort of thing. She had a knack for it, what she called an aptitude.

Despite the scent of the Airfix glue, the sweetish odour of decay was creeping across the room, getting stronger by the day.

'We need to tell someone about Grandpa. We should have told someone already. We'll get into trouble. You're supposed to tell the authorities when a person dies.'

'It's not like we killed him, Pete. He died in his sleep. In his own bed. He was dead when we went in and found him.'

'We should have reported it when it happened.'

His sister smiled. In a dreamy voice, she said, 'The unrestful dead isn't the half of it.'

'What the hell does that mean?'

She nodded at the book. 'There's a formula in there for bringing people back. Properly. Wholly.'

'He's rotting up there, Dawn. Not to mention the fact that his soul has departed his body.'

'Spoken like a bloody altar boy.'

'I am a bloody altar boy.'

'It's probably been done before,' Dawn said. 'This book is centuries old.'

'What does that prove?'

'That it won't be the end of the world?'

'If you did bring him back, he'd be mad at us.'

'What for?'

'For using his debit card without his permission.'

'We've got to eat.'

'For going into the attic when he forbade it.'

'Only to cover up his own father's war crimes. If he was standing here now, Pete, he'd be pretty sheepish about that.'

'It's sacrilegious.'

'Big word. I mean, by your standards.'

'And because I'm an altar boy I understand its meaning.'

Dawn folded her hands across her chest, pursed her lips, cocked her head to one side and quietly said, 'There's a reason I was given the language skills to understand that text. Sometimes things happen simply because they're meant to. I believe this is one of those times.'

Peter stared at his unfinished model. Scabs of glue had hardened, frosty and jewel-like, around some of the cannon. He'd done a crap job, really, of constructing the *Victory*.

'What's going through what passes for your mind, Pete?'

'Nothing,' he said. But this wasn't true. He was thinking of their mum and dad. You got pretty mangled up when your car lost an argument with an HGV on the motorway. Just that morning, he'd expressed a preference for cremation over burial in a conversation he'd had with Andy Baxter. But his parents hadn't been cremated after their fatal accident back in January. They had been buried, in the same plot.

Peter and Dawn never spoke about their dead parents. On his part this was simply because it would be too soon and too painful. The grief was still too raw. Now he wondered, how much did his sister miss their folks? What would she do to have the chance to see them again? He thought the answer to this rhetorical question was probably, *Anything*. They'd delighted in their clever daughter. Even more than her teachers at school, they'd spoiled her. She probably missed that.

Over against the wall, in their fish tank, Freddy the terrapin slipped while climbing blindly and plopped back into the water with a noise that sounded to Peter as emphatic as the full stop at the end of a closing sentence. He'd never win an argument with Dawn. It just wasn't possible.

FOUR

The boat was rigged up to look like a paddle steamer. But the substantial wheels on its sides didn't house real instruments of propulsion. They turned, or more accurately churned, only for show. The boat was powered, in actuality, by twin diesel-powered screws fixed at the stern and sited well beneath the waterline.

Like all Thames passenger craft in the post-*Marchioness* world, the *Esmeralda* was scrupulously maintained. The safety checks were bi-annual, rigorous, and she always passed them with flying colours. She was licensed to take eighty passengers, had a crew of ten and on this bright Sunday morning at the beginning of June was carrying her full complement when she cast off from Westminster Pier on a voyage along the river that was scheduled to end at a berth just short of the entrance to Hampton Court Palace.

The boat was packed, probably as a consequence of the lovely early June weather. The sky was an unsullied blue so bright above the water that it almost appeared turquoise. The water shimmered, reflecting the sky. The temperature was in the mid-seventies by eleven a.m., the *Esmeralda*'s departure time. There was a slight, pleasant, cooling breeze for those passengers to enjoy who chose to voyage on the deck rather than in the long single cabin beneath it.

In that cabin, as the boat passed under Chelsea Bridge, the weekend festivities were soundtracked by the chink of beer and wine glasses and chortles of carefree laughter – familiar noises generated by the happy celebrants of an English summer.

Adam Porter wasn't drinking. Adam was a reluctant weekend dad, the reluctance prompted by the fact that he would have preferred to see his beloved seven-year-old son Josh every day rather than for a mere two days every fortnight. He thought the custody arrangements involved in divorce settlements thoughtless and close to arbitrary in the way they were decided. They discriminated against a loving father. But he had Josh today and he squatted beside him, face paled by factor fifty sun cream, expression totally relaxed, mouth fully engaged in the eating of a double ninety-nine with strawberry sauce which Adam knew the boy would never have persuaded out of his organic-minded mother.

'Happy?' Adam said to his son, knowing the question was redundant.

Josh nodded from behind the twin chocolate towers of the Cadbury's Flakes anchored in his ice cream. 'Excited, Dad,' he said.

There was a funfair scheduled to be staged that day in the grounds at Hampton Court Palace. There was to be hog roast and archery and mead tasting. There was going to be a tombola and a coconut shy. You could ride on a donkey or take part in a space hopper race. Best of all, there was a jousting tournament, horsemen in full armour riding full pelt at one another with lances in a re-enactment of what had given the palace's Tiltyard its name back when a Tudor monarch named Henry had got through six wives. Sometimes bloodily.

One marriage had been enough for Adam Porter, he reflected now as his son ate through a week's sugar ration in one go. The boat churned serenely through the water as they reached Putney Bridge and the capital began to slip away while the buildings beyond the banks of the river began to look less iconic and more suburban. One wife had been enough; the one who broke his heart and took him to the cleaners in a court of law and then deprived him too regularly of the company of his only child.

Adam looked around him at his fellow passengers. There was a group of pensioner men, jolly in flannels and striped blazers and boaters straight out of Jerome K. Jerome. A fit-looking middle-aged couple in matching denim he took to be tourists; possibly Dutch or Austrian, but without hearing them speak, he'd have bet money they were German. She wore her hair short and severely cut and he wore a Rolex Explorer wristwatch glittering on its steel bracelet on his left wrist.

There was a group of hipsters, heavily bearded and tattooed, which made Adam speculate on the correct collective noun for the species. A micro-brewery of hipsters? An inking of hipsters? The thought amused him. His son saw him smile and smiled back, ice cream smeared across his happy little face. Adam ruffled his son's blond mop of hair and felt a surge of love for the boy so strong it made his chest swell physically and caught the breath momentarily in his throat so that a cough was forced out of him.

'OK, Dad?'

'More than, Josh,' he said.

There was a group of women, piercings and tattoos, retro gypsy-themed clothing reminiscent of what Stevie Nicks had worn onstage and on album covers, and probably in life, when Fleetwood Mac had been at the height of their Seventies fame. Adam thought that they were a good thematic match for the hipster men as the two groups converged and began to chat to one another. At that moment, if asked, he would have said that the mood aboard the boat was better than happy. It was, actually, blissful.

They'd just passed Kingston and the island landmark of Raven's Ait and were more or less at the centre of the river, when the boat began to sink. There was no warning or preamble. There was no collision, no judder of sudden impact or tearing of metal or splintering of wood. There wasn't even time for panic. Matters descended into tragedy before any of the passengers could even reach for a life jacket.

The hull slipped beneath the surface and almost a hundred bodies were all at once in the water; thrashing, screaming, tight-packed together in a riot of summer colour for the brief second before cramp or current began to thin them out.

Adam clawed at water, eyes searching desperately for Josh. People were sinking from the surface, disappearing with a surprised gulp, as though hauled under by strong, demonic hands.

'Josh,' he screamed, 'Josh!'

There was no reply to this. There had to be fewer than twenty people now with heads still above the water, none of those heads that of a blond boy. None of them someone he knew and cherished. No one seemed to have made it to either bank. Bubbles rose and

broke through the viscous sheen of spilled engine oil from pockets
of trapped air aboard the sunken *Esmeralda*.

Adam went under then. He went down as though jerked hard,
astonished at his own velocity, incredulous at the depth to which
he was being dragged, lungs iron-bound, robbed of the light, but
strangely relieved because this had become impossible and he knew
he was only dreaming. A bad dream, sure, but one he was certain,
even as his life ebbed away, that he would wake from in the morning.

Juliet Harrington heard about the tragedy on the afternoon of
the same day. Everyone did. The news reporters who rushed to
the scene used the same phraseology in every bulletin. It was an
event 'unprecedented in the UK in modern times'. And all the
experts invited to offer sound bites said the same: it was completely
inexplicable.

A benign stretch of river. No obstacles to hit and cause the craft
to founder. A substantial and river-worthy vessel that witnesses
watching on the Thames towpath said sank so rapidly it looked
like some ghastly conjuring trick. 'Like a special effect in a movie,'
said one traumatized ten-year-old girl who braked her bicycle on
Barge Walk to watch the horror unfold.

And no survivors. Not one person capable of swimming through
warm slack water to the safety of either bank. It was shocking. It
was mysterious. It seemed, to some of the river authorities,
impossible.

The following day, Juliet read all the stories about the sinking
in all of Monday's serious newspapers. She studied the sectioned
plan of the *Esmeralda*. She learned about the jobs and backgrounds
of the first few passengers to be identified. She read too about the
vessel's crew. She did all this as she did after every major plane
crash or earthquake or avalanche, and not out of mere morbid
curiosity. She did so looking for a pattern, asking herself, Is this
a portent?

After a good deal of rumination, just before turning in on
Monday evening, she took out the notebook she only ever used in
connection with her speculative research. The only subject matter
ever discussed in its confidential pages was the *Almanac of
Forbidden Wisdom*. She sat with the notebook open on the bureau

in her bedroom and her pen poised. She stayed like that for a long moment as though uncertain about the gravity, the sheer irrevocable seriousness, of committing her thoughts to words.

Then she wrote:

> *The Almanac really does exist.*
> *Someone has newly discovered it.*
> *They have used it to work a spell involving water.*
> *And so yesterday, as a consequence, the Auguries began.*

But that was wrong, wasn't it? That partial eclipse no astronomer had predicted had been the Augury, the sign that some calamity or tragedy was about to occur. Something catastrophic. The price inevitably paid when the Almanac was used, magic wrought from its antique pages by someone ignorant of the consequences.

Or someone, Juliet thought, who simply didn't care about the cost of what they did.

FIVE

Early on Tuesday evening, as he did habitually each month, Andrew Baxter confessed his sins to Father Gould. The veteran priest didn't think these transgressions amounted to very much. An apple taken from his younger brother's lunch box. A white lie concerning the location of some missing homework. A promise to sweep the drive of their house made to his mother that he hadn't so far kept. Thomas Gould had heard far worse in a long and eventful priestly career. And that career had honed his instinct to the point where he knew that Andrew was troubled by something far graver than the sins he believed himself to have committed.

'Is there anything that you haven't told me? Perhaps something you'd like to share?'

'It isn't a sin, Father.'

'But it's a problem, Andrew. And you'll be familiar with the old saying that a problem shared is a problem halved.'

On the other side of the confessional grille blinding them to the sight of one another, there was a silence Father Gould thought to be eloquent. Then Andrew said, 'At the cemetery the other day, I think we might have buried someone still alive.'

'That's impossible, Andrew.'

'I heard movement. It was definitely coming from inside the coffin. Pete Jackson said it was probably a rat, but it couldn't have been. Not that quickly. Unless the rat ate its way into the coffin while the coffin was still in the church, which someone would have noticed. There'd have been sawdust.'

The boy had clearly been pondering on this, worrying at it in his young mind since the burial. 'Pete Jackson heard this coffin sound?'

'No, he didn't, Father.'

'And neither did I.'

'Except that I didn't imagine it.'

A phrase insinuated its way just then into the old priest's head. He didn't know what it meant and had no idea of from where it came. A jackdaw moment. A magpie's shiny find. The phrase was *the unrestful dead.*

Father Gould's tone was gentle when he spoke next. 'The unfortunate fellow we buried the other day had sustained injuries no one could have survived, Andrew. The cause of death was smoke inhalation, which was a blessed mercy for him because his body was subsequently burned beyond recognition. He'd lost an arm and most of his lower limbs. The best you can do is to pray for his soul.'

'I will, Father.'

Father Gould absolved Andrew Baxter and the boy left the confessional and went to unchain his bike and ride it the distance home. But that phrase nagged at the priest maddeningly. He knew that he could fire up his old desktop computer and search the internet for its origin and its implications. Google was a powerful tool. But his preferred method was to consult someone human. Forty years earlier he'd been at the seminary as a novitiate with the colleague and friend who was now bishop of his diocese. He'd still never come across a more knowledgeable man or anyone of either sex with a finer mind. And so, it was the bishop whom he rang.

'Your Grace?'

'Mark, to you, Tom. Let's have no unnecessary ceremony.'

'I'm being haunted by a phrase, Mark. Though "haunted" might be a slight exaggeration. I'm trying to place it, to find a context for it, and I can't.'

'I'm intrigued, Tom. Let's hear it.'

'"The unrestful dead"?'

The bishop was silent. It was now just before nine p.m. in early June, so light was still left in the day. 'You're what, Tom, twenty minutes away?'

'Probably less than that, at this time of night, by car.'

'Take a cab, Tom. Expense it to the diocese. You're not driving. This is a face-to-face discussion over something a lot more potent than coffee or tea.'

It was whisky. It was the single malt, Oban. And the only mixer the bishop had was the purist's choice of soda water. No ice. The bishop believed whisky a drink properly consumed only at room temperature.

They swapped the usual pleasantries. And then the bishop cleared his throat with a cough. Unlike his visitor, white-haired and ascetically thin, the bishop was bald and short and prosperously plump.

'"The unrestful dead" is a phrase I've come across formally only in a monograph written by an Oxford academic named Juliet Harrington. Professor Harrington is an authority on sixteenth-century mysticism. The phenomenon of the unrestful dead is as much side effect as affliction, according to her speculations. It's a direct consequence of coming into contact with the *Almanac of Forbidden Wisdom*.'

'You mean dabbling in magic? Working spells?'

'No. It's just a temporary disruption to the norm. Using the Almanac's spells has far more serious physical consequences. They're known as the Auguries.'

'I still can't recall where I came across that phrase,' Father Gould said.

'The subject of the Almanac came up briefly at a seminar we both attended more than forty years ago. You'd have heard about the unrestful dead then, but it's no surprise that after all this time you can't remember.'

'Pretty ghoulish stuff.'

'Very. In what connection did it come up?'

Father Gould told his friend. The bishop turned pale and poured them fresh drinks. Stiff ones, Father Gould observed.

'Is this a fanciful boy?'

'Not usually. And he's served on my altar for six years. Everything about funeral ritual is familiar to him. There was nothing particularly to provoke his imagination.'

'Then he must have misheard. He must have been mistaken.'

The two men were silent, sipping whisky, both, Father Gould knew, contemplating the alternative. He had remembered another detail from that last funeral service. The incense used in the requiem mass had seemed unusually pungent, the smoke acrid and darker than it should have been. The whole familiar ritual, now he recalled it, had seemed strangely out of kilter.

Eventually the bishop said, 'Awful business with that pleasure boat at the weekend.'

'Lost two parishioners. Not a single survivor. Beggars belief.'

'The sort of pointless calamity that costs people their faith, Tom.'

But Father Gould hadn't finished with their earlier topic. 'I'd thought the legend of the *Almanac of Forbidden Wisdom* apocryphal. Somewhere between a fable and a cautionary tale.'

The bishop shook his head, slowly. He said, 'You should read her monograph. Professor Harrington thinks it real enough. She speculates on its contributors. The Vatican believed in its existence strongly enough to put a bounty on it at the end of the eighteenth century. Find it so it could be ceremonially destroyed, and you'd earn your weight in gold bullion.'

'I didn't know that.'

'It isn't common knowledge. Rome has always been good at secrets. The only people who did know were the agents charged with the mission of the book's recovery. And they failed.'

'Do you have a copy of Professor Harrington's monograph?'

'Here, in the library. I'll get it for you.'

Half an hour later, Father Gould was dropped by his taxi outside the gates of the cemetery where he prayed the subject of his most recent burial service still peacefully reposed. The gates were locked, but he was a relatively agile man emboldened by two large whiskies and the wall was old and time-pocked and therefore easily scalable.

It had grown dark, but the paler gravestones were navigable landmarks and he was able to find the plot he wanted to examine straightforwardly enough.

Turf had been laid in neatly cut squares about a foot in length. The job had been done in haste by the look of it because the gaps between the turf squares were uneven in size. This was noticeable even in darkness, once the priest's eyes had adjusted to his surroundings.

He raised his eyes from their study of the ground and looked around. He was a man in a black gabardine suit and a white clerical collar with an occult-themed monograph in his jacket pocket who thought he would have quite a bit of explaining to do should an official of any sort discover him there. But there was no one around. Or at least, there was no one living around. This was a necropolis, a city of the dead. He had plenty of companionship, all of it mouldering. There was a sense in which they were all the unrestful dead.

After a moment's hesitation, Father Gould knelt on the turf on the grave and then got on to all fours and prostrated himself on the ground. He turned his head so that his left cheek prickled against the close-cut grass blades and he felt the cooling earth against his skin, listening for some signal or clue from under the recently turned soil beneath the sods.

Nothing. No sound except for night wind soughing through leaf-burdened trees around the empty chapel a hundred feet away from where he lay. And his own breathing, shallower and less regular than he thought it should have been. After a few minutes he got to his feet somewhat wearily and headed off, intent on reading into the night.

SIX

I'm frightened of that damned book. It has power and the power is baleful. And potent. So potent that I've had to overcome my recent desire to destroy it. I fear the repercussions should I attempt to do so. It's my strong belief that steps have been taken to protect its contents from physical harm. Attempt to destroy that compendium of evil and malice and perversion and I might very well be destroying myself in consequence.

I suppose I could attempt to sell it. There must be a market for antiquarian texts on every subject and as far as I've been able to determine, my copy of the Almanac of Hidden Wisdom *is the only one in existence. The existence of even a single copy of the book has been debated down the centuries, sometimes believed, more often scoffed at as a mere conspiracy, a baseless tale, a bit of irreligious propaganda. But I think to sell it would bring terrible misfortune. That's my instinct, which I tend to trust and follow.*

So, it sits with my other keepsakes. With the pistol I took from the German officer I shot dead in a skirmish in the Ardennes forest in the weeks following D-Day. With the collection of gold coins I had the good fortune to liberate from an Italian monastery. With the paintings I had the devil's own job smuggling back after taking them from a grand house during the fall of Berlin.

I discovered the book in the library of a chateau about ten miles north of Paris. The chateau had been abandoned, the book left in a glass case and its most recent owner, so far as I could ascertain, in a tomb in the crypt below. I should have realized straight away that it wouldn't bring with it good fortune. But even with my schoolboy Latin I could see that the subject matter was sensational. All I could think about was its rarity and potential value. I was blinded, not for the first time, by greed.

The book has real occult power. I would never attempt a spell or curse or create a formula or enact one of the rituals from its pages. But you only have to be in its proximity for it to inflict its contaminating effect. And it's extremely disturbing, this party trick the book facilitates in its owners.

The book was in my knapsack on the first occasion this occurred. I was alone, at the wheel of a requisitioned jeep, scouting ambush locations, when I stumbled into the aftermath of one at dusk. The bodies were all about, bullet-riddled, their uniforms telling me they were Italian, all with the slumped posture of the recently and violently deceased. I braked and got out of the vehicle, intent on wallets and wristwatches. But as I began to pass among them, the bodies began to twitch and writhe. One, shot in the chest, exhaled slowly through punctured lungs. It was a ghastly sound and they were a surreal and frightening sight for the few seconds before they became still again.

It was the first occult experience I had, but it wasn't the last. That occurred in a hospital when I went to visit my commanding officer a few weeks before being demobbed back in Blighty. He'd taken a shrapnel wound to the foot and some boot leather had infected the wound.

He was cheerful, and on the mend, when I saw him. It was a visit jocular enough. Then at the end, in a bid to avoid all the miles and miles of hospital corridors I'd tramped through on my route to the major's bedside, I took a shortcut to the hospital's rear entrance.

This was a mistake. Because it brought me through the mortuary. And I was treated to the thump and slap of the corpses in their metal drawers as the contamination I carried briefly animated them. It was a trapped, frenzied sound that made an orderly scream before he dead-fainted to the floor.

I think that this only happens when you've handled the book recently. I have it safely under lock and key in the attic and, thank God, there's been no repetition. I never want to experience anything like it again. It's a waking nightmare that makes a man's skin crawl and feels like an icicle thrust through the heart. It also makes you doubt your sanity.

Peter Jackson didn't know whether to call this a letter, note, boast, confession or warning. It was written in black fountain pen ink over three sheets of lined paper which had then been bound together by a single staple at the top left-hand corner. There was no date on the note, but the ink was faded and the handwriting sort of old-fashioned. And a phrase like 'on the mend' struck Peter as terribly dated. And who, these days, used words like 'ghastly'?

He'd found the document rummaging through the bureau in Grandpa's study. He'd actually been searching for cash. There was a healthy enough balance on Grandpa's debit card, but they got funny looks, like the cashiers knew it wasn't theirs, when they used it in the supermarket. They'd taken to using the self-checkout, but cash was a less risky proposition altogether.

He thought it quite cool to have shot a German officer dead in a French forest in the war, but a bit shabby to try to take personal belongings from the bodies of ambushed soldiers. He'd always thought of brave people as heroes and now knew that his light-fingered great-granddad, despite being brave, had not been heroic at all.

Peter read the note with all the windows open, having the previous evening finally persuaded Dawn that they had to shift what was left of Grandpa before he liquified in the summer sunshine and slid off the bed in a stinking puddle of decomposition. He'd done some recent internet reading on what happens to dead people and 'decomposition' was a word new to him which he thought rather cool.

Grandpa had not been rather cool. He'd been smelly, and softer under the armpits than he should have been, when they carried him down the stairs. Sort of sticky, there. But he'd been a small man and quite thin and wasn't heavy, which was something. They'd folded him into the chest freezer kept in the garage as a back-up and then plugged it in and heard it chug softly into life. It wasn't perfect. They'd have to thaw him out for Dawn to attempt to bring him back, but in the meantime he wouldn't get any worse.

What he had just read had confirmed Peter's existing suspicion that the proximity of the Almanac gave him a bit of a problem. And he was in its proximity, all the time, because Dawn carried the bloody thing around like a toddler with a comfort blanket. It meant that going anywhere near a coffin with a body in it was for him, just then, impossible.

Nobody would know it was happening because of him and it wasn't something he'd ever do deliberately. What worried him was the effect it would have on the mourners. He was supposed to serve at a requiem a week away, a funeral mass for one of the drowning victims of the *Esmeralda* disaster. It was a seven-year-old boy.

And it brought a whole new meaning to the term 'death-rattle'. Peter didn't want the boy's coffin toppling off its trolley as he jerked around inside it in the church.

It had been quite subtle the last time. It hadn't happened until the graveside and only Handy Andy Baxter had been aware of anything amiss. But he'd been around the Almanac for a lot longer now.

And he couldn't destroy it. Great-grandpa had been right about that. You only had to look at that flesh-coloured vellum cover to sense that the book protected itself. And he didn't think he could hide it away. If he did that, Dawn would know straight away that it had been him and she would make him bring it back, and then what would she do?

She'd punish him, was what she'd do. She'd use these new powers she was learning to possess and punish him in some awful way. Peter turned to look at their fish tank. They'd need a new one soon. Freddy the terrapin had got bigger since his death. Bigger and paler. Sort of jelly-like. And kind of see-through. You could see his innards, under his rotting shell, as though bringing him back hadn't been a total success. He was still just small enough to flush away down the loo and without a head he didn't have a mouth either to nip. But Dawn liked this physical proof of her new powers, the endless, sightless, circular swim.

Peter had realized that, depressingly, he was actually frightened of his sister. And possibly becoming more so. All the jokes about her being on the spectrum had been tolerated, but no more than that. In tolerating them, she was actually just humouring him, but those cracks were as far as he would go because they were as far as his twin would let him. With the adults gone, she was very much the person making the important decisions in their lives. And she was armed now with the Almanac.

'A cold,' Peter said, aloud. In a week's time, to miss that requiem, he'd develop a cold of the sort that had always served him well enough on occasions when he hadn't done his school homework and needed to delay going back by a day.

Freddy, propelled by his swollen flippers, provided a constant, sloppy soundtrack to his thoughts. He lifted his head and saw his sister standing at the study door.

'Working on Grandpa, sis?'

'Grandpa's complicated. I need a fresh model to start with. Still an apprentice at this.'

She was standing with her hands behind her back. It was an

unusually coy posture for Dawn, he thought, uncharacteristic of someone as generally confident as she was. It was almost endearing.

'Are you OK?'

'I'm fine and dandy,' she said. She brought her right hand from behind her back and raised the attic Luger and shot her brother squarely in the centre of the forehead. He didn't fall from the armchair in which he'd done his reading. He just sat back as though asleep. Except that his eyes, glazed now in death, remained open.

'No time to waste, Peter,' his sister said, placing the pistol delicately on top of her grandfather's bureau. 'Let's get this done.'

SEVEN

They were almost at the end of term. There were late essays to mark and assessments still to do, but the seminars and lectures had pretty much wrapped up and most of the academic staff were simply looking forward to the long vacation and holidays they'd booked back in December and January. Her guard was down, she was feeling relaxed, and that was probably why it was a sickening shock on Wednesday morning for Juliet Harrington to get a formal summons to sit before a disciplinary panel over comments a journalist had attributed to her in the recent interview she'd given but hadn't yet bothered to read.

It would be Martin Doyle's doing, she knew. And it wasn't just their differing philosophies on what constituted proper research. She thought that the truth was he'd been gunning for her ever since a faculty cocktail party almost eighteen months earlier at which he'd asked her out on a date and she'd declined.

She'd done so diplomatically. She had been polite and even friendly in saying no. But Martin was a results-based individual and 'no', however sugar-coated, had been the direct opposite of the answer he'd wanted to hear. Tactful rejection was still rejection.

He hadn't persisted in trying to woo her. Instead, he'd sulked. And then he'd turned hostile. Not openly so; he was too skilful a politician to allow people generally to think he had any kind of personal agenda. But his criticism of her academic interests and even her methodology had been persistent and corrosive. It had undermined her reputation and hurt her personally. It was undeserved. What it actually was, however subtly done, was bullying.

Prior to her appearance before the panel, she read the piece. She sounded more emphatic quoted on the page than she remembered being on the phone. The claims she made concerning the *Almanac of Forbidden Wisdom* seemed wilder. The panel would comprise the vice-chancellor, her head of faculty and the senior manager from human resources. Two of the three were perfectly reasonable people. She thought that with a bit of luck and a lot of nerve, she could ride this one out. She did not want to be forced to resign over something so relatively trivial. She liked her job.

Reflecting on just how much she liked her job, seated outside the meeting room awaiting her summons, Juliet had time to reflect upon her life generally. Her marriage had ended acrimoniously when she'd uncovered her ex-husband's ongoing affair, two years ago now. Recovery from the betrayal and its fallout had been slow and difficult. A subsequent experiment in internet dating had been almost farcically unsuccessful.

Objectively, she knew that she wasn't physically unattractive. And she was a youthful enough thirty-five-year-old for students sometimes to try to hit on her. But her life suffered from the lack of the commitment that comes only with a partner and children. There was no romance and precious little love in it.

What else? There was the growing suspicion that the world might be seriously out of kilter. Juliet was aware that her day-to-day life lacked thrills. She was also aware of the old Chinese curse about living in interesting times.

The door in front of her opened and their HR manager popped her bespectacled face around it and signalled with a jerk of her head that Juliet's moment had arrived.

'What's the evidential basis for your belief that the *Almanac of Forbidden Wisdom* is anything other than a preposterous myth?'

The question, typically passive–aggressive, came, of course, from Martin Doyle. Martin Doyle, PhD, Juliet reminded herself: Dr Martin Doyle.

I believe it because of an unexpected astronomical event, Juliet thought. I believe it because an inexplicable catastrophe claimed every life it could. I believe it because the Auguries are upon us.

What she said was, 'During the eighteenth century, agents of the Catholic Church were incentivized with a huge reward to find the Almanac, simply so that it could be destroyed. This was a specific instruction. The relevant paperwork is marked by the papal seal. I sourced it myself while doing research at the Vatican a few years ago. I was permitted to make a photocopy, which I can show all three of you.'

'Gullibility and the Catholic Church are not mutually exclusive, and never have been,' Martin said.

'I believe the Almanac to have been compiled in 1530,' Juliet said. 'There was a three-month period when half a dozen of the most eminent occult practitioners in Europe were all in London. They came from Germany, Italy and Holland. They came for a reason. Our home-grown participant was a woman, Mary Nye.'

'This is very speculative,' the vice-chancellor said.

'Speculation is a large part of what we do,' Juliet said.

'And that newspaper article struck me as quite sensationalist.'

'I didn't write the article and so didn't determine its character. And some of my quotes were exaggerated.'

'Completely unrepentant,' Martin said.

Juliet shrugged, a gesture she immediately regretted.

Martin Doyle raised a forefinger for emphasis. He said, 'You're in danger of bringing the academic credibility of this institution into disrepute with this ridiculous obsession with hocus-pocus. So here's a reasonable compromise. Until you can provide concrete proof of the existence of that book, you refrain from all future public mention of the subject. Agreed?'

'Agreed,' Juliet said.

On either side of Martin, the two female panel members nodded sagely.

Juliet felt quite relieved. But she knew that her card had been marked. She glanced at her wristwatch. It was five minutes to ten in the morning and she had no further appointments that day. She decided that she would drive to Kingston upon Thames, to the river, to see for herself the site of Sunday's tragedy. She didn't think doing so would provide her with the answer to anything, much less any solid proof. She didn't think her motives prurient or ghoulish either, though. She felt compelled by instinct to go. The drive took just over an hour and a half. She parked and walked over Kingston Bridge to the towpath on the Bushy Park side. She'd changed out of the suit and heels she'd worn for her dressing-down, into jeans and a canvas jacket and her hiking boots. The fine weather was holding on, a day a happy boatload of assorted souls had never lived to see.

The first sign of the tragedy was the litter of wreaths washed up against the solid obstacle of Raven's Ait by the river's gentle flow. Further on, at the spot itself, there was a marker buoy. It was a navigation point, she supposed, for the police or salvage divers. In due course the wreck would be raised.

The opaque water of the river itself offered no clues about what had happened there. And whatever debris had washed up on the river bank had been taken away. It was almost as though the incident itself, not just the people involved in it, had been effaced. Its legacy was the pain in the hearts of those who grieved, and Juliet suspected that would last a lifetime.

She went back to the bridge and crossed it and walked along Kingston Riverside to Queen's Promenade and the Riverside Café. It was now one o'clock in the afternoon of a so far eventful day, but she couldn't discover much appetite for food. She needed to eat, though, to have the stamina and concentration for the drive back. So she sat at one of the café's little metal tables and forced down a toasted cheese and tuna ciabatta sandwich that on another day would have tasted delicious, washed down by a Diet Coke.

The river sparkled benignly under sunlight. The world was generally indifferent to what went on in it. You could despoil and pollute or overheat it, but it didn't behave with deliberate malice. The malice came from mankind and mankind's infernal dabbling.

There had been a boy aboard the boat. They'd run a human-interest story in the follow-ups in the papers, filled with poignant detail. His name had been Joshua Porter and he was seven years old. He'd been with his weekend dad. He'd been excited, said his bereft mother, about a funfair he was going to with his dad at Hampton Court. He'd been talking about this event for weeks. Most of all he'd been looking forward to the jousting.

Was this really the start of the Auguries, this inexplicable tragedy, that unexpected eclipse? Juliet thought that she would need another sign before she really began to believe that. But if it did happen, she didn't have the first clue as to what she would do about it.

She already had colleagues who thought her obsessive and possibly even a bit unbalanced. Naive, gullible, easily taken in, credulous to a fault, a bit of a professional embarrassment. A gusher.

Was that really who she was?

She sat at a table on the Thames outside a pretty café and thought about it hard, but without coming to any firm conclusions about herself. She couldn't exonerate, but neither could she condemn. She just didn't possess the necessary objectivity.

EIGHT

D awn thought the revived Peter a bit of a disappointment. He'd never been the sharpest knife in the drawer, but now he seemed barely able to communicate. His walk was a slow shuffle and he seemed to have a problem with the concept of walls. He'd walk towards a wall and then try to keep going, a bit like someone treading water in a swimming pool, or a stupid wind-up toy.

The most impressive bit of the procedure had been the way his head wound healed. The bullet hole had completely gone. There wasn't even a scar. But he didn't have the energy that her headless terrapin had come back with. Animation, Dawn thought, was the characteristic that her brother now lacked.

Though Freddy, if she was really honest with herself, was developing problems of his own. His shell had become a soft and gluey mess. Under it, his body had turned loathsomely translucent. You could see organs pulsing and blood beating along intricately patterned arteries. It was like the biology lesson from hell, now that he'd grown to about the size of an overfilled hot water bottle. She'd resolved to find a spell in the book to make Freddy disappear. He was no fun at all any more.

She was beginning to think her brother, though always dim-witted, might have been on to something talking about the hazards of coming back without a soul. When he didn't think she was looking, he'd stare at her with an expression of pure malice she'd never seen him wear before she shot him. It could be quite unnerving, particularly now that he didn't seem to require sleep. Before she'd killed him, you could easily have confused Peter with a hibernating animal, so much sleep did he seem to rely upon. But that situation had changed completely. This version didn't seem to need a minute's shut-eye.

His conversation now, if you could even call it that, was pretty random. It was like turning the knob on a really old-fashioned radio, such as the one Grandpa still owned. Different frequencies. Different voices. Different subjects, a babble of languages, all slurred, all projected, the way she knew a skilled ventriloquist could project their voice. She'd enjoyed the novelty of it at first, but now she was bored with it and wished he'd shut up.

The school had become a problem. She was still going in, obviously. But they'd taken her to task about Peter's non-attendance and kept trying to reach their grandpa by phone. They basically wanted to see a doctor's note confirming what Dawn had told them, which was that her brother had meningitis.

She had thought about killing him again and burying him in the back garden and that way having the problem literally vanish. But she wasn't confident that he would stay dead. She thought that he might just revive and dig his way out. The magic seemed to be in some ways stubborn and strong and difficult to control.

Then there were the headaches. After bringing Freddy back she had required an extra-strength paracetamol. After bringing her brother back she had needed two.

Dawn did all the shopping now, obviously. And even that was proving to be more difficult since the experiment involving her brother. He'd come back with this disgusting appetite for raw meat. He'd killed and eaten two cats that had strayed into Grandpa's garden. It was just a good job for both of them that Grandpa's garden wasn't overlooked by nosy neighbours.

Some of the spells in the book were really interesting and she was discovering more every day. One of her favourites involved copying an odd geometric shape on to a plain sheet of paper. You folded it and put it into an envelope and said the relevant spell aloud. Then you addressed it, and when the person it was addressed to opened it and looked at the shape, they became permanently blind. Dawn had drawn up a list of the people she wanted to target with this very cool bit of sorcery.

Another that had impressed her was a musical spell. You had to have a picture of the person for this one. Dawn knew that in the olden days that would have been a sketched or painted portrait, but she was sure that a photograph would be a more than practical substitute. There was a lullaby printed on one page of the book. Four verses, each of four lines in length, and no chorus. This lullaby reminded Dawn a bit of a nursery rhyme. Anyway, you propped up the picture and stared at the subject and sang the lullaby out loud. And the person pictured died in their sleep *that very night.*

Dawn wondered whether this spell would work with a group shot. A bride and groom, say. A school hockey team. Would it work with a selfie someone had posted on to their Facebook page? She couldn't think of a good reason why it wouldn't, and she could think of several people who probably had that coming. Though dying in your sleep was quite a nice way to go and some of them deserved a far worse fate.

Not all of the spells were anything like as practical as those two. If you wanted someone to lose a hand or a foot you needed to burn a bit of their fingernail or toenail as you recited the relevant words. Dawn didn't think this terribly realistic. Access would be too much of a challenge. But she also thought the lopping off of limbs generally a bit medieval. To her mind, this was a spell that had dated rather badly.

It was six o'clock in the evening. Dawn had lured Peter down the steps to the cellar and locked him in as he did his treading water thing against the wall opposite the door. He could probably break out. She had a hunch that he had come back a great deal stronger than he'd been before, but he might like it down there in the damp and darkness and having him there increased cat safety in their locality by 100 per cent.

The reason she thought him stronger now was the way in which she had seen him kill the second cat. Saliva had dribbled down his chin as he anticipated his feast. With just his bare hands, her brother had ripped off the limbs and the head of the cat and then skinned it.

Dawn switched on the television. One of the reasons that she knew she wasn't on the spectrum was that she liked to keep abreast of world events. People who were really on the spectrum were indifferent to current affairs. Dawn wasn't.

The lead item was about statues. Before turning up the sound, it looked to Dawn as if some serious vandalism had been done to some of London's most familiar landmarks. They were all male statues. There was the famous one of the Duke of Wellington on his horse and the Churchill statue in Parliament Square and the one of Richard the Lionheart around the corner from that. The Peter Pan outside Great Ormond Street Hospital's main entrance. Red paint trickled out of their eye sockets and mouths. Someone had even got to the top of the column in Trafalgar Square and done it to Lord Nelson.

Dawn turned up the volume. A moment later, she was incredulous at what she was hearing. The reporter on the scene at Parliament Square was saying the substance wasn't paint, but blood. All over the capital, the statues were bleeding.

Incredulity was turned to sadness as she watched. The statue of Nelson had reminded her of Peter's modelling and particularly of his recent project to build HMS *Victory* from a kit. It wouldn't ever be completed now. The version of Peter she had returned to life would never do anything like that. He was a base and clumsy creature, a consumer of uncooked carcasses who liked them best still warm.

The bulletin ended, and Dawn switched off the TV. She had zero interest in *Emmerdale*. Later, she would learn how to make things disappear. Not become invisible like in Harry Potter, but cease to exist altogether. She would consult the book, try it on Freddy and, if it worked successfully, get rid of her brother.

In the meantime, she had to create something diversionary to stop the school pressuring her over Peter. She thought that the sudden death of a beloved teacher would do it. She got up and switched on her laptop, confident that somewhere on the internet she'd find a photo of Peter's form teacher, Mrs Mahoney.

NINE

On Monday morning, Juliet went into college only to empty her pigeon hole and pick up her gym kit to launder it. It was five days since what she retrospectively regarded as her pointlessly whimsical visit to Kingston. And it was the morning after the strangest news bulletins she had ever seen transmitted on television. They had turned all her vague and insecure doubts into crushing certainties.

Statues didn't bleed.

The Auguries had begun. Someone was using the *Almanac of Forbidden Wisdom*. The book existed, all right. And she further thought she now understood its real purpose. It had been created to trigger the biblical apocalypse known in the gospels as the End Times.

Like many people with empty personal lives, Juliet suffered the irony of being an early riser. So she was at college at nine a.m., where a surprise greeted her outside her office door in the shape of a sheepish-looking Martin Doyle. How long had he been standing there? If there was urgency here, why hadn't he called? It wasn't as if he didn't have her number.

'You've visitors,' he said. His voice was little above a whisper. 'A delegation. A deputation. I don't know which of those is the most accurate description. There are three of them in there.'

'Don't the best things always come in threes?'

'My criticism of you last week may have been somewhat premature and a little heavy-handed.' He hesitated. He bit his lip and shifted his feet – rather, Juliet thought, like someone dribbling an invisible football. She'd never seen her department head so discomfited. 'I know it's your office, Juliet, but given the exalted status of the people waiting to see you, I'd be inclined to knock before entering.'

She didn't do that. She was too territorial, and this was her space, her nest and sanctuary. They were two men and one woman. She recognized each of the trio. The men were the Home Secretary and the Archbishop of Canterbury. The woman was the Metropolitan Police Commissioner. Somewhat redundantly, they introduced themselves. Ordinarily she had three chairs in here, her own and two for visitors. A fourth had been provided, probably by the newly humble Martin Doyle.

It was the Home Secretary who spoke. 'We want you to tell us about the Auguries.'

'You'd think me a crank.'

He smiled and glanced to left and right at his two colleagues. 'We have a partial solar eclipse no astronomer predicted. We have the inexplicable sinking of a watertight boat. And then yesterday statues bled, which bronze and marble aren't supposed to. Physically, biomechanically, biologically, it's impossible. Yet it happened.'

The Commissioner spoke next. She said, 'An event like the Raven's Ait tragedy can affect the national psyche in a way that's corrosive. Morale is damaged because the sheer number of casualties seems morally wrong. But when something unprecedented like the phenomenon of the bleeding statues occurs, it induces mass panic. We're obliged to take a holistic approach. In common with my two colleagues, I read the *Telegraph* piece. Tell us about the Auguries.'

Juliet took a deep breath and then began to speak. 'Five hundred years ago an occult compendium was put together by a cabal of knowledgeable practitioners of magic. It was called the *Almanac of Forbidden Wisdom*. The Auguries occur when the book is used. I don't think their nature can be predicted. But I do know an eclipse prophesied calamity in the medieval world.'

The Archbishop said, 'You think it signalled the Raven's Ait tragedy?'

'It's just a theory.'

'Then what calamity do the bleeding statues represent?'

Juliet said, 'If I'm right, and I hope I'm not, we'll know soon enough.'

'You really believe that someone in this country is using the Almanac?'

'Going on the locations of Raven's Ait and the statues, I'd say someone in Greater London is using it.'

'How do we find them?' asked the woman.

'You tell me,' Juliet said. 'You're the Met Commissioner.'

'Help us with the profile.'

'I assumed for a long time that the Almanac would have been written in English because it was compiled in London. I now think, because the contributors were from all over Europe, that Latin is likelier. We're looking for someone with good linguistic skills because even if it's not a Latin text, Middle English isn't straightforward.'

'Anything else?'

'They're going to be good at cracking codes and puzzles. Much of the text will be codified. They'd need to be numerate.'

'So, someone clever?'

'Someone contradictory,' Juliet said. 'Extremely bright, but morally bankrupt. Anyone with the remotest ethical sensibility would know that dabbling in this stuff is fundamentally wrong. You just don't risk the consequences of messing with the natural order of things.'

'Unless it's a precocious child,' the Home Secretary said. 'Someone with an adolescent sensibility characterized by spite, resentment and a desire to get even. A person like that wouldn't really care about the natural order.'

Juliet said, 'The Almanac would be God's gift to the character you've just described.'

The Archbishop said, 'This has nothing to do with God.'

'Amen,' the Met Commissioner said.

It hadn't occurred to Juliet Harrington that the Almanac could have fallen into the hands of someone intelligent enough to use it but too immature properly to understand the ramifications of dabbling in magic. The Home Secretary was spot on. In a perverse way the book would suit an adolescent mindset. Most adults, even sceptical adults, would be too afraid to use it.

She became aware that the Home Secretary was staring at her. He said, 'Magic exacts a price.'

'Always,' she said, 'traditionally. Whether you believe in it or you don't. All the tales are cautionary. There's always a catch.'

'If there is another calamity,' he said, 'we'll be coming back to you.'

'I don't see what I could do.'

'You strike me as a resourceful woman. I'm confident you'll think of something.'

Juliet sat at her desk after her deputation had departed and pondered on whether she could actually do anything. The trail of the *Almanac of Forbidden Wisdom* was secretive, clandestine, clouded by obscurity and, at 500 years old, extremely cold. Original ownership had never been claimed because anywhere in the Europe of the sixteenth century it would have earned a death sentence carried out in the most brutal manner.

She supposed she could travel to Hanover and take a thorough look at what survived of Gunter Keller's papers. She had never before had the sanction to do that because her head of department would have seen it as a deliberate provocation as well as an absolute waste of time and money. But his attitude seemed to have changed quite a lot. And if she was doing it at the behest of the Home Secretary, she thought Martin Doyle would use every ounce of his academic clout to get her full access.

This left Juliet feeling slightly conflicted. On the one hand, she had dreamed for years of being granted access to the Keller archive. On the other, she didn't want some catastrophic event to deliver her that wish.

The phone on her desk began to ring. It was the Home Secretary. He said, 'Is this a secure line?'

It was too soon for him to be back at Whitehall. She thought he must be phoning from his car. A bad sign. She said, 'I've absolutely no idea what that means.'

'Probably doesn't matter, but old habits and all that. I'll call you back on your mobile in five minutes. Take the call outside and out of anyone's earshot.'

'You don't have my mobile number.'

'Of course I have your bloody mobile number.'

On her way out of the building, she remembered that he had come into politics late. His background was a spook's background. He'd worked at MI5.

'There's been an outbreak.'

'Go on.'

'Over a hundred cases presented this morning, swamping A&E departments at four major London hospitals which have gone into crisis mode as a direct consequence. We've had to declare a major incident. We might have to declare a state of emergency. More than half of those cases are critical.'

'What's wrong with them?'

'Bubonic plague.'

'The bleeding statues.'

A bark of sardonic laughter. 'Indeed. The one UK consultant with experience of plague says he's never seen it spread so fast or with such virulence. The most seriously afflicted generally get attacks to their lungs and last a couple of days. He says some of these victims will be dead within hours.'

'Oh, God.'

'What can you do for us, Professor Harrington?'

'A German alchemist named Gunter Keller was one of the people who compiled the Almanac. I've always had a hunch that he was its mastermind.'

'A hunch?'

'An informed guess. An intuition.'

'I'm listening.'

'I could go to Hanover and look at his papers. If there was a way to begin this, logic suggests there should be a key to stopping it.'

'What was Keller's overall motive? Money? Notoriety?'

'Bigger than either. I think he wanted to trigger the End Times.'

'Then that might be a one-way street.'

'You don't think I should bother?'

'I think you should go home for your passport and pack a bag. We'll have you on a flight this afternoon. We'll book a hotel room, wire you expenses money. And my next call will be to Dr Doyle. He's going to do everything in his power to smooth that path for you over there, academically.'

Juliet took a breath. She said, 'We don't really see eye to eye, me and my head of department.'

'Irrelevant, frankly. If he doesn't cooperate fully, I'll personally see to it that by the end of the week he'll be sweeping gutters for a living.'

'Do you really believe a book is doing this?'

'We told you this morning, we take a holistic approach. The army is on full alert, all leave cancelled. We've a COBRA committee meeting due to begin as soon as this car reaches Downing Street. Our sociologists and psychological people are saying riots are imminent.'

'Bloody hell.'

'And in answer to your question, no, I don't believe a book is doing this. But I've yet to be convinced that it isn't being done by the person using that book.'

Juliet did as she'd been instructed; she went home and packed a bag and retrieved her passport. A text message told her she was booked into a hotel at the other end. The Keller archive was housed at the Humboldt University in Berlin, rather than in Hanover. There was a university in Hanover, but it famously specialized in technology, which hadn't really been Gunter Keller's thing. The wisdom he had revelled in was ancient wisdom. He was someone who had never done anything other than go forward by looking back.

She was in her department head's office having a final discussion with him about the project prior to driving to Heathrow, when a call came through for her.

'I'm a Catholic priest named Thomas Gould. I'd like to speak with you about the monograph you wrote.'

She didn't really think she had anything useful about the monograph to discuss with a clergyman. He was probably just looking for an argument. And anyway, now wasn't the time.

'I'm leaving on an unscheduled trip,' she said. 'I'll have to contact you when I get back, Father Gould.'

That wasn't ideal, he said, sounding somewhat disgruntled. But he supposed it would have to do.

TEN

The school wasn't closed because of the sudden and, to Andrew Baxter, shocking death of popular teacher Mrs Bernadette Mahoney. It was closed because all the schools were closing until what they were calling the 'public health crisis' was resolved by the government. Though it was Handy Andy's personal opinion that it was the NHS which would resolve the crisis, rather than the ministers putting on frowns and their gravest voices delivering sound bites on the telly.

Bubonic plague was infectious. Andrew had studied the Black Death in a series of history lessons he'd really enjoyed. Some estimates claimed that 60 per cent of the world's population had perished. Whole villages and even towns had died. Crops had gone unharvested in the fields for lack of labourers to carry out the work. Basically, there'd been chaos, and it had taken the world's population 250 years to recover to pre-plague levels.

Bubonic plague was infectious. So was meningitis, if it was viral meningitis. But Andrew, for a fourteen-year-old boy, was a conscientious soul. He believed that good over bad was about actions rather than words. It was why he served on the altar. It was why he was going to knock on Sneaky Pete Jackson's grandfather's door this afternoon. Pete's mobile seemed to be off, which was understandable. There was his slightly weird twin sister, but Andrew wasn't even sure she had a phone – very weird when you thought about that. And of course, he didn't have a number for Pete's grandpa.

He'd asked his mum about visiting Pete, if he was successful in finding out which hospital he was in. And his mum had sat him down with a concerned look on her face and said that London's hospitals weren't particularly safe places just at that moment, even if Pete's meningitis wasn't viral.

Andrew had nodded. He got this. He wondered whether being a bit dirty encouraged diseases such as meningitis. Sneaky Pete's personal hygiene had been all over the place since the accident that killed his folks.

'Just find out what hospital and which ward he's on and send him a nice card,' Andrew's mum had said to her son. 'Something funny that will make him smile or chuckle. WH Smith do an excellent range and they're reasonable value.'

So here he now was, outside the house where he knew Pete Jackson lived with his gramps and his dippy twin sister, whose name he would have to remember in case she was the one who opened the door to him. And when she did open it in response to his knock she was pale and quite wide-eyed, wearing a large bandage on her bare right upper arm.

'Dawn,' Andrew said. 'What happened to you?'

'Handy Andy,' she said. Then, 'Dog bite.'

Andrew blushed at her use of the nickname. He said, 'You're quite tall. Must have been a big dog. Unless it jumped?'

'Great Dane,' she said. 'Like in *Scooby-Doo*.'

'Thought they were friendly,' he said, 'like in *Scooby-Doo*.'

She raised her eyes skywards in a gesture of exasperation. They were bright green eyes and, actually, very pretty. 'It's never the dogs, Andy. It's always the owners.'

Andrew nodded, more sagely than he felt. He didn't really know what she meant. The bandage had blood seeping through it. He remembered his own tetanus jab. The random thought came into his mind that most soldiers wounded in the Great War died of tetanus rather than the wound itself. Dirt got into them from the trench mud and it was full of bacteria.

'Why don't you come in for a minute? Tell me what it is you want.'

Dawn didn't speak like most fourteen-year-old girls Andrew knew. Her perfect grammar made her sound like someone older. She'd won the German prize at school two years running.

They went into the kitchen. It smelled stagnant from a fish tank Andrew saw was empty and slightly green with sediment. There was an unfinished model of HMS *Victory* on the table-top. Andrew knew that Sneaky Pete (who wasn't truthfully sneaky at all) always spent his requiem tips on Airfix kits.

'What's that noise?'

There was a rhythmic, booming sound coming from somewhere below them.

'Next door,' Dawn said. 'Remedial work. What do you want?'

Andrew didn't know what remedial meant. He just knew that next door's work sounded pretty close. He said, 'I'd like the name of the hospital and ward Pete's in. I want to send him a card.'

'Have you got the card on you?'

'Haven't bought it yet.'

'When you do, bring it round. I'll take it on my next visit, save you the postage.'

'That's kind of you, Dawn.'

'I know. I'm all heart.'

Except that Dawn didn't look all heart to Andrew. She looked shrewd and suspicious and maybe also slightly amused. She was also much easier on the eye than he'd ever previously noticed. Noticing now made it a bit difficult to concentrate. He was having the sort of thoughts about her he would end up having to confess to Father Gould.

'Terrible about Mrs Mahoney,' Andrew said.

'Tragic,' Dawn said. 'But she was quite overweight.'

There'd been a note about the death of Mrs Mahoney taped to the locked school gate that morning to the right of the notice announcing the school's closure. On it had been a xeroxed snapshot of the teacher. It had looked to Andrew like a holiday snap.

The remedial work, whatever that meant, continued. It sounded like one of those pneumatic hammers used by council workmen to pound pavements flat. Dawn hadn't sat, and Andrew hadn't been invited to do so. He didn't really want to be offered a cold drink from the fridge or a cup of tea or coffee. The kitchen had a sort of derelict look. And that fish tank smelled more rank the longer he stayed. And though Dawn was generally much more alluring than he remembered, the bandage oozing blood on her upper arm was undeniably gross.

There was a funny atmosphere in Pete and Dawn's grandpa's place. Though Andrew thought 'peculiar' a better word than 'funny'. It gave him a feeling he had only ever experienced when a fast lift descended from one of the upper floors of a tall building. It was a sinking feeling in the pit of his stomach that had him clenching his bum and his fists. It was uncomfortable, and he couldn't make it go away or stop. And he was beginning to feel confined in there. Trapped, even.

'I'd better go, Dawn. My mum's expecting me back.'

'Of course she is, Andy. Drop that card around at ten o'clock tomorrow morning, will you? WH Smith do a nice range and they open at eight a.m. so you'll have plenty of time to choose.'

'I'll just stick it through your letterbox. Don't really want to trouble you again.'

'Whatever.'

Dawn Jackson showed him to the door.

She closed it on him with a sigh. The Great Dane had been her brother Pete, who had moved with unexpected and ferocious speed in taking a chunk out of her right bicep and then swallowing the flesh. She'd managed to lure him into the cellar afterwards only by dangling a raw lump of beefsteak and walking backwards down the stairs in case he pounced again.

She'd dropped the meat on to the cellar floor. He'd dropped on to all fours to eat it and she'd yanked out a hank of his hair, which he hadn't even seemed to notice. Then, as he ate, she'd barricaded the cellar door with a chair, its back wedged under the doorknob.

She'd still had that hank of her dead brother's hair in her hand when Handy Andy knocked, on his touching quest to earn a bit of breathing space from damnation. He was an altar boy like her brother had been, and so of course went in for all that pious crap. Though she was now totally convinced that Pete had been bang to rights about bringing people back without a soul. At best, they were disappointingly incomplete.

Now she went to get the hair from where she'd hastily hidden it, in an unused sugar bowl in the cupboard. She was going to burn it and recite the spell that caused people to lose parts of their body. That bite was going to cost her brother his head. That was her intention, anyway. Pete might carry on living, headless, as the Freddy precedent had proven was possible. But headless, he wouldn't be able to bite her again.

It was all a bit of a bore, Dawn thought; the novelty of magic wore off rather rapidly. There were unexpected repercussions. That said, she was a bit like a learner driver at the wheel of a car, wasn't she? The perfect three-point-turn or precise angle necessary for parallel parking came only with practice. And she was buoyed by the death of Mrs Mahoney. But for the two-paracetamol headache after singing the deadly lullaby and the accompanying feeling of weariness, that, she considered, had been completely and utterly cool.

She went to fetch the book from the place where she now habitually hid it. Once she'd performed the lopping-off spell, she'd look for another that would heal her bitten arm. It was throbbing and still oozing blood under the bandage. And she was running a temperature that would only get higher without intervention. The wound was infected. But she was confident that the book would work much more quickly than a course of antibiotics.

ELEVEN

Juliet reached her hotel room at just after nine thirty in the evening. She ordered a room service dinner and bottle of lager to wash it down with. Her preferred tipple was white wine, her habitual choice Chablis, but she needed a clear head the following morning, not the self-inflicted handicap of a hangover. And the Germans did happen to do lager rather well.

She switched on the TV and tuned it to Sky News in English. Pockets of rioting had broken out in London. There'd been a sprinkling of arson attacks on shops and cars, and some looting. Juliet didn't think this an Augury. This was just the response of a frightened and frustrated population to events over which they had no control and for which they could find no rational explanation. It was an unhelpful response, but rioters were disinclined to see things that way.

The rioting wasn't an Augury. But Juliet thought that what had impeded the rioting – and then stopped it altogether – was. A fog had covered London. It had spread as far as those parts of Surrey nearest the capital. It was thick and noxious, a dirty yellowish colour, sulphurous and choking, almost like a chemical spillage, the news reporter was saying into a microphone from behind the handkerchief tied bandit-fashion around the lower half of his face.

Meteorologically, it was so far inexplicable. It hadn't descended on the city. Witnesses to the start of it were saying it had ascended, and spread, from the river.

Juliet had been lucky. All flights from London City and Heathrow and Gatwick had now been grounded indefinitely. She'd felt quite alone before hearing that, in the cab taking her from the airport to her hotel. But hearing it now increased her sense of isolation still further.

What fresh calamity would follow the fog once it lifted? How long would it take for people generally to start linking these weird phenomena with the toll on human lives that followed? The bad news was that fifty-six of the plague outbreak victims had died. The good news was that the rest were responding to treatment and the epidemiologists had the spread under control. But at a price, in that the whole of Whitechapel had been quarantined. There was now no getting in – or out – of one of the most vibrant and prosperous areas of the capital.

There was already an End Times character to what some of the more prominent clergy, particularly the evangelicals, were saying publicly. And people were leaving London. Nobody could say accurately how many had gone. But the tube trains and buses rolled along empty. Work absenteeism had risen by 40 per cent. Tourists were cancelling by the thousands, maybe by the millions. Plague outbreaks and sightseeing didn't exactly go hand in hand. The only people readily taking to the streets now, it seemed, were those intent on mischief.

Two hours after seeing that first bulletin Juliet got into bed, more tired than she could ever remember having felt before. She thought about the following morning and the Keller archive. Her own German was pretty rudimentary, but they were sending along a German national who worked at the British Embassy to translate for her. Half of what Keller had written had been done in Latin. But this translator was an expert linguist. She hoped he was also a nice man, someone easy to get along with. She'd had enough over the past eighteen months of fractious men such as Martin fucking Doyle.

Just before she fell asleep, Juliet's last conscious thought concerned the *Marchioness* disaster. She'd been six years old when that occurred but still remembered the anguished mood of the time, the outpouring of public grief and widespread anger and bewilderment. She'd been at school then in Wandsworth. She thought about that seven-year-old boy, Joshua Porter, aboard the *Esmeralda*. She thought about an A&E department swamped with the sick and dying. And she wondered what would next befall the capital, unable to guess but gloomily sure that it would be something terrible.

Just what that was, she discovered the following morning as soon as she woke and tuned into Sky News. The fog had cleared, so the carnage at the scene was vividly apparent through the camera lens in a chilling tracking shot and then a devastating close-up. Because of the fog, the riots had petered out the previous

evening. But it would not now be remembered for that. All flights
out of the region's airports had been grounded. But there were
still the incoming flights, and one of those hadn't turned back.

Something had gone wrong with the aircraft's electronics, and
communication with it from the ground hadn't been possible.
Perhaps it hadn't had the fuel to turn back by the point in its
flight when the fault was discovered. Probably continuing on its
journey had been a calculated gamble. If so, it was a gamble that
hadn't paid off.

The aircraft was a 747, a Jumbo Jet. It had strayed off course
and descended too low. Without a fully functioning flight
computer, the pilot must have flown into the fog completely blind.
At least the passengers would have had no warning, Juliet
reasoned. At least there would have been no fear or panic, or even
any trepidation, before that moment of colossal impact.

Flight 201 from Chicago had crashed into the Thames Barrier.
The aircraft and the central section of the barrier were both virtually unrecognizable as what they'd been. The area now was just a
tangle of metal and flung debris, still smoking from the inferno
of flame sparked by the collision. The shiny metal of the barrier
– where it still stood – was smoke-blackened, despoiled, like huge,
rotten teeth, giant human molars gaping out of the water.

'A flood will follow,' Juliet said to the TV. It was early summer,
June, and the English weather was predictably fine, but if the
curious, petulant, profoundly self-interested soul using the Almanac
continued to do so, she thought, the rains would come, and they'd
persist. The tide would surge and London would drown, consumed
by water. And people would drown, and those that didn't drown
would panic and it would seem with this litany of catastrophe that
the End Times really were upon them. And prophecies were self-
fulfilling, weren't they?

She switched off the TV and showered and dressed casually. She
had an early breakfast meeting with Paul Beck, her translator.
She would brief him fully on what it was they were looking for.

When she got to the café that was their rendezvous point and
first shared destination, it had only just opened and there was a
solitary customer, a rangy man of about thirty, sunglasses pushed
up into his longish blond hair and wearing a leather jacket and
jeans and a pair of engineer boots. She thought a professional

footballer or track athlete, one who would have no trouble attracting the advertising endorsements. She looked at her wristwatch. Her embassy translator was late. It wasn't an auspicious start.

Until the blond man got up from his table and strolled across to her smiling. He held out his hand to shake hers in formal greeting and introduced himself as Paul Beck.

TWELVE

Provisionally, they'd said that her school would reopen a week after the plague outbreak that had closed all London schools. On this basis, Dawn Jackson realized that she needed to take a break from the book of spells she had discovered in her grandfather's attic. She had English literature essays to write on the fiction of C.S. Lewis and Robert Louis Stevenson. She had a maths paper to prepare for, the specific subject geometry. A vocabulary test had been scheduled in Spanish, a language with far fewer words than English boasted, but a subject she had rather neglected. She was proud of being a part of the school's Special Study Group and didn't want to jeopardize that status.

Her private thinking on the Narnia books was that they were sentimental slop and that *Treasure Island* wasn't very much better, Long John Silver too much of a wuss to be a proper pirate. But the public Dawn would enthuse about these works rather than confound her teacher's expectations. Trial and error had taught her that people generally were too soft-hearted to respond well to what they saw as negativity.

She hadn't visited the cellar since completing the lopping-off spell intended to prevent her dead brother from being able to bite her again. She had successfully restored her arm to how it had been before. The headache afterwards had been relatively minor and the fatigue only a dull and temporary ache. She had stolen down to the cellar door and heard scuttling movement, so assumed he was still animate in some way. But the hammering at the door had stopped completely.

There was food down there. Dawn assumed this was as a

consequence of her grandpa's having lived as a young child through the Second World War. He had experienced rationing and this, at an impressionable age, had made him a hoarder in adulthood. There were cans of boiled ham and corned beef and sardines and pilchards down there, the sort of vile produce old people ate. And there were piled pallets of bottles of bitter lemon and lemonade. Probably past their sell-by dates. And quite how someone without a head would eat, Dawn didn't really know. But the scuttling sounds from behind the cellar door suggested that what remained of Pete was surviving, at least for the time being. And no longer trying to get out, which was a relief. After seeing what became of Freddy the terrapin, she really didn't want to see what had become now of her brother.

Had she made him a monster? She thought that she probably had. But she'd put the silent kitchen-table rebuke of his unfinished Airfix model in the bin and felt much better for no longer having to look at it.

She'd had to chuck away the get-well card duly delivered by Handy Andy Baxter first thing that morning. That too had given her guilt pangs about Pete and what she'd done to him. She'd shot him only on a whim, out of curiosity to see just how powerful the spell book was. He hadn't been the perfect brother, he'd been too dull intellectually to be that. But he'd been company, however lacklustre, and with Grandpa gone she felt alone in a way that didn't feel terribly pleasant.

There was a passage long enough to register as a chapter in the spell book about *making* a companion. It was a bit vague about the shape this companion would take and not terribly clear as to its actual origin. Or its character. Or, to be honest, its intentions once you brought it into the world. Despite the setbacks with Freddy and Pete, Dawn remained optimistic. Her arm had healed completely and without apparent side effects. Mrs Mahoney had died neatly and emphatically in her sleep as planned. The pros and cons were probably, so far at least, about even.

Dawn had noticed that London had recently become rather accident prone. Because she absolutely wasn't on the spectrum, because she took an interest in the exterior world, she was aware of the *Esmeralda* tragedy. She'd taken an interest in the plague outbreak. The Jumbo air crash was all over the news. In a sense, these events provided welcome distractions. They preoccupied people generally. In this climate, questions about her brother's continued absenteeism were not going to be at the forefront of the meddlers' minds when school reopened.

With less to distract them, she thought that the neighbours might have noticed by now that her grandfather no longer seemed to be around. In ordinary circumstances, she thought that a social worker might have knocked on the door as the consequence of a tip-off. But the circumstances were far from ordinary and personally, Dawn felt grateful for that.

She went out and paid for a thick sheet of polythene and a role of strong adhesive tape from a hardware store. She very carefully wrapped the spell book when she got home. Then she fetched a spade from the garden shed and dug a hole at the centre of the lawn her grandfather had so assiduously tended before his death. She dug to a depth of about two feet and tamped the base of the hole flat, placed the book in it and filled the hole in.

Dawn had been careful to cut and roll back the turf rather than damage it with the spade, so that when she replaced it, only a slight depression in the ground at the spot signalled that anything had been done there at all.

Dawn didn't feel denuded of power, as she'd expected to, in the absence of the spell book. This was because she now knew some of her favourite spells by heart and didn't need a prompt or reference to put them into effect. Should it become necessary to blind someone or have someone die in their sleep, she could do that now entirely independent of the book.

There was one slight anomaly she hadn't understood. After she had shot her brother dead and was seated on the floor in front of his corpse studying the ritual that would revive him, he'd suddenly and quite spontaneously started to writhe like an eel, his limbs sort of juddering and breath whistling out of his dead lungs. It had stopped after less than a minute, this movement, but had still struck her as strange.

And then she'd remembered the phenomenon of the unrestful dead and what had happened at the graveside at the funeral at which Pete had served. This happened around corpses when you'd been in contact with the book. Like radioactivity or something.

Her school was a small one and all the pupils above the age of twelve had been invited to attend Mrs Mahoney's funeral. In ordinary circumstances, Dawn would have gone. She liked funerals. Grief wasn't supposed to be a spectator sport, but she enjoyed seeing those ungovernable outpourings of emotion loss provoked. They were strange and interesting.

She'd have to give this one a miss, though. She didn't want to provoke Mrs Mahoney into dancing in her coffin like Beyoncé did onstage. It wasn't something suited to the occasion. Funerals were supposed to be dignified, even solemn, events.

Dawn got the TV remote and turned the news channel on. They were starting to release the names of some of the passengers who'd died aboard the crashed Jumbo. They included an eighty-strong child choir on their way to St Paul's Cathedral for some sort of religious festival. One pundit said it was the sort of occurrence that made people doubt their faith.

Dawn could not remember ever having had any faith to doubt. Though having magic demonstrably proven to her as something real and even practical had recently made her think hard about matters beyond the physical world. Intellectually, she understood the concepts of good and bad. But she honestly had more of an interest in what was achievable and what wasn't.

Magic was tricky. She'd already had a couple of setbacks. But her car-driver analogy held true. Even a Grand Prix champion started at the beginning with L-plates and an instructor.

She would become better and, eventually, she would become an expert. It would become second nature and then would transform into instinct and when that happened, she'd have the world at her feet. And by then, it would be a world she'd be shaping.

But for now, it was revision. She switched off the TV. She went and got her school bag and took it into the kitchen and sat at the table, thinking she ought to empty that smelly fish tank. There was a clatter from the bottom of the stairs as her brother, presumably unseeing now, collided with a pile of cans of something in the cellar. She could empty the fish tank later. The smell was tolerable, for now. She rummaged in her bag for her Spanish grammar and then opened it with a sigh.

THIRTEEN

The Keller archive was kept under lock and key. Pages almost 500 years old were fragile. They had to be handled in a sterile environment and wearing cotton gloves so that secretions from the pads of a person's fingers didn't damage them. It didn't contain the stuff that had sent him to the stake. That had been torn to shreds and thrown like heretical confetti on to the bunched faggots at his feet as the fire that would consume him began to take hold and he roared curses at his judge and executioners, at the jeering hoard of onlookers, on the country that had condemned him and on Lower Saxony's statutes and its principles and its religious convictions.

Keller's death was not delivered quickly. Earlier rain had dampened the wood fuelling the flames. Witnesses said the whole bottom half of him had burned away before he finally succumbed a full hour after the pyre was first lit.

This was interpreted in contemporary accounts as God's doing, and as only an earthly precursor to the suffering Keller the heretic would endure in hell. It seemed he hadn't been merely unpopular so much as enthusiastically loathed. In the unlikely event that his trial had resulted in an acquittal, it was Juliet Harrington's considered opinion that he would have been publicly lynched, torn limb from limb or trampled by an angry mob in the street.

There were parchment-covered notebooks in the archive and they were obviously incriminatory, because they were written in the style favoured at the time by men with rebellious intellects: in code. There was a sketch-book with larger pages and those pages were covered in diagrams and tables and mathematical calculations.

The biggest item was ledger-sized and about fifty pages long. It was handwritten in Latin and Paul Beck pored over it for about half an hour as Juliet sat beside him unwilling to interrupt his study or break his concentration.

Eventually he turned to her, closing the big, thick, leather-bound volume with a small, dusty thud. Everything in the room bar the archive was a pristine white – walls, floor, furniture. The air conditioning was a frigid hum. When Paul spoke, the acoustics made his voice crystalline. And it was 'Paul'; he'd insisted in the café on Christian names, on an un-embassy-like absence of formal protocol. Juliet had liked him from the moment he spoke, insisting on buying her breakfast. 'A big breakfast,' he'd said. 'I suspect we're in for a long day. And we'll need our brains on full alert. High stakes, right?'

'I don't think they could be any higher, Paul,' she'd said.

His English was idiomatic, unaccented. She'd put this down to his linguistic expertise.

Now he said, 'This is a sort of diary, or journal. I think the only reason it isn't codified too is the word-volume. That sort of discretion with this quantity of material would have taken up too much of his time. So he took a risk with it, which is to our benefit. I can read this fluently and, if you like, I can read it aloud.'

Juliet nodded at the codified notebooks. 'What about them?'

'We'll get to them. I'm quite good at code breaking. Not Bletchley Park standard, but not too shabby.'

'You speak English perfectly.'

He grinned at that. 'German national with an English mum. Contrary to Aryan mythology, it's from her I got the blond hair and the blue eyes.'

'And the code-breaking skills?'

'A maternal grandmother who *did* work at Bletchley Park. Alan Turing quite rightly gets the plaudits, but most of the staff there were Oxbridge-educated women. Anyway, if I can't crack Gunter Keller's code, we've a specialist at the embassy who can. But one thing at a time, Juliet. Let's start with the journal.'

Paul Beck was reminding Juliet Harrington powerfully of just how much she'd enjoyed the company of men before her marriage break-up disillusioned her. If his intellect was an asset, his looks were a terrific bonus. It was early days, obviously, but she liked his character too, the bit she'd so far got to know of it. There was bound to be a partner. Children too, probably, if he was straight. But the significant thing was that she thought he was someone she was going to enjoy working with.

'He starts off in the spring of 1528, so a full two years before what you believe to be the publication date of the *Almanac of Forbidden Wisdom*. He's living in Hanover, struggling, he says, with poverty. He's above the breadline, but not by much. He's twenty-nine years old and claims to be working as an apothecary. But he wouldn't admit to alchemy, because alchemy was stigmatized in that place and at that time as little better than witchcraft.

'I'd say, judging from his grammar and vocabulary, that he's self-educated. He's intellectually arrogant and writes as if he believes the world owes him a living. Socially, with or without justification, he's a snob. He makes no mention of women socially and comes across as fairly indifferent to your gender, so perhaps he's asexual. Shall I begin?'

'Be my guest,' Juliet said, settling back into her white-painted hardwood chair.

FOURTEEN

Hanover, April 10, 1528

The commission comes from an English nobleman of financial means so vast they are almost incalculable. His interest in matters esoteric is already impressively learned for an amateur. His ambition, though, is quite breathtaking. He seeks to combine every proven magical rite, ritual and formula in a single volume. Such a book has never existed in the modern world. Not since ancient times, before the destruction of the Library of Alexandria, has the world been able to boast of anything approaching this. Not since Alexandria, or perhaps Thebes, has there existed such an ambitious accumulation of secret and powerful knowledge.

It is to be forged by several practitioners working as one, each of them eminent in his or her own right. I know all of them by reputation but for the English soothsayer Mary Nye. My new patron vouches for her personally, having availed himself twice of talents he insists are genuine.

The practice of magic exacts a heavy toll. There is a price to be paid for every successful spell. Man cannot confound the natural order without nature exacting a kind of revenge or retribution, sometimes with savage consequence. The more successful the magic, the greater the consequence, a paradox with which my noble new master is familiar.

When this almanac is completed, its power will be enormous. But that power will also be inert until its pages are put to practical use. I will endeavour to make it as potent as possible in the belief that it can fulfil my own secret and heartfelt ambition.

It is my great desire to bring about the End Times. I wish to provoke the apocalypse. The Christian world perpetuates a cruel intellectual and physical tyranny I wish to see destroyed utterly. The triumph of Lucifer predicted in the Bible can be orchestrated, encouraged, brought about more swiftly than fate intends. If I succeed, mankind's greatest achievement will be mine. And minds and spirits like my own will be ungoverned and free and, crucially, free of the fear that haunts and censors and persecutes us.

That sounds boastful, I know. But I speak as a man who five years ago defied mortality. I perfected a ritual in which the essence of a man – his spoor – can return him to life after death. I succeeded in doing this with a wealthy merchant, the recently drowned master of a Baltic fishing fleet. But he returned requiring a human host from which to feed. And he was able to summon his dead wife and brother, and even his dead son, out of the ground in a spectral contagion which outraged people and was described by them as a plague of the dead.

One by one, these mortal miracles which I had gifted with a second life were destroyed. For several months I was the subject of suspicion, of pointed fingers and barely veiled hostility. But when it was put to me that I had dabbled in the Devil's work, I simply denied it and demanded that my accusers either desist or demonstrate proof. 'Only God has the power to endow life,' I said. 'To suggest otherwise is blasphemy.'

And thus were my accusers silenced. For blasphemy is a grave offence which earns a brutal punishment.

I am not so boastful or deluded as to claim that the dead recalled by my ritual were perfect specimens. They came back with crude appetites. They had a rank odour about them no amount of bathing could sluice away. They could be cruel and furtive. They were greedy for the company of their own kind.

It was said by the people of my restored merchant's village on the Baltic coast that they were like this because they possessed no souls. A nonsense, this, a belief no better than the crude witch-craft of charms and familiars. I am a scientist. If I push at the boundaries of the possible, it is because that is where my talents and inclinations lie. Without men like me in the world, there is no possibility of progress.

The biggest impediment to progress is the Church. It is the yoke which hinders scientific advancement. That magic can reduce it to ashes and unlamented memory is the great irony of our age. But it can be done. This book is my vehicle for bringing it about. There will never be a better opportunity.

There is much work to be done before its completion, of course. I must list and collate and continue to experiment. I am still accu-mulating knowledge, still working on perfecting my formulae and methodology. It will take at least a year to gather together every-thing I need to make my crucial, influential, perhaps defining contribution to this almanac, to this great and noble project.

My blue-blooded English patron has dispatched his emissary with the generous funds which will put paid in gold to this scrimping life I've wished so ardently, for so long, to escape entirely.

That wish is about to come true. Already, I am grateful and energized by this new direction and prosperity. It will enable me to buy the costly materials for my experimentation.

This changed state of affairs will not breed any carelessness in me. I very well appreciate that there are spies and informers everywhere and that I am already the subject of much suspicion. Everything must be done discreetly, even clandestinely. But secrecy is a habit I mastered a long time ago. Discretion to men like me is life and death. Sometimes I dream about the manacles glowing white hot around my burning wrists as the pyre rages with my poor body bound against the stake at its centre. It is not a fate I wish to encourage through arrogance or carelessness.

I am debating with myself whether to include my greatest scientific achievement in the almanac of which there is no doubt that I will be the principal architect. A part of me wishes to keep that knowledge for myself alone. But there is no question that if someone were actually to conjure what I conjured briefly just weeks ago, it would accelerate the process of bringing about the End Times.

The ritual itself is surprisingly simple. It is only a slight exaggeration to say that a child could do it. But a child could not undo it, as I managed to only after the most prodigious and exhausting struggle. Every ounce of my occult ingenuity was used in what our Arabian friends of a few centuries ago would have termed 'putting the genie back into the bottle'. It was the most difficult experience I have ever undergone, and I believe it came close to costing me my life.

I created a creature from nothing. Unless I coaxed it out of the dreamscape, that abstract dimension that exists just beyond our five senses. But it was born with the most ferocious hunger, the most appalling appetite. And it grew with venomous speed.

Was it a monster, coaxed from our deepest common fears, made corporeal only by a combination of will and enchantment? Was it something transported from the stars by my spell? I do not know. I do know that I felt a shift, a shudder through the universe, in reaction to a man doing the business of a god. I might have felt the wrath of our Creator, scolded from the very Heavens for doing something no one human should. No matter. I am here to tell the tale.

I am to meet my new patron's emissary in a few days, when he has crossed the German Sea carrying the purse he will present to me. The signal that he has arrived will be a small brass tack newly pressed into the wood of my front door. I am embarrassed about the hovel in which circumstance has obliged me to live and would rather he did not see it, even from the outside. I was reluctant to give my address to the baron in our clandestine correspondence. But how else will his man find me without the spies being party to our meeting?

On the evening of the day the tack is pressed home I am to meet this emissary at a tavern where neither of us is known. Care and discretion are essential in such matters. Greatness summons me. Perhaps a kind of immortality. On the one hand, that sounds like nothing more than the hot air of a braggart. On the other, thoughts like those are useful in giving me purpose and calming nerves the pointing fingers have left badly frayed.

FIFTEEN

Juliet's mobile rang. Paul got up to get a drink from the water cooler in the corner. Her caller was the Home Secretary.

'How are you getting on? Any progress?'

'Not really. Gunter Keller really liked the sound of his own voice. A lot of hot air and bragging about one spell in particular that seems to have affronted nature.'

'What did he do?'

'He claims to have created a life. Sounds like he conjured something demonic.'

'Things have rather escalated this morning, professor. The Foreign Secretary has gone public on a theory that the plague outbreak and the miasmic fog were deliberate acts of aggression carried out by a foreign power.'

'Sounds a lot more plausible than the Almanac.'

'That's the problem. Despite zero evidence, it sounds extremely plausible.'

'Which foreign power?'

'I'm sure you can guess that without any hints from me.'

'What's been the reaction?'

'Immediate and emphatic calls for retaliation. They've broken off diplomatic relations. A majority of the population here is extremely angry. The Americans have weighed in rather heavily. Two hundred and seventy of the three hundred and fifty fatalities when that aircraft obliterated the central section of the Thames Barrier were their citizens, eighty of them twelve-year-old children from a Chicago choir. Their parents are naturally anguished.'

'Anything else?'

'As it happens, yes. It's raining here. Heavily. And we're expecting the highest tide of the year. The army are sandbagging buildings. We look like we're at war already, which we're not, but no one is ruling out the possibility that we may be quite soon.'

'If London floods, people can hardly blame the Russians.'

'On the contrary. If it hadn't been for the fog they're being blamed for, we'd still have a flood barrier.'

For no reason she could really have explained, Juliet then remembered the cold-calling Catholic priest, Father Thomas Gould. Perhaps she remembered him because just at that moment, it seemed a miracle was needed. And not a miracle like those of which Gunter Keller routinely boasted.

'How are you getting along with our embassy Adonis?'

'Companionably.'

'I'm sure.'

'I'll call you just as soon as we come across something of practical use.'

'Practical magic,' he said. 'Not a phrase I ever thought I'd use.'

She ended the call. Paul was still over by the water cooler, sipping his second or third helping from a conical paper cup. They didn't hold much and clearly reading aloud had made him thirsty. She told him about the escalation in London.

He was quiet for a moment. Then he dropped the cup into the pedal bin at his feet. He said, 'Five hundred years after his grisly execution, Gunter Keller finally gets his apocalypse.'

'Diplomacy has usually worked in the past.'

'Not in 1914. And not in 1939. And they've all got bigger toys now to throw out of their prams.'

'What are you making of Keller?'

'Either seriously deluded, or very much the real deal. I'd bet there's something in the chronicles about the plague of the dead in that Baltic village. That doesn't sound like a bundle of laughs.'

'For all his talk of caution, his occult dabbling was extremely reckless.'

'Drunk on power?'

Juliet shook her head slowly. 'His agenda,' she said. 'The greater the volatility, the more significant the reverberations, the closer he believed he got to triggering the End Times.'

'And the Almanac is his best shot.'

'He's being well paid for compiling it too. From Keller's perspective, what's not to like?'

May 15, 1528

I am to travel south to meet the Spanish sorceress Cordelia Cortez. She has agreed to give a demonstration of her powers, her worthiness, if you will, to qualify as a contributor to the *Almanac of Forbidden Wisdom*. Her skills are predominantly aquatic, or in her own phraseology, oceanic. Or so she claims. We shall see.

My new English patron employs a network of agents, emissaries, couriers and mercenary men-at-arms throughout Europe. Thus have I been able to communicate efficiently with the woman. She is a great beauty, by common account, which will impress me not in the slightest since I have never been remotely moved by the pleasures of the flesh. More impressive is her claim that if I wear the amulet she has sent me, my voyage across the seas to Spain will be entirely without hazard. Since she resides on the Atlantic coast, this is a comfort to me. The Atlantic is a treacherous wilderness of water to a non-sailor such as I.

Cortez is of noble birth, a countess who lives in a marble palace built on a high promontory where she can entertain herself with the endless briny vistas to be seen from its balconies. Her powers, however authentic, are a well-kept secret, of course. Spain is a papist country and her title would not protect her were it to be whispered in Church circles that she is an occult practitioner. She would be put to the torture. At the conclusion of that ordeal, once a confession had been extracted from her by her expert interrogators, she would hang, or more likely burn.

Even a few weeks ago a journey such as I am about to undertake would have been inconceivable to me. I would not have had the means to charter a craft. I would have been too ashamed of my mean and shabby attire. I would have possessed no motive to forge an alliance with someone else with esoteric skills. Probably I would have seen them as a rival or a threat. But the Almanac can only be realized to its fullest potential if the most powerful practitioners in Europe unite in order to achieve it.

The amulet is gold and exquisitely engraved with an image of a sea serpent coiled around the hull and rigging of a warship. This symbolic beast is gigantic. Its scales do not look as though cannon fire would penetrate. I believe the vessel in the engraving to be doomed. It is an odd sort of charm, perhaps an ironic pun, but

I am inclined to believe the claim made by the countess that it
will keep me safe. Why otherwise would she risk its loss at sea?
It is heavy and ornate and unique. It must be very valuable.

June 16, 1528

I am newly returned from my journey to Spain. I was the guest
of the countess for three eventful days. She was a gracious hostess.
We communicated in Latin. She was better read than I imagine
most women are and better informed about events internationally.
She was bold for her sex in the sense that she was more forthright
in expressing opinions than any other woman I have met. Not that
I have known, or cared to know, very many.

She exercised the necessary discretion when her staff were
present. In my presence alone, she performed a spell in which the
flow from the spout of a pump drawing well water in her palace
grounds became a solid pillar of ice. On a sweltering summer day,
this was an impressive trick.

She told me that she could drown a man on dry land, achieving
this as he lay in his bed by inflicting a dream upon his sleeping
mind in which the victim is engulfed in water. She told me a priest
who'd accused her of witchcraft had died this way before having
the opportunity of making the accusation public. But of course, I
saw no proof that she could genuinely do what she claimed in this
regard.

I saw her reverse the flow of a stream. I saw her step across a
deep drainage ditch as though its surface were as solid as glass.
She explained to me that this was possible because she was practised at levitation. So, on the second evening, I challenged her to
step off the exterior balcony on the uppermost floor of her palace,
which she did without hesitation or mishap, hovering, suspended,
supported by nothing more solid than the air invisible in the void
beneath her expensively shod feet.

She saved the best until last, and the final evening of my stay,
when she invited me to take a walk with her on the clifftop not
far from her home. I anticipated more of the levitation, but was
mistaken in this assumption.

The sun was setting out over the sea. The orb was crimson and the water like fire or blood, reflecting it. The surface was calm, cleaved only by a single vessel perhaps half a mile distant from the spot at which we stood. My nautical knowledge is scant, my maritime ignorance almost total, but this boat or ship may have been a privateer, because I was sufficiently keen-eyed to see that it was armed with cannon.

I half expected then to see the great leviathan engraved on her amulet rise in life from the depths and embrace this vessel in destruction. But that did not happen. I was, I confess, profoundly unprepared for what did.

The countess stood close to the cliff edge and brought out her hands stretched to either side of her like a bird about to take wing. She choked out sounds in a voice I would not have recognized as hers. Then she raised, or rather jerked both arms upward with a speed which suggested that the movement was less willed by her than compelled by some exterior force.

A grey cloud in the sky above the boat shaped a pointed finger of vapour which reached downward towards the sea. And the sea rose to greet it in a glittering, gaseous pillar till the elements met and merged in a great, spinning waterspout that shrieked aloud as its base hit the boat and the boat was plucked upward, perhaps a hundred feet, before crashing back down and disappearing beneath a litter of debris made by its own shattered timbers.

I turned to my hostess, who looked exultant at what she had accomplished.

'You have impressive powers, my lady,' I felt obliged to remark.

'They come only at a price,' she told me.

And I believe that price was paid two days later, when it was reported that a coastal village only a league or so away from the spot at which we stood was overwhelmed by a tidal wave. The destruction wrought was complete. Not a man, woman or child survived the deluge. Ninety innocent souls. But true magic always takes its toll and it was proof that I wasn't charmed or hypnotized by a guileful fraud. I witnessed what I did in Spain only because it really occurred.

Before we parted I asked her why a woman with her worldly riches wished to participate in our joint quest. I knew it could not be for mere money.

She looked at me, pale-skinned, obsidian-eyed, cold under the straight black helm of her hair, a slender and imperious woman exuding a powerful sense of wilful cruelty. Not barbaric, this, but quite the opposite. Cultured and refined. She said, 'I want to put my tilt upon the world, Herr Keller.' She smiled then and glanced beyond me, seeing the future. 'I suspect I wish to achieve the same consequence you do.' I merely nodded in reply. Words were unnecessary. The accord was quite plain, our ambition entirely shared.

SIXTEEN

July 30, 1528

My travels have taken me recently to the Tyrol, where the demonstration I witnessed was organized in circumstances of needful secrecy by the black magician Lorenz Hood. Hood lives in thrall to Lucifer, from whom he gains those baleful insights that enable him to formulate his potent spells. The spells themselves have a solid methodology which means that, in theory, they can be practised by anyone literate and disciplined enough to enact their rituals and recite their liturgy.

But this is never the story in its entirety. Experience has taught me that in the same way some religious preachers have great power, so do some practitioners have more capacity for magic than others. There is no word for this talent in any language I have come across. It is the occult equivalent of divinity. Hood has it, the price he might yet pay for it eternal damnation. But the man I met in the village where he lives in happy anonymity seemed in no mood for repentance.

He is aged about forty, broad-shouldered and well over six feet tall, and resembles a man-at-arms more than he does a spell-master. He is taciturn and a dour demeanour masks a mordant wit expressed in exaggeratedly pessimistic remarks.

I arrived at his door late, well after darkness had fallen. We supped at his generous enough table and he asked me questions about the commission, which evidently intrigued him. Mulling over my answers he fell silent. With strong fingers he tore a chunk from the loaf of black bread on its platter between us and chewed thoughtfully.

Eventually he said, 'Are you as fit and agile as you look, Keller?'

Only for a few recent weeks had I been able to eat and drink on the basis of choice, rather than necessity. But I am not by nature an indulgent man physically.

'I'm fit enough,' I answered.

'Have you a head for heights?'

'I'm an alchemist, Hood, not a steeplejack.'

'We need to reach the snowline.'

'The snowline's high at this time of year.'

He made a face at that. 'More of a scramble than a climb,' he said. 'And Hannibal crossed the Alps with elephants.'

'I've always had trouble believing that.'

'Tread carefully tomorrow, Keller.'

'What do you intend to do?'

'I intend to revive a corpse.' He grinned. 'Take care on the mountain. I don't want it to be yours.'

'Your concern for me is touching,' I said.

'My concern is for the Almanac and your Englishman's purse,' he said.

We set off at first light the following morning. Hood believes that magic is always more potent practised in darkness and I think that true enough. But making this attempt without daylight would have been self-murder. The route was difficult, hazardous and in some places dizzying. And the little I knew about mountains included the advice that coming down is more dangerous than going up. By then you are both fatigued and confident, a sometimes disastrous combination.

We had the higher slopes entirely to ourselves and climbed towards the snowline wordlessly in solitude. As we ascended in altitude and the air thinned I needed all my energy just to breathe.

It was obvious to me that my companion was familiar with the route we travelled. He was completely sure-footed and unhesitating. He did not look for handholds where we needed them; he knew from experience and habit where they were.

The first snow we encountered was in truth slush, heated by the rays of the summer sun and hard going in the boots Hood had lent me, which were of heavy leather and hobnailed and only slightly too big. Then we came to proper snow and the going became easier, the surface more solid underfoot, though dazzlingly white when I looked up from under the brim of my hat.

We reached a shallow dip or gully, the snow deeper here, and something about his posture told me we had arrived at where Hood had wanted to get to. He sat astride a boulder and wiped sweat from his brow with his sleeve. Then he took out a flask and wrenched out the cork stopper with his teeth and offered it to me. It was cognac. I took a swallow and then scooped snow up from the ground to slake my thirst.

Hood nodded towards an arrangement of stones that looked composed by man rather than by nature. They would have attracted the attention of a curious soul, but none ascended this high. This was Lorenz Hood's private place of mischief. It was his desolate domain. What he did here had gone unwitnessed, I was sure, until now.

The previous evening, I had told him about my own efforts at the revival of the dead and he had grunted, unimpressed.

'Haphazard,' he'd said. 'Much can go wrong with such an approach.'

'Much did,' I confessed.

Now he shaped the stone markers into a small cairn a few feet from where they'd lain and then reached around in the snow that had been beneath them, scooping until he revealed a pair of feet shod in clogs. Small feet; those of either a woman or a child.

Hood grabbed the ankles and simultaneously grunted and hauled. And a woman was revealed, snow powdering her clothing and making rigid her blond hair. She was slender and comely and emphatically dead and, though bare-headed, was clothed in the black and white habit of a nun.

Three things had made themselves immediately apparent to me. The first was that the snow had preserved the inanimate corpse. The second was that this young woman had died, abducted from her priory, at Lorenz Hood's hands. The third was that he came up here to pleasure himself physically at her expense.

He sat her up to work his spell. She was long past rigor, but the cold to which her body was subjected kept her torso rigid. She was warming quickly, though, the snow in her lashes and her hair crystalline and prismatic with vibrant colour in the high sunlight.

Hood sprinkled his victim with a small quantity of light powder from a drawstring purse he produced with the rapid sleight-of-hand skill I would more usually associate with an illusionist. He recited his spell.

The young nun's eyes snapped open. Comprehension dawned in her expression, which then registered dismay that was transformed into dawning horror. She choked out a sob and whispered, 'God help me.'

'Too late for that,' Hood said, laughing. He quickly reversed his spell and the corpse, warm now, slumped sideways. He buried her again and put back the stones that signalled the spot.

'Is there any point,' I said, 'in returning someone to life so reluctant to live?'

'It might seem a contradiction,' Hood admitted. 'But it's an art that requires a degree of practice and the sister provides that. And coming up here once a week in the summer months conditions me. I enjoy the solitude on the route.'

'And the reverberations?'

'That's why I can't do it in the winter, Keller. The risk that doing it will trigger an avalanche and kill me.'

'And the summer reverberations?'

He pointed down to the village where he lived, impossibly distant and small from this ghoulish eyrie of his. He said, 'Reviving her is less costly than reviving and then taking her. But one or two newborns will die in their cots tonight.' He shrugged. 'There's always a price.'

'Always,' I said.

I knew that this was a man with whom I could work. He effected his magic with no pomp and little fuss. And there was no question his ability was considerable in its potency. His ruthlessness was total, but I liked his honesty and thought he would be a dependable ally in framing the Almanac. I knew he had once been a priest. Probably that perverse fact enhanced his powers.

But I wasn't, by that moment, really thinking about Lorenz Hood's qualities. I was thinking instead about our descent. The sun was at its zenith by then and the steep white world glittering all around me was treacherous. I survived it though without mishap, these words the proof.

SEVENTEEN

Handy Andy Baxter didn't feel as he'd hoped he would after delivering his get-well card to Sneaky Pete Jackson's grandfather's door. He felt fobbed off by Pete's weirdo sister. He wasn't even convinced that she'd delivered Pete the card. Unless Pete was at death's door, he would have at least texted a smile emoji in acknowledgement.

Andy had been doing a bit of reading on the internet about meningitis. It was a pretty serious illness in all its forms, but if it was going to kill you, that usually happened sooner rather than later. And if it had happened, they would have announced it at the school assembly straight away, which they hadn't, at least prior to the plague outbreak's closing all the schools for a week.

Andy couldn't shake the suspicion that something fishy was going on here. And not just with that smelly and oddly vacant fish tank in Pete's grandpa's kitchen. The more he thought about it, the odder and less convincing he thought Dawn Jackson had seemed.

And there'd been that banging noise, that piledriver rhythm from below. Not work of any kind being done next door, as Dawn had claimed, but actually underneath their feet, like someone was tunnelling or something.

Andy was thinking all this at home. School wasn't back yet, it was pissing down with rain outside and he was bored. They were saying on the news that London was at its greatest risk of flooding for almost a century. The graphics were good the first time you saw them, the CGI really giving a vivid picture of the scale and scope of this possible catastrophe, but the bulletins were repetitious, just the flood risk and the diplomatic crisis. The major nations involved were having 'talks about talks about talks, through intermediaries'. That sounded like a long-winded process to him.

Andy's dad was at work. Andy's mum was out. She was a volunteer librarian and today she had a shift. She'd explained when she'd started doing this that without a volunteer workforce the library would close as a consequence of council cuts caused in turn by the government's programme of austerity. Andy figured that the austerity had been going on for as long as he personally was able to remember.

But it meant that he was free to do as he pleased. And he knew where sneaky Pete kept his front door key, under a painted pebble in his grandfather's front garden. Dawn might be in. Pete might have taken his key with him to the hospital. But Andy was becoming less and less convinced that Pete was in hospital at all. And Dawn might not be in, she might be out.

Pete had told him she spent a lot of time on academic work for this Special Study Group she belonged to on account of being so weirdly bright. With their school still closed, Dawn could revise at home. Or she could revise in the library, where his mum had mentioned seeing her poring over her textbooks on her last shift. His mum hadn't known Dawn. But she'd known Pete was a twin and had spotted the resemblance, and she'd approached Dawn and asked.

'Such a polite, studious girl,' his mum had said; she'd asked after Pete and been treated to the in-hospital-on-the-mend line.

Andy would walk to Pete's grandfather's house, he decided. It was just too wet to ride his bike. His paper round had taught him that you got much wetter riding a bike in the rain than you ever did walking. Setting off, with the hood up on his cagoule, he thought the streets unusually quiet. The plague had panicked a lot of people who lived there into getting out and had put the tourists off completely. The flood risk had made even more people leave. Andy thought the only people enjoying any of it were the burglars. Break-ins would be off the scale and the police couldn't cope because there weren't enough of them. Austerity again, his dad had told him.

Andy had on his Mountain Warehouse waterproof boots. The weather was a good test for them, and as he walked to Pete's he was gratified they were passing it. He only counted one or two pedestrians on the entire route. None of them police officers, which sort of proved his dad's point. He'd heard on the news that most of the Met police force was deployed at the big shopping centres to prevent the looting epidemic that the flood was predicted to bring.

It was all a bit biblical really. His dad had used a word over dinner the previous evening. 'Apocalyptic,' his dad had said and, impressed, Andy had asked his dad the word's meaning. 'Plagues and floods we can deal with, son,' his dad had said. 'The world's a resilient place. Nuclear war, though, I'm rather less confident about.'

He was there. He looked at the façade of the house. It was large, three storeys above the ground, three windows to each floor, altogether a much grander place than where Andy lived. There'd been no problem about Pete's grandfather having the room to house his grandchildren. Just a problem, apparently, with things like soap and detergent and shoe polish and an ironing board. And Head & Shoulders shampoo for Sneaky Pete's dandruff.

Andy stood in the rain and studied the house, waiting for a curtain to twitch at one of the windows and give Dawn away, doing her creepy sentinel thing. But there was no movement at all. So he rang the bell, and when that didn't summon anyone he knocked on the heavy brass knocker, which he noticed was badly tarnished. It wasn't just Pete his grandpa neglected.

And come to think of it, where was Pete's grandpa? You got the sprightly pensioners and you got the ones who sat around looking unwell. And Pete's grandfather was very much in the latter category. He'd been badly wounded serving at somewhere called Aden in the army about fifty years ago, according to Pete. He'd been an officer and when he'd been left with a limp they'd chucked him out.

Andy retrieved Pete's key from under its pink-painted rock. Andy had teased him that keeping your door key under a rock that colour was a bit girly, but Pete wasn't the sort of character who let that kind of remark bother him in the slightest. He'd either laugh it off, or he'd retaliate with a crack of his own. Andy realized then, with a feeling of slight surprise, that he missed his friend. Of course he did; it was why he was there.

With the key held between the thumb and forefinger of his left hand, Andy gave the door knocker a final rat-tat-tat before transferring the key from his left hand to his right and letting himself in.

Dawn hadn't bothered emptying the fish tank in the kitchen. The ground floor of this house was spacious, with the kitchen at the back, and Andy could tell that from just inside the front door. The smell had grown both staler and stronger. He thought it strong enough now to permeate the fabric of soft furnishings and carpets. You might never completely get rid of it. It was almost strong enough to make you gag.

He went through into the kitchen holding his breath. And he noticed two things straight away. The first was that the green water in the fish tank was moving, sort of rippling. The second was that the get-well card he'd bought for Pete, ripped into a dozen pieces, was in the waste-paper basket under the table.

It had one of those black and white archive photos on its cover. A caption comically at odds with the image itself. It had cost him £2.75, and she had ripped it to spiteful shreds.

Still holding his breath, red-faced he knew with the effort, Andy went over to the fish tank and saw that its contents seethed with life. Tiny terrapins, hundreds of them, perhaps thousands, none bigger than his little fingernail and feasting on each other in a loathsome frenzy.

Unable to hold his breath any longer, Andy gasped it out and then inhaled because his lungs weren't giving him any choice. The stink assaulted his senses and he gagged and puked into the fish tank, adding his half-digested breakfast to the roiling mess in there.

Andy heard that jackhammer boom from below then; ponderous, stolidly rhythmic, implausibly loud. And then it stopped. And he heard a bellow of raw fury that wasn't at all a human sound. He fled the place, clawing at the front door in his blind panic to get out before the thing at the bottom of the steps to the basement got its strong and unshakeable grip on him.

On the street outside, it was still raining hard. Harder, if anything. He trudged home through it, expecting at every turn to be confronted by a returning and indignant Dawn. But the library wasn't even in the same direction as his home.

He'd left no clue that he'd been there, apart from the puke, which the terrapins would nibble at with the same avid hunger with which they nibbled at one another. Andy thought he'd seen how extinction worked, and it had frightened him.

Not to the same extent, though, that he was frightened of Dawn Jackson. He was beginning to think that she might have done some harm to Pete. The contempt with which she had discarded his get-well card pointed at someone not just callous, but deliberately nasty. Had she done something too to her grandfather?

Wildly, for a moment, Andy thought about an anonymous call to the police. But it wouldn't stay anonymous, would it? They'd had the technology to trace mobile calls to their numbers and locations for years. Even if he found a working payphone they'd get that number, and these days they could extract DNA. If Dawn was up to something, they'd want to find and question him. If Dawn was completely innocent, they'd want to find him and prosecute him for wasting police time.

Andy didn't want to speculate on what manner of beast lurked in the basement or the cellar of that house. He didn't want to try to imagine the physical nature of the creature responsible for that monstrous sound he'd heard. All the way back home through the pouring rain he endured it again, playing on repeat in his head, as though he would be incapable now of ever forgetting it.

He decided to detour to the library. He wanted to see his mum, wanted the reassurance of her smile as she ruffled his hair. Even the perfumed scent of her was a comfort to her son. But he stopped, dead in his tracks, half a block on. There was every chance that Dawn Jackson was swotting at a library table. And if she was, she would know. She'd subject him to one of her cool, appraising, green-eyed gazes and she'd know everything. Right down to the Alpen muesli and full-fat milk helping fill her fish tank, along with a sample of his stomach acid.

EIGHTEEN

D awn had studied Malthusian theory as part of her Special Study Group economics lessons. She didn't take to every historical figure but thought Thomas Malthus had expressed some very interesting ideas about population control, back at the beginning of the nineteenth century.

It was the positive checks on population control Dawn particularly warmed to, and the fact that Malthus referred to them as positive at all. They included famine, disease and war and they kicked in when populations became too big for existing resources to sustain them.

There was no famine in London currently, but an incidence of bubonic plague had probably got closer to epidemic proportions than anyone was prepared to admit. And the world seemed to be on the brink of full-scale war. Dawn knew this because she took the interest in world affairs that proved so emphatically that she wasn't on any kind of spectrum, though her dead brother, when alive, had tediously insisted that she was.

The Foreign Secretary had said that the recent fog had been chemically induced by agents of a hostile foreign power. He had pointed an accusatory finger at Russia and, to use a terrible pun, was sticking to his guns. The flood threat was a direct consequence of an aviation catastrophe that would not have occurred without the fog, so that was being blamed on Russia too. And the Russians were reacting with typical fury. Or untypical fury, because Dawn knew her twentieth-century history and didn't think they had been this hot and bothered since the height of the Cold War. Maybe not even then. And at that time they hadn't possessed anything like the inter-continental ballistic weapons that they did today.

Her clever head was full of Malthus until the moment she got home. As soon as she opened the door, she knew someone had been there. It was only an intuition, no evidence to support the belief, but to Dawn it was a certainty. She wondered whether they were still there, down in the cellar partying with what was left of her brother, subject to his insatiable hunger and new-found passion for warm-blooded raw meat. Good luck to them, if they were.

Dawn hadn't been down to look, but didn't think the lopping-off spell could have been wholly effective in depriving her brother of a head. He was still ambulatory, still roaring out the sort of occasional noises for which people depended on vocal chords and still, presumably, eating from Grandpa's stockpile of cans of vile food – his corned beef, his boiled ham, his Spam and bloody pilchards. Revolting sardines with a key that rolled back the lid. Only stale, flat bitter lemon to drink. But then beggars couldn't be choosers, could they?

The terrapin explosion pleased Dawn as much as it had distressed Handy Andy. Like him, she thought it looked like a world on its way to extinction in microcosm, which was a word Dawn knew and Andy didn't. But the sight delighted rather than repelling her and she was growing accustomed to the smell. The smell was, to her, just the olfactory equivalent of an acquired taste. She thought there was a Malthusian character to the squirming mass of tiny creatures as they busily devoured one another. There were too many and they were demonstrating population control in a positive manner.

She didn't honestly know how they'd been spawned. She knew vaguely that terrapins usually came into the world as eggs. These hadn't, they'd appeared spontaneously. They were an approximation of terrapins rather than the real things, created by magic, she thought, more than by nature. *Provoked* by magic. This signified that she wasn't fully in control of the magic. Unless there was a spontaneous quality to it, a sort of life of its own she'd sparked unintentionally.

She couldn't honestly devote the necessary degree of thought to what the terrapin explosion implied. Chaos? Confusion? Anarchy? She still had tests to revise for and they were currently at the forefront of her bright and energetic mind. If the avid little amphibians got bigger, she'd just perform the vanishing spell that had worked so well on their predecessor. And then she'd have the fish tank vanish too.

A thought occurred to Dawn. She walked back through the house and out of the front door, leaving it ajar behind her. She lifted the pink pebble under which she knew her dead brother's front door key should have reposed. It wasn't there. Someone had done the vanishing spell on it. Except that no one but she was capable of real magic, because she was the only person with the book. So not magic, but basic, bland, earthly mischief.

'Handy Andy Baxter,' Dawn said, aloud. She smiled at the thought that he would have seen his carefully chosen, affectionately written card torn up in the kitchen waste bin. When school started again, he might mention her brother's continued absence to a teacher; reminding them, stirring up fresh trouble for her. And a visit from the truancy officer would be a disaster. She might have to have another diversionary incident where a teacher died in their sleep. Someone as popular generally as the late and much lamented Mrs Mahoney had been. Or someone with a crucial role like the head of year or the headmaster.

Handy Andy she would deal with at her leisure. Dawn considered retribution a very satisfying activity for which she was proving to have a real and growing talent, thanks to her possession of the spell book. The revision was a bit of an intermission in her personal and private magic show, but there would be a second act. And she was aware of the old saying that revenge is a dish best eaten cold.

She looked up at the sky, blinking through persistent rain. She didn't think it would flood in her grandpa's part of town. Their house was in Crouch End, which was hilly, and they were at an address a substantial distance above sea level. And she was confident that the way she'd wrapped it would protect the book against damp, safeguard it against the seepage of rain through the turf of the garden.

She went and looked out of the kitchen window at the lawn. The depression at the spot where she had dug was so slight it hadn't even puddled. Unless you knew it was there, you really wouldn't notice it. She thought her secret completely secure and safe.

Well, one of her secrets, she conceded to herself, with a resigned sigh. The other secret, the one in the cellar, needed checking on.

She wouldn't do that personally. It was just too dangerous after the way Pete had moved when he'd bitten her. It had been a cobra strike of suddenness and cold savagery and speed. She was not a match for him physically and didn't want to risk another attack. But her study of the spell book had provided her with another way.

In the book it required an incantation and then a camera obscura kind of arrangement involving a box with a pinprick at its centre. This tiny light source projected the image you wanted to see on to a screen or wall. Except that Dawn wouldn't do it like that. She didn't see the need for the obsolete technology. She had too much faith in the potency of the magic. She would incant what she'd learned by heart with her mind intent on those Latin words and their charged meaning, their occult power. Then she'd switch on the television and see what resulted.

She pressed the change-channel button nine times before she recognized her grandfather's cellar. The light wasn't very good. Discarded empty meat and fish cans littered the floor, glimmering slightly in what scant illumination there was.

Her dead brother was a large, still shape slumped darkly in one corner, breathing audibly in big, gusty lungfuls of the cellar's dank air, crooning softly to himself.

Then he seemed to sense this fresh scrutiny. He tensed, his whole body taking on a coiled posture, as though ready to pounce. He sprang up abruptly and scuttled forward into close-up.

He still had his head. An ear and an eye were missing, and his skull had taken on a sort of concave look, but it was still there on his shoulders. And something had happened to his mouth. It was shaped in a leer stretched across the whole bottom half of his face and barbed, crowded, with an array of sharp and uneven teeth. More of a maw than a mouth. It reminded her of a shark.

'You're a dentist's nightmare, bro,' Dawn said quietly at the screen. But what she truthfully thought was that he was a nightmare altogether. She'd misused the lopping-off spell. It was meant only for hands and feet. These fresh deformities were the consequence.

She'd taken further precautions with the cellar door. It was strengthened and welded shut by thought spells she believed made the cellar itself inescapable. One extra-strength Nurofen had sorted out the resulting headache. But eventually she'd have to do something about Pete. There was some sort of contamination at work there. He was changing, transforming, degenerating into a monster. The truth was, he was already a monster.

But it was a problem really for another day. Revision beckoned. Dawn liked an academic challenge and was aiming eventually for straight As in her grades. She switched off the television and the thing her brother had become vanished from the screen and from her mind. She went to fetch her textbooks.

NINETEEN

September 1, 1528

I have spent almost the whole of the last month languishing in a prison cell, the victim of rumour and innuendo, put to the torture with heated irons and the rack, stewing in the heat of the height of summer in a stinking cell with a bed of straw to sleep on, deprived of materials with which to write or even a solitary book to divert me from discomfort and severe pain and constant, gnawing

hunger. The only blessing is that I retain my sanity. And that I
have had a month to reflect in the abstract on the Almanac, the
shape it will take and what steps to take to render it ineffective
should it fall into the wrong hands.

A malicious neighbour must have informed on me to the authorities. Suspicions, rather than anything resembling hard evidence of
occult practice. Proof would have sent me to the gallows, at best.

The burghers of the city sent pike-men to my handsome new
lodgings in the small hours at the beginning of August. Perhaps
my new-found material wealth was the spur. Gains are always
ill-gotten in the minds of the envious. I was questioned by candlelight at an ungodly hour, still in my night-shirt. My inquisitors
were masked to conceal their identities, I suspect for fear of occult
reprisal should my rumoured powers prove real and authentic.

'You do the Devil's work, apothecary.'

'My calling is medicinal.'

'Liar.'

'An unsupportable accusation.'

'Unless we force you to confess.'

And so on. Mary Nye is here, dispatched by my English lord
to lodgings not half a mile away. A mixed blessing. On the one
hand she represents a risk; on the other, her poultices have eased
the pain searing my joints. I have enjoyed the nourishment of her
fortifying cordials. We shared a discussion about pain generally.
She has the power to put an end to physical discomfort entirely
but has also a reluctance to use it.

'It seems futile, mistress, to harbour power you choose to ignore,'
I remarked.

'If pain were an end in itself, sir, I would not hesitate.'

'What is pain, if not a conclusion or result?'

'It is a warning. Pain chastises us for our carelessness. It signals
illnesses for which we summon physicians. To be without it is
extremely dangerous.'

I had not expected philosophizing from a woman so unprepossessing in manner and drab in appearance as she. But her salves
were effective enough.

I asked her about the second sight. She cannot see her own
future, which is veiled to her. So I asked her if she would kindly
look into mine. She sat opposite me and concentrated on a small

mirror shard she uses for the purpose. Then she turned pale and winced, which did not seem to me a welcome indication.

'What do you see?'

'Recognition. Success. Reward. Wealth. All of these will come to you in the short term, Herr Keller. This is your destiny over coming years.'

'And in the longer term?'

'The longer term is closed to me at present.'

I did not believe her. I think she could see my future as vividly as words written in black ink boldly on a white page. But she would not share what she saw. Perhaps some grisly fate awaits me further along the road I travel. But it matters not. She saw only one possible outcome, I think. I believe we write our own destiny. At every crossroads, we choose a path. No man's fate is written in stone while still a mewling infant. That is not at all the manner in which the world functions.

Most interesting was what Mistress Nye had to say about my English lord and patron. He is regarded as the greatest swordsman in Christendom, having killed a dozen men in duels with rapiers he has fashioned at extravagant cost from Toledo steel worked in Spain by the best craftsmen money can commission.

He has a perpetual motion machine made by the artist and inventor da Vinci some years ago. Physical laws claim that energy is finite and eventually exhausts itself; but Mistress Nye insists that our master's infernal machine is relentless in its ceaseless industry.

He is a collector of physical trophies. In a water pool hewn from the ground beneath his castle, these are said to include a siren of the sea, half woman and half fish, her lower portion entirely scaled and with a tail fin shaped horizontally in common with the mammals of the oceans.

'Have you seen this creature?'

'I have heard her singing,' Mistress Nye told me. 'It is not a sound, sir, you would quickly forget.'

'Is our new master cruel? He has killed a dozen men.'

'None in cold blood. All affairs of honour. He would not kill you. You are of common birth and so would not qualify to cross swords with him.'

Both a rebuke and a comfort to me.

'Has he a wife? Children?'

'Both a wife and heirs. A bastard or two is possible. He likes women, in contrast to yourself.'

'Your manner borders on insolence.'

'In matters esoteric, Herr Keller, we are equals.'

'Prove that to me.'

She asked for paper and a pen. I fetched her parchment and a quill and a fresh pot of ink. I sat feeling the dull throb of my tortured limbs as she scratched away, a dreamy, preoccupied look across her unimpressive features. Presently, she stopped writing and held up the single sheet upon which she had worked.

'This is a list of your recent inquisitors. These are the burghers who disguised themselves in your presence for fear of vengeance.'

'How do you know?'

'I see things. Trust me. These are the men who had you arrested and imprisoned.'

'What is the purpose of this list?'

'Retribution,' she said. 'Choose a name. Its owner will die tonight.'

'How?'

'I will sketch their likeness and sing them a lullaby and their heart will stop. Their sleep will become cold and eternal.'

'You know what they look like?'

'Masks do not obscure second sight.'

I pondered on this, impressed. I said, 'Sketch a likeness of each. Sing them all a lullaby.'

Mistress Nye shook her head. 'A connection would be made. A finger would be pointed. You would be re-arrested and would not survive the subsequent questioning.'

She was right, of course. It did not require second sight to see that. I pointed at a name on her list, one I recognized, a wealthy corn merchant and generous commissioner of religious artworks in the city's churches, a lay preacher and enthusiastic advocate of the flaying whip, the thumbscrews and the rack. A man I believed to have a brood of seven children under the age of twelve, whose loss would reverberate after his demise.

He duly died that night and, after a four-day period of public lamentation, was put to rest with lavish ceremony in an elaborately sculpted tomb. By that time, Mistress Nye had set off across the German Sea on her journey back to her English home. A woman of churlish character and unremarkable appearance, by the time of her departure she had nevertheless earned my respect. And some degree also of gratitude for her timely intervention into my own troubles.

Something simple would be the best antidote to the Almanac, something that could defuse it as a bomb can be defused before the carnage its explosion can inflict. I need to create a fitting spell for this. Something such as a grain of sand or a single crystal of salt placed between its pages to make it cease to manufacture magic. It need only be a symbolic thing, something readily available. And of course it must, to be of any use, be irreversible. I will work on it. It is far from beyond me. My new master has furnished me with a full laboratory. Its location remains secret, despite the agony of my recent ordeal. Its survival is testament, I suppose, to my own dedication.

TWENTY

'It would be interesting to know what he meant by the "wrong hands",' Juliet said, 'given that he wanted the Almanac to trigger apocalypse.'

'Someone good,' Paul said. 'Someone who wanted to see an end to famine and encourage a pacific mood in the world. They weren't at all Keller's objectives.'

'I'm beginning to wonder about the objectives of the man who commissioned it,' Juliet said.

'The serial-killer swordsman?'

'Don't make the mistake of judging him by the standards of a time half a millennium away from his.'

'He still sounds as though his feathers were easily ruffled.'

'If we knew his identity, we might be closer to the Almanac's present location. We'd at least have some clues. Aristocrats have a lineage.'

'Mistress Nye says heirs,' Paul said.

'No guarantee they survived him. Infant mortality was extremely high then. We can't take this material out of its specific time and context.'

'Spoken like an academic.'

'Well, I am an academic.'

Paul grinned. 'You don't look like one.'

'What does that mean?'

'It's a compliment, Juliet. Lighten up.'

'I'll lighten up when we've found the Almanac and put it to bed with sand or salt. Wish he'd been more specific about that.'

Paul closed the ledger and hovered a hand over Keller's note-books, fingers spread. He said, 'I'm going to have a crack at these this afternoon. But I need some lunch first and a break from translating Latin aloud.'

'Interesting stories,' Juliet said, 'if unenlightening.'

'Pretty dark,' Paul said. 'Do you believe it all?'

Juliet thought about this. She said, 'I saw the solar eclipse. I read about the *Esmeralda*. I avoided the fog by a few hours and know that as a direct consequence of that weird period of weather, London is about to flood. I can't remember a time when the superpowers have been more at one another's throats.'

'And this book's responsible?'

'The *Almanac of Forbidden Wisdom* was never neutralized in the way Gunter Keller suggested it could be. It's in the hands of someone vindictive, immature and completely reckless. We've speculated on an adolescent child. We have to find them.'

Paul gestured again at the notebooks. He said, 'I think these are formulations, the spells in coded longhand which he'd have boiled down for the Almanac. I think the whole point of the spell book was that an amateur could use it. That way Keller could see it used most effectively to trigger the End Times. I don't think any of this material is going to help us with its present location.'

'An English aristocrat who was also a notorious duellist shouldn't be all that difficult to identify.'

'There could be more than one candidate.'

'How many who had their rapiers forged from Toledo steel? How many regarded as the best swordsman in Europe?'

'How many with a pet mermaid?' Paul said.

Juliet smiled. She said, 'I'm assuming that particular claim to be dubious at best.'

'Mary Nye takes a practical approach to magic generally. She's pragmatic, almost dour about it.'

'She couldn't have been all that pragmatic, Paul. Less than four years after this encounter she was strung up at Tyburn for witchcraft.'

'And four years after it Keller burned. Hazardous hobbies.'

'They weren't hobbies. They were the same vocation. Keller, Cortez, Hood, Nye; it sounds like a compulsion with all of them. If the rewards were enormous, so were the risks. But they don't seem to have been able to stop themselves.'

'Do you think the Almanac's present owner shares that compulsion?'

'We have to hope not, but the answer's probably yes.'

'If Keller's aim is apocalypse, why the preoccupation with material luxury? Isn't that contradictory?'

'He hints at the answer to that himself, Paul. After a lifetime of near penury, he just wants to sample the alternative. He just wants a taste of the affluent life.'

Paul Beck shivered. The air conditioning in that sterile reading room made it chilly. But Juliet thought it more a shudder of horror than a simple reaction to the cold.

'Let's go and get some food,' he said.

They walked three blocks to a café with pavement tables. They could have eaten at the university canteen. Whatever Martin Doyle had done from Oxford had seen them warmly welcomed in Berlin. But the day was bright and warm and the work grimly important and it seemed sensible to make the best of their short break from it. Besides, Juliet thought, they were enjoying one another's company to the point where she privately wished the circumstances were very different. She'd have preferred a less stressful agenda and a Paul who was unattached. Once they'd found a table and ordered, Juliet busied herself sending a text.

'Anything I should know about?'

'I'm speaking to an Oxford colleague. She's a Tudor specialist. I want her to try to pinpoint her likeliest candidate for the man who commissioned the Almanac.'

'Good idea. My instinct tells me we'll get nowhere with the Keller archive. I mean it's an interesting insight into occult rites and amoral characters, but I don't think it's going to turn into a concrete lead.'

Juliet was quiet. Paul said, 'What?'

'I was just thinking that I wish you were free to work with me on this. I rather wish you weren't based in Berlin.'

'I'm in England as of next week, Juliet. Specifically, in London.'

'Why? How?'

He'd been maintaining eye contact throughout their conversation. Now, as their waiter approached their table with drinks, he looked down as though studying his cutlery. He didn't answer her until their waiter had retreated back inside, out of earshot.

'I requested and have been granted a three-month leave of absence.'

'Why three months?'

'Because that's the most time they'll give me and the least it's likely to take me to recover.'

'You've been ill?'

'Only if you count heartsick.'

'Divorce?'

'Fiancée broke it off ten days ago, which was a fortnight before the wedding was supposed to take place.'

'Why?'

He shrugged. 'Better offer.'

Juliet said, 'To be perfectly honest, you strike me as a bit of a catch.'

'It's like you said earlier, Juliet. Context is everything.'

'Meaning?'

'I'm a linguist. I'm a translator. I can't compete with a love rival who plays football for Bayern Munich. Terrible pun, but that's out of my league.'

'When I first saw you this morning, that's what I thought *you* were. A footballer.'

'She goes for a particular physical type. But I have neither the playing skills nor the bank balance to compete.'

'I'm sorry.'

'I'm not,' Paul said, 'not really. She's shown her true colours, is all. It's a bit disillusioning. But you're better off knowing that kind of thing sooner rather than later.'

The waiter reappeared, this time with their food. Juliet noticed that Paul hadn't yet started his drink. His soft drink; they were both on Diet Coke. The Keller archive might be a cul-de-sac, but they had to be sure. And the sand/salt revelation was something, especially if the afternoon provided some information to confirm which of those it was.

Paul Beck no longer looked to Juliet like a man particularly interested in the food presented on the plate in front of him. He was elsewhere, momentarily in the company of someone else. She thought there was an obvious discrepancy between his words and his feelings. The English phrase for it was 'putting on a brave face', something he would certainly know.

Then he surprised her by saying, 'Tell me about you. The second thing I noticed about you was that you don't wear a wedding ring.'

'And the first thing?'

The eye contact had returned. He was looking at her coolly, openly. 'How lovely you are to look at,' he said. 'Tell me about you.'

Juliet thought briefly about using the hoary old line about being married to her work. But she didn't do that. Instead, she told him the truth about her divorce and the farce of her subsequent internet dating experience. He laughed, not cruelly, but in the appropriate places.

When they'd finished, Juliet insisted on paying with some of her Whitehall expenses money. Their conversation had reminded her that she was a believer in fate. And she thought they got up from their table different people to the two who had only an hour earlier sat down.

TWENTY-ONE

At three o'clock that Tuesday afternoon, Juliet Harrington was listening to her Tudor specialist Oxford contact, taking notes on the phone, while Paul Beck worked through the coded notebooks Gunter Keller had filled, trying to make sense of them.

In London, at five past three that afternoon, the combination of heavy rain travelling down the Thames and a surge-tide coming up the river forced the surface to rise and swell above the height of its embankments and flood most of the West End and the City to an average depth of six feet. The commercial damage was both immediate and incalculable. No one in political office would put a price on the harm done to property and infrastructure. The metropolis was crippled. Raw sewage exploded to the surface, streets become canals and then transformed into runnels of filth and, potentially, of disease.

The cultural impact was equally immediate. And devastating. And of course, irreversible. Theatres and galleries and cinemas awash with polluted water, precious artworks destroyed by a ruinous and stinking elemental catastrophe. Trade simply and suddenly froze. Survivors overwhelmed the heights of Hampstead and Primrose Hill in a fleeing horde. Floating bodies littered the surface lower down, too many to count, let alone to gather up and bury.

The emergency services and the military were quickly and predictably overwhelmed. Gangs of youths in stolen RIBs began an ungovernable spree of looting. Thousands of people trapped in the upper floors of their homes or workplaces waved handkerchiefs at windows in a futile bid to be noticed and rescued.

The rest of the country continued to be governed. The Cabinet sat exiled from the capital at Windsor Castle, having been taken there in two Chinooks by Royal Marine pilots when the event became inevitable a few days prior to the actual deluge.

The international crisis inevitably worsened. Londoners blamed the Russians for the fog and the fog for the air crash that had disabled their proud and precious flood barrier. The few dissenting voices in government were considered weak, vacillating and gullible. They weren't just deluded pacifists. They were appeasers in a wounded country crying out for retaliation.

Dawn Jackson, from the relatively safe altitude of Crouch End, watched the news bulletins wondering whether the bodies decaying quickly in the flood waters would bring the cholera epidemic some medical experts were predicting.

She thought that Thomas Malthus would have enjoyed the TV coverage. It was Malthusian theory in practice: nature seeking a positive way to thin the population of an overcrowded city and succeeding ingeniously.

She wondered at the wider impact on her studies. She knew that exam boards were regional and thought hers might struggle to find invigilators and enough school premises remaining unscathed to make her Special Studies exams a realistic proposition. It would be a great shame, she thought, if they didn't now happen. They would be the concrete proof of her academic precocity. Accolades were important to Dawn.

The rain finally stopped at five fifteen p.m. Twice the average rainfall for the month of October had fallen in twenty hours in June. The surge-tide slowed, stopped and receded. By five thirty p.m., the water level in Oxford Street had fallen by a full foot. Dawn thought that if it kept on falling at that rate, the streets would be under puddles only by midnight. But morning would reveal the aftermath. The buildings smeared with mud and shit and silt. The waterlogged furniture and spoiled food stocks and contaminated water supply. The thousands, maybe millions of cars that would have to be written off. The likelihood, in the absence of the flood barrier, that all this was destined to happen again.

And the bodies. There were too many to count, let alone clean up to a timetable that was logistically safe. One commentator had said that there were too many bodies to contemplate, but Dawn enjoyed contemplation, regarding it as one of her many intellectual skills. Her dead brother had always been too shallow-minded for contemplation. She was an altogether deeper thinking individual.

There was talk of mass burial of the flood victims. And there was contrasting talk of drying them out and burning them on huge bonfires. If they did that, the smoke would be black from body fat and it would smell like a giant barbecue. Dawn couldn't really see it, though.

One ingenious idea was to tow the dead out as cargo aboard barges and bury them at sea. But there was a practical problem with that in that there weren't many barges left intact on the river. They illustrated this on TV with footage of a barge on George Street, which was the high street in Richmond upon Thames. It was berthed in the House of Fraser window it had smashed its way through. There was another adrift in Parliament Square, where Dawn remembered the statue of Churchill had bled from the eyes and mouth not long ago. A third was canted at an odd angle on the river-lapped steps of St Paul's Cathedral. That one still had most of its cargo of industrial coke, the ballast that had moored it where it had finally ended up.

No politicians were talking about casualties, but Sky News had got a statistician in who knew about population density. He said that in his rough estimation, the death toll would be in the hundreds of thousands. For many of the drowned, the flood had just been too deep and rapid to escape.

Dawn liked that phrase, *rough estimation*. She liked it so much that she wrote it down, wondering whether she could find a context for it in her own written work.

Dawn's secret ambition was to become a writer. She knew she had a good, if rather dark, imagination. She suspected that she might lack a little bit of empathy, but even the most gifted writers didn't have everything in their creative arsenal. And she could fake empathy, she thought. There was plenty of room for manoeuvre, after all, as to where the fiction started, and where it finally stopped.

She heard a clatter above her head and then a soft thump in her grandpa's garden and went out through the kitchen door to see what had caused the commotion. There was a large bright unnatural fabric thing collapsed on the lawn, which she quickly realized was actually a small parachute. It was made of nylon, or something similar. Some polymer anyway, light and tough.

Dawn gathered up the parachute and saw that there was a wooden crate underneath it. She went and fetched her frozen grandpa's Swiss Army knife and pried open the crate. It was filled tightly with water bottles and tins of food and packets of dried soup and stew. No brand names on the packaging. From that she assumed army rations.

She had done a big shop only the previous day. She thought the public-spirited thing to do would be to knock on doors and hand this stuff out to neighbours with fewer provisions than she had. But Dawn didn't know the neighbours and didn't wish to get to know them. She didn't really do neighbourliness. And she didn't want them to get to know about the secrets stored in her cellar and garage. There was still room in her kitchen cupboards. And though there was still a couple of thousand pounds in Grandpa's account, his debit card would not go on working for ever.

Standing there in the garden, Dawn was extremely tempted to dig up her spell book and go to work on Grandpa. She was curious to see what could be achieved with him. He'd been a bit crotchety sometimes, and never in the best of health because of the war wound and the smoking. But he'd been much more intelligent than she'd ever thought her brother to be. She thought he might come back closer to the full shilling than her brother had. And he wouldn't bite her. His false teeth would fall out if he tried.

But sore as the temptation was, she didn't dig up her spell book. Instead she stored the army provisions away neatly in the kitchen cupboards. She put the water bottles in the fridge, slightly amazed that she still had electric power. There was no point distracting herself with the spell book until she had clarification one way or the other about her school tests.

Dawn revised until seven p.m., when the power did go off. Her big concern when that happened was whether it would be restored before her grandfather had time to thaw out. Light wasn't a particular problem because, like most old people, Grandpa had a stock of candles – big, waxy, wicked cylinders she'd seen in a kitchen drawer with a full box of Swan Vesta matches. And it was almost the longest day, so it wouldn't be dark anyway for all that much of the night.

She closed her Spanish vocab textbook with a snap and fetched and lit a candle, just for the flame and the scent of melting wax and the atmosphere. She went to turn on the TV and catch up on the flood news, but remembered that without power, the TV wouldn't work either. Unless she wanted to watch the Pete channel, which she didn't, particularly.

She sat instead in the candlelight and thought of ways in which she could get even with Handy Andy Baxter. It wasn't at the top of it, but it definitely featured on her list of things to do.

Behind her, in water which, in the absence of electric light, glowed with phosphorescence, the surviving terrapins roiled and slathered. They were down to twenty or so, snapping hungrily at one another. And the survivors had grown. It was natural selection, the survival of the fittest, which was Darwin rather than Malthus, but still something Dawn knew about. She was oblivious now, though, to the cannibalistic conflict being waged at her back. Her mind was wholly on Andy.

TWENTY-TWO

October 15, 1528

am returned from Jerusalem, a hazardous place to travel to by land and sea, but I still possess the amulet given me by Cordelia Cortez and saw enough of what the countess is capable of to believe wholly in the power to protect with which she invested it.

I went there in search of treasure. The talisman I sought is perhaps the most highly prized in Christendom. It is the fragment of the One True Cross seized by Saladin at the calamitous Battle of Hattin in the Second Crusade.

This relic, in Muslim hands, was subsequently lost to history. But Mary Nye saw it in one of the black visions that sometimes assail her and apprised me of where it might be found. Soaked in the sacred blood of Christ, used properly – or rather, improperly – it possesses enormous power. And my journey was worthwhile, for I found the item where she said I would, in a small casket secreted in a chiselled hollow shaped for it on the rear side of a stone fronting a section of the old city wall. This sheltered casket, hinged and fashioned from gold, had kept the priceless wooden fragment perfectly preserved.

I recovered it in the small hours and thus in darkness, armed with a sketch demonstrating the correct section of wall. I would not have attempted to do it by day. But the stars are bright in the East and the sketch formidably detailed. I found what I was looking for after just over an hour's search.

Blasphemy is a great spur to occult power if the blasphemer has the courage and willingness to go to true extremes of degradation. I will use this relic more than once in rituals I have yet to devise. They will be an insult both to the crucified Christ and to Christianity itself. I take my sacrilegious acts as seriously as, conversely, I take my acts of worship.

On the way back to Hanover I diverted to the Netherlands to press Tiberius van Vaunt into contributing his arcane knowledge to the eventual creation of the Almanac. I had no need for a demonstration of van Vaunt's prowess at the esoteric arts. For seven years, in my own youth, he was the master and I was his pupil.

The one criticism I would make of my former tutor is that it is to him that I owe my own unfortunate habit of tinkering sometimes with the dead. Neither of us has the talent for this that Lorenz Hood, in the Tyrol, proved to possess. Though Hood has the advantage of the cold to preserve his corpses. And at least I am innocent of Hood's lustfully unsavoury motives for reanimation.

Tiberius van Vaunt was intrigued by the proposition of the Almanac, by its ambition and by the quality of its contributors. He had heard of Cordelia Cortez and Mary Nye and Lorenz Hood. There is an occult underground, necessarily secretive and mostly encoded. But it is there and its whispers carry and resonate throughout the continent.

And of course he knew about me. 'My most talented and distinguished pupil,' he said, 'always the bravest in the extremes of your experimentation.' This last observation was as much admonishment I think as praise, but I was still proud to hear it from someone with his powers.

I did not require him to provide me with proof, as I had the others. I knew the potent extent of what my old master could accomplish. But I was treated to a demonstration nevertheless.

My new-found prosperity was probably what prompted this. We walked from van Vaunt's Amsterdam home for dinner at a tavern he said was safe from prying eyes. The food was good and the beer even better and we gave nothing away to anyone eavesdropping on our blandly innocent conversation. But my clothing now is rich enough in cloth and cut to make me look a prosperous man, and when I insisted on paying the reckoning for our repast I brought forth my purse, fairly bulging with coins.

We were not immediately aware of being followed out of the door. But followed we were, by three ruffians armed with stout clubs and a short maritime cutlass. All three had knives in their belts and enough scarring on their faces in the bright moonlight to suggest a familiarity with street and tavern brawls.

They said nothing. They were skilled enough thieves to confront us at an isolated spot, late, with a high wall blocking any hope of retreat or escape. We were cornered. There was a leer on each of their faces and the one armed with the cutlass gestured with the fingers of his free hand for us to surrender our valuables.

I reached resignedly for my purse, wondering whether our attackers would beat us after robbing us, just for the sport. I looked around for a missile. One of my skills is to move objects with my mind at considerable velocity. A brick or pebble, a piece of cartwheel, a plank of discarded timber or clay flowerpot would have made a destructive weapon. A loose cobble I could pry from its bed using the power of thought; but there was literally nothing to hand.

My old tutor pulled out a pocket watch. He held it forth by its chain in front of him. It was heavily engraved across both sides with what looked to me like runic symbols. It began to spin, gaining in the speed of its revolutions until it was a glimmering moonlit blur. And then van Vaunt began to chant something in a language that sounded coarse and ancient.

I expected one of our assailants to snatch the watch. I thought it likely that it was the work of Peter Henlein, the master locksmith and clockmaker of Nuremberg, the man credited with inventing these small and elegant timepieces about four or five years ago. Items of such intricate rarity are almost priceless. But no move was made to take it. The three would-be thieves simply stood transfixed. Then they simultaneously dropped their weapons to the ground.

A cutlass and two clubs clattered to the cobbles. Their knives followed. The watch continued spinning, my old master continued incanting in that strangely broken monotone. Then the men began to sob, almost like a trio of tearful children. And then at once, they turned from us and walked away, each with the same identical gait to their movement. Almost as strung puppets depending from invisible strings, their feet appearing weightless across the ground.

'Why did they weep?'

'Self-indulgence, Gunter. They were grieving their own deaths.'

'Where are they going?'

'To the canal. Into the canal.'

I waited to hear three splashes. But of course, there was only one. They went in together.

'Was it hypnotism? How did they follow what you said?'

'It wasn't hypnotism. I merely robbed them of their will and then commanded them. I was speaking Dutch but had to make the language alien to your ears, so you wouldn't be compelled to go too.'

'Will you teach me to do that?'

'The enchantment, or the cloaked language?'

'Both.'

'Tomorrow. The beer and the spell casting have conspired to make me tired.'

'How deep is the canal?'

Van Vaunt laughed. 'Deep enough,' he said.

'I didn't know you profited from your work to the degree that enables a purchase such as that timepiece of yours.'

'The watch was a gift from someone grateful for what I did for his eight-year-old daughter. Cholera, Keller.'

'Ah.'

I didn't ask whether the disease had been arrested, or the child revived. My old tutor had many talents, but he was no physician. Sometimes discretion is called for and this was such a moment. And so we strolled, unmolested, back to his comfortable home.

I do not know precisely what price was paid for the magic that delivered us from our would-be attackers. But I believe it might be one rich in irony. It transpired that they were sailors from a merchant vessel. Their deaths made the ship short-handed and it was delayed putting to sea, I later heard, while their replacements were recruited. When finally she did embark, the *Esmeralda* sank with all hands three days into her voyage.

I have decided on salt. A single salt crystal placed between each of its pages will divest the *Almanac of Forbidden Wisdom* of all power. Sometimes I am too reckless. There will be no recklessness concerning the Almanac. It cannot fall into the hands of someone intent on using its power in a bountiful or compassionate way. Christ's miracle with the loaves and fishes will remain a legend of the gospels, not something to be repeated by an individual armed with ideals and the power to summon magic. The sole and secret purpose of the Almanac will be to provoke apocalypse. I am intent upon it.

* * *

It was the last entry. Paul Beck read it aloud, ten minutes before the university library was due to close. By then he'd decoded the notebooks; his earlier supposition that they were spells and formulae Keller would boil down for the Almanac had proven correct. Their exhausting day had given them not a single clue about the book's possible location at the present time.

'What now?' he said.

Juliet blew a loose strand of hair away from her face. 'Honestly?' she said. 'I feel like getting drunk.'

They had not yet heard about London. Fifteen minutes later, utterly incredulous, they would see the carnage from their bar stools on a wall-mounted flatscreen TV.

TWENTY-THREE

They were on their second beer and pretty much in shock when Juliet took a call from the Home Secretary, desperate, to go by the sound of his voice, for some glad tidings. She had to confess that there weren't any of those coming from her direction.

'What do you know about the Blitz, Juliet?'

'Not my period,' she said.

'Several facts about it aren't really discussed. Everyone knew by the late 1930s that Nazi arms escalation was making war inevitable and that it would be an aerial war, a war of bombing. Yet the British built no air raid shelters. Do you know why?'

'No.'

'Because our psychologists said that a population sheltering safely from bombing raids would never come back up to retaliate. The people denied shelters weren't invited into the Underground, either. That's a cosy myth. The Underground was stormed by civilians with nowhere else to go.'

'I see.'

'Sheer good fortune that a line under the Thames wasn't bombed. The Bakerloo line. Carnage.'

'Where is this going?'

'The Germans had psychologists too. They were consulted by the Luftwaffe. The first bombs used were firebombs, small and dropped in clusters to ignite a seriously combustible city. Everything burned, from the horsehair stuffing the furniture to the paraffin in the stoves. But it didn't work.'

'I'm sure there's a point here, sir.'

'My point is what came next. The psychologists said, if you bomb their landmark buildings to rubble, they'll forget what they are fighting for and give up. Level St Paul's and the Houses of Parliament, bomb Tower Bridge into oblivion, and they'll lose their national identity. Without those reminders, they'll no longer know who they are.'

'And that's happening now?'

'The flood waters are receding. But much of London is irreparable, including some of its most treasured and iconic buildings. Have you seen Nelson's Column yet?'

'No, sir.'

'Came down half an hour ago. Subsidence at the base, caused by the flood waters. It was pushed to an angle where the engineers said it could no longer support its own weight. It's in three pieces, and the man it celebrates is now in two halves.'

'Jesus.'

'How's Romeo?'

'How's who? Oh, I see. Paul's fine, sir. We didn't get anywhere today, but that's through no lack of effort or willingness on his part. He cracked Keller's code. Did you know his grandmother was at Bletchley Park?'

'Of course I did. I want you back here tomorrow, both of you, if he's going to be useful. There's an army base you can fly from; I'll send you directions. You'll come back aboard a Hercules.'

'Why a military plane? Seems a bit unnecessary. Flying into where?'

'Flying into Heathrow. Heathrow's been requisitioned by the military. All civilian flights have been cancelled. The country's in a state of emergency.'

'I won't be bringing Romeo, sir. He's got a leave of absence.'

'I think not, Juliet. I think you'll find he'll volunteer for this.'

She had walked out of the bar to take the call. Inside, through the picture window facing the street, she could see neon signage and subtle lighting and Paul Beck watching the images shot in London earlier in the day on the flatscreen above the bar. London didn't resemble Venice, under the water. The water was mud-coloured and looked as if it would stink. Bodies floated inert in it among an impossible litter of other debris. The images were surreal until your mind made sense of their magnitude and chaos. Then they became apocalyptic.

'How close are we to war, Home Secretary?'

A mirthless laugh was emitted from her phone. He said, 'You need a cocktail of anger and indignation and hatred to declare a war. You require optimism to win one. Right now, we have precious little of that. The situation in the South East of England is close to anarchic. You'd think an enemy power would take advantage. I doubt, from an enemy point of view, there's ever been a more advantageous time.'

'The country on its knees?'

'On the ropes,' he said. 'Always a puncher's chance, Juliet.'

'That stuff you told me about the Blitz?'

'Yes?'

'Not my period, like I told you. But I know quite a lot about medieval history. By some accounts, the Black Death claimed the lives of sixty per cent of Europe's population. Famine was widespread in northern Europe in the aftermath, because there weren't the peasants left to gather the grain harvest, so people had no bread.'

'People thought it was the End Times,' he said.

'The Western world at least was on the brink,' Juliet said. 'There's a tipping point. There's a moment when people lose faith.'

'And it's contagious,' he said. 'I think we were very close to it in the autumn of 1940. I've never experienced it in my lifetime. But I'm feeling something of it now.'

'There will be people who'll think a war would be a good thing,' Juliet said. 'Dispel the gloom, everyone pulling together.'

'Which is exactly how some of my Cabinet colleagues feel,' he said. 'Fortunately, they're not in the majority.'

'Not yet.'

'No. Not yet.'

When the call ended, Juliet went back inside. The London flood images were still being televised, on what she thought must be the loop-tape from hell. She drained her by now tepid beer and apprised Paul of her conversation.

'I know him slightly. There's a family connection. Bit patrician, bone-dry sense of humour. Essentially a good guy.'

'That how he knew you'd volunteer?'

'What's his take on all this?'

'Holistic,' Juliet said.

'What does that mean?'

'Agnostic and a believer at the same time. He doesn't really believe a book is doing this, but still wants me to stop whoever's using it.'

'Well, he's a politician,' Paul said. 'They like things both ways. Contradictions to them are just compromises. Paradoxes become principles.'

Juliet looked up at the screen just as a body welled to the surface somewhere she thought she recognized as Bond Street. Fenwicks department store, its glass obliterated by weight of water, window display mannequins neck deep in it, the caption crawling across the bottom of the screen saying that this was shot at just after four in the afternoon.

She'd seen enough. She grabbed Paul by the hand and hauled him outside on to the pavement.

'What's happening?'

'I need to walk in the fresh air, Paul. Then we need to try to eat.'

'Good luck with that.'

'We can neither of us run on empty.'

'And then what?'

'There are two things you need to know about me. The first is that I don't do one-night stands. The second is that I really don't want to sleep alone tonight.'

'You're a Londoner, aren't you?'

'I was brought up in Wandsworth. Went to school there. This is all very personal to me.'

'I had no intention of leaving you on your own tonight,' he said. 'It's not in my nature to behave so callously.'

She kissed him. She didn't know she was going to do it until it was done. She thought it took them both by surprise. And then they held one another, which seemed completely natural to Juliet. And also exactly what the moment required.

TWENTY-FOUR

D awn Jackson awoke the following morning and, when she walked into the kitchen, became aware that the power had been restored. The fridge was humming loudly, working hard to restore its low ambient temperature, the power presumably not having been back on for all that long.

Dawn took this as a sign. It signalled that she should revive her grandfather that very day. Yes, he could grump sometimes for England. And he'd probably go bonkers about the appalling state of the fish tank. And he always smelled strongly of tobacco smoke. But she wanted company apart from that which her feral, leering, ever-hungry dead brother now provided. She wanted *proper* company. And maybe Grandpa would have lost his interest in smoking. Maybe old habits died hard only if the person possessing them hadn't literally died themselves. Just a thought, thought Dawn. Just a bit of pre-breakfast philosophizing.

He'd been a bit, well, mushy, had Grandpa, when they'd carried him down the stairs. He'd been overripe, in all honesty. But Dawn believed strongly in both practice and persistence, and thought she would do a more polished job with Grandpa than she had with Pete. Pete was actually what manufacturers called a prototype. You got the kinks out with the prototype before you began the production run proper. Everyone in industry knew that.

Reviving Grandpa would probably come at a cost. But the pain from his old war wound had been chronic and the mirrored cabinets in both bathrooms were crammed with both over-the-counter and prescription painkillers. There was plentiful generic aspirin and paracetamol. Brands included extra-strength Nurofen. And for the real humdinger headaches, there was Naproxen and Diazepam. The cabinet above the sink in Grandpa's bathroom was practically a pharmacy.

By now, Dawn considered she was all over her trickier Special Study Group test subjects. She was on top of Spanish vocab, well up on *Treasure Island* and Narnia. London was in such a state of ongoing chaos that she didn't even know yet whether the tests would be staged. There was no information, which was bad. But no one was showing any curiosity about her dead brother's whereabouts any longer, which was good. Well, nobody other than Andy Baxter. But Dawn had plans down the line for Handy Andy. Instinct, or intuition, told Dawn that even though she knew it by heart, the revival spell would work best with the book to hand. So immediately after switching off the chest freezer containing Grandpa, she took the spade from the shed in the garden and went and dug the book up, careful to roll the turf and heap the soil and preserve the polythene wrapping intact so that she could bury it again later once her mission had been accomplished.

The revival spell required an artefact with which the subject had been physically intimate. She had used Pete's toothbrush. Thinking along similar lines, she went and fetched her grandfather's upper dentures from the glass on his bedside table in which both sets reposed. The water had all long evaporated and the glass was white at the bottom with residue from the dissolved tablet that cleaned the false teeth. They looked a bit dusty, so Dawn ran them under the tap.

This particular spell worked only in darkness. The sun had to have gone down. There was some explanation in the book about waking the dead from their slumber which made the night-time bit sound more symbolic than real to Dawn, but after what she considered her flawed experimentation with her brother, she was prepared to toe the line as far as the instructions were concerned. She didn't really want another monster on her hands.

The artefact meant that she could do the spell remotely. She didn't have to go into the garage at all. She didn't even have to unlock the freezer's heavy lid, since only gravity kept it closed. Presumably Grandpa would wake up, or come around, or whatever. And then he'd climb out. 'Clamber' might be a better word, she thought, for this part of the process. Grandpa was sort of stringy build-wise but, like most old people, a bit stiff and uncoordinated in his movement. And of course there was his dodgy knee.

Dawn performed the spell just after full dark, at almost a quarter to ten at night. Then she watched a bit of the news on the television. The crisis was worsening. Two Royal Navy fighter planes had been scrambled from the deck of the aircraft carrier HMS

Nemesis. They'd been in a dogfight over the Solent with a Russian fighter-bomber and had shot it down. The Russian aircraft's pilot had ejected and been picked up uninjured in an onion field on the Isle of Wight, but his navigator was missing presumed dead. Moscow was calling it a very grave escalation. So was the British government.

'Handbags,' Dawn said, flatly, to the TV screen. Her own idea of a grave escalation was a nuclear bomb levelling a city.

London didn't need a nuclear bomb. The streets were littered with wrecked cars and black cabs going nowhere and buses on their sides. All the shop frontages were smashed in and the stock ruined. Lavatories overflowed with raw sewage when householders tried to flush them. In every London suburb the streets were a kaleidoscopic riot of pulled-up and dumped carpets. A warning about graphic content flashed on the screen before footage of flood victims being bulldozed into high piles of bodies at a junction somewhere. And there was a typhus outbreak.

A bit bored with the flood coverage, Dawn switched to the Pete channel.

'Bloody hell, you must be hungry,' she said to the screen.

Pete was seated down there in the gloom, cross-legged on the cellar floor, surrounded by empty corned beef and pilchard tins, most of his left arm now missing. He was gnawing at the stump.

He looked up sharply when she made the remark, giving a hint of the preternatural speed of reflex he now possessed in what remained of him. He grinned and winked with his one good eye. And then his tongue protruded, palely serpent-like, and he licked blood lovingly from exposed bone.

There was a feathery tap at the sitting room window. Dawn went to the front door and opened it. Her grandfather stood in front of her in striped pyjama bottoms and the white singlet soiled yellow under the armpits where he had started to ooze as he'd lain upstairs, dead in his bed in the summer heat. He'd felt gluey there, when they'd carried him down the stairs.

'Hello, Dawn.'

His voice was an echoey rasp and when he grinned at her he looked different from how she remembered him. Wolfish, somehow. There was a proper word for that, wasn't there? Dawn knew she'd have it in a second, and then she did. The word was 'lupine'.

It was the teeth that were different. Grandpa had his own teeth now, and they were long and discoloured and sharp looking. He must have grown the teeth in death. Unless he'd got them as part of the revival process.

'I'm hungry, Dawn,' her grandpa said.

And Dawn thought, Here we go.

He walked stiffly into the house and through to the kitchen and Dawn saw with a stab of disgust that he'd soiled himself. Well, understandable. Grandpa had waited a long time for that pee, hadn't he? Elderly men. Prostate problems. Ugh.

She followed him and opened a cupboard and perused the rations parachuted into their garden the previous day.

But when she looked, he was eying the fish tank and its energetic contents, avidly.

'I'll have the seafood, Dawn,' he said. He was drooling saliva in a glistening string from his chin. And Dawn was feeling a bit regretful, thinking her brother might have some company in their cellar quite soon.

She grimaced. 'How will you eat them?'

'Easily. I'll suck them from their shells,' her grandfather said.

Two birds with one stone, Dawn thought. He'd probably lick out the tank afterwards. She could feel the thump at her temples of an oncoming humdinger of a headache. She felt more than tired, she felt suddenly bone weary. And saliva was filling her mouth, sour, like it does just before you puke. This didn't feel, to Dawn, like a moment of triumph.

The rumble of earthquake made the surface of the green sludge filling the tank ripple and shiver as her grandfather groped through the slime for a terrapin and began his impromptu meal. It would loosen a few slates on their roof and inflict a crack in an interior wall. But Crouch End mostly got away with a tremor or two. Central London did not. In Bloomsbury and Clerkenwell, in Islington and Camden Town, it was a nine on the Richter scale. It was mass death and utter devastation.

In their shared hotel room on Park Lane, Paul Beck and Juliet Harrington rushed to the window in time to see a large floodlit statue topple opposite. Someone big and mythological, cast in bronze. Someone with a sword and shield, prone now, plucked from his plinth by the spasms jerking the earth. Achilles, Juliet remembered.

'They're active again, Paul,' she said, 'using the Almanac. This is the Auguries. This is the world out of kilter. This is the universe wronged.'

Their hotel room window juddered, panes of glass smashing one by one as though plucked from their frames. They retreated as far as the bed and held one another until the earth's delinquent movement altogether ceased.

TWENTY-FIVE

The military base was at Paderborn, a 300-mile drive in a hire car from Berlin but the only place from which they could fly to the UK in the state of emergency that had downed all civilian flights in and out of the country. They'd set off early and reached the base at ten a.m. on Wednesday morning, Paul averaging over a hundred miles per hour at the wheel on the route. He might not have been a top-flight footballer, Juliet thought, but as far as his white-knuckled passenger was concerned, he certainly drove like one.

A Hercules aircraft was big, loud, prop-driven and, as Juliet discovered, completely free of creature comforts. It was five p.m. before they were picked up by a ministerial car at Heathrow and driven to their hotel. Juliet showered and changed, and Paul ordered a room service meal for each of them while she switched on her laptop and researched the man her Tudor specialist Oxford contact had told her was the likeliest to have commissioned Gunter Keller to mastermind the Almanac.

His name was Edmund Fleury and he was a baron. His lineage was Norman, an ancestor a knight and formidable warrior and one of the barons who had helped William the Conqueror achieve the victory at Hastings that gained him the English throne. In return for this service, Jean-Luc Fleury had been handed as his English estate a large slice of what was now Dorset. Almost 500 years later his direct descendant, Edmund, inherited as the eldest son.

Even by the standards of Tudor aristocracy, Edmund Fleury's wealth was vast.

And he seemed to have been a true Renaissance man. He was an accomplished writer of sonnets. He'd designed buildings on his estate. He'd played and composed for the clavichord. And he'd been extremely enthusiastic about astronomy.

'Not to mention running a variety of duellist opponents clean through with his pricey rapier,' Paul said from behind her shoulder.

'He didn't need to run them through. He just needed to draw blood to settle an affair of honour. He was so handy with a sword he could apparently nick an opponent at will. Even he couldn't have killed someone with impunity in peacetime. You needed to be the monarch to get away with that.'

'And you needed the semblance of a trial,' Paul said. 'Thomas More. Anne Boleyn.'

'You know your history.'

'I just enjoy movies.'

Juliet read some more. Then she said, 'Edmund Fleury isn't quite adding up.'

'He's just your average clever blue-blooded psychopath,' Paul said. 'They were a fairly common breed, weren't they? A bit of jousting, a bit of calculus, a dash of womanizing, some occasional warfare. I mean, there's a theory Henry the Eighth wrote "Greensleeves".'

'What I mean is, he seems too rational to be the man who paid a fortune to have the Almanac compiled.'

'I don't know, Juliet. John Dee didn't much differentiate between science and magic. Were there really any lines of demarcation before the Enlightenment?'

'No. But there was an intolerance, religious and legal, of blasphemy, witchcraft and heresy. This is a cultured and intelligent man who inherited more wealth than he could ever squander. His is a very proud and profoundly Christian heritage. His younger brother renounced his own wealth and titles to become a Franciscan monk. He had ancestors who became Crusaders. One of them earned a place in the chronicles for his valour at the Siege of Jerusalem. Why does a man with his noble lineage want to create the *Almanac of Forbidden Wisdom*? He had a wife to whom he was devoted. He was a loving father to three children. Why take the enormous risk of dabbling in that sort of mischief? What on earth did he stand to gain from it that he didn't already possess?'

'Maybe he can tell you himself. He sounds like the sort of man who would have written things down. Clever people have a habit of expressing themselves. Even if they feel obliged to do it in code. Did he leave any papers?'

'According to my Tudor authority, they're in the Bodleian Library.'

'Oxford. Sounds like fate to me, Juliet.'

'They're no likelier to tell us where the Almanac is now than the Keller archive was.'

'Without the Keller archive you and I would never have met.'

'That's true. Plus, there's the fact that we've nowhere else to look.'

Juliet's phone began to ring. She didn't recognize the number on the display. She took the call anyway, knowing it might be important.

'You're back in the country. I can tell from the dial tone.'

She didn't recognize the voice, deep and male, perhaps just the hint of an Irish brogue. 'Who is this?'

'My name is Thomas Gould. I'm a Catholic priest. We spoke briefly before your departure. I wanted to speak to you. I still want to speak to you.'

'About my monograph.'

'Specifically, about the *Almanac of Forbidden Wisdom* and the phenomenon of the unrestful dead. I think I may have experienced the latter.'

'I think you'd know for certain if you had. And to experience the latter, you need to have come into contact with the former. Have you?'

'This is completely unsatisfactory, Professor Harrington. We need to have this discussion face to face.'

'How did you even get my mobile number?'

'Dr Doyle gave it to me. Not everyone shares your apparent contempt for the clergy.'

'On matters clerical, Father Gould, where do you stand on the End Times?'

'I know from your monograph that you think the Almanac was Gunter Keller's attempt to bring them about. I know from your university head of department that you think it's been rediscovered by someone currently using it. I don't think the string of catastrophes we're enduring is either a test of faith or a coincidence. I need to see you, professor.'

Juliet took the phone from the side of her head and tapped it with her free hand, thinking. She was an Oxford-based academic with a ministerial backer. The Bodleian was a great deal easier for her to access than the Humboldt library had been. As Paul had implied, it was her home turf. But it was closed now and wouldn't open again until the morning.

'Where are you, Father Gould?'

'Crouch End.'

She looked at her wristwatch. It was just after six. 'How long would it take you to get to Park Lane?'

'If I can pick a route reasonably free of flood-damaged cars I can cycle there in an hour. An hour and a half, tops.' He sounded relieved. Something had really bothered this man. Was still bothering him. If she gave him an hour of her time, she could still turn in before nine p.m., nine thirty at the latest. She couldn't remember having felt more tired. She needed to be rested and alert in the morning for whatever the Baron Fleury had left for them to read about his life and motivations.

'You don't sound young.'

'Until bowing out last year I was a member of the London Dynamos. A veteran member, but I can ride a bike.'

'Fair enough.'

She told Father Gould where they were staying. She asked him to ring up from reception when he arrived.

But Father Gould never did arrive. Just under an hour after this conversation was completed, the glass in the window of the room they were in had danced its shattered path, some of it on to their carpet, some of it seven storeys further down to the street outside.

And Father Gould, having had a puncture on the bike he'd subsequently abandoned, was kneeling in a rubble-strewn train carriage on one of the handful of Overground lines restored after the flooding, clutching his missal, administering the last rites by the light of the torch on someone's iPhone to one of three dying passengers crushed by stone shaken from the roof of the road tunnel they were under.

TWENTY-SIX

The hotel had to be evacuated. The risk of structural collapse was just too great for any other option. Juliet and Paul grabbed the duvet and pillows and joined the rabble army of hotel guests from all along Park Lane and headed for Hyde Park. Darkness fell on a white-wrapped litter of prone bodies, maybe 2,000 people too stunned to speak or even move as the aftershocks rippled through the still sodden grass beneath them.

Juliet woke at first light and roused Paul and they picked a careful path through the sleeping throng until they reached a park gate, from where they could see that the mass exodus from the capital had started, with gridlocked traffic on the road in both directions and pedestrians like a shuffling somnambulist procession burdened by suitcases and rucksacks and sullen, silent, fearful children.

Smoke rose, black pillars of it reaching skyward from burning buildings in every direction. No one raised a human voice above the heaving throb of traffic beneath its exhaust haze and heat-ripple.

'The End Times,' Paul said. 'Oxford might be impossible now.'

Juliet went back into the park to find a quiet spot to make a phone call. Assuming the network hadn't crashed. Assuming she could still raise a signal.

The Home Secretary answered before she had time to hear it ring at his end.

'Where are you, Professor Harrington?'

'Central London.'

'Beck?'

'With me.'

'Both intact?'

'So far, yes. We need to get to Oxford.'

'I'll have a chopper scrambled. Where are you precisely?'

'Park Lane.'

'Good. Find an intact hotel. One with a helipad. Call me when you're there and I'll relay your location to your air crew.'

Juliet thought 'intact' a relative term. Though getting into the hotels wasn't a problem through yesterday's glassed-in foyers, now smashed to pieces and therefore open to the world. Their own hotel had been open to guests despite the slime-smeared carpet in the vestibule, the non-functioning lifts, the walls on the ground floor discoloured to head height by recently receded flood water. 'The Blitz spirit,' the concierge had said. Juliet thought the Blitz spirit now evaporating fast.

Their helipad, when they found it, was twelve floors up and gave them a panoramic view of the devastation. Fires raged unchecked. Fissures several feet wide scarred roads. Almost no building seemed unscathed. The sleepers in their hotel sheets looked like corpses in their winding shrouds laid out on the park's summer grass, which was damp and starting to steam under a strengthening sun in a vista rendered totally surreal. Elsewhere below them, looters ran here and there in the streets like swarms of ants.

Juliet rang the Home Secretary and gave him their location. 'Not a single seismologist or geologist predicted last night's quake,' he said. 'But then no meteorologist predicted the fog. And no epidemiologist could explain the plague outbreak. What's happening simply isn't normal or even explicable.'

'We need to locate the Almanac.'

'I think it might be too late,' he said. 'Is Oxford a decent lead?'

'Oxford's our only lead, sir.'

'Then Godspeed, Juliet. Godspeed.'

She remembered the priest then, a man steeped in the rites of organized religion, a cleric with a claim concerning the phenomenon of the unrestful dead. Another lead? Another cul-de-sac? She retrieved and called his number, but heard only silence.

They were in Oxford by eleven a.m. After the sensory assault of an apocalyptic London, it looked as perfect in the summer sunshine as a film set might. Grass was verdantly green, the Cherwell sparkled prettily and the spires dreamed on oblivious to the carnage occurring only sixty miles away.

They'd been given a thoughtful pack of field rations as breakfast for their journey, washed down with a rejuvenating brew of strong coffee from a vacuum flask. Juliet could have done with a shower, but compared to the people they had left sleeping in the park that morning, she thought neither she nor Paul had any real cause for complaint. London had become a place of fleeing refugees. The unthinkable had happened to the capital. And it looked likely to continue to happen.

They walked through the tourist throng in the Bodleian's courtyard and into the scholarly hush of the library itself like two people walking into another century: mullioned, burnished, leather-bound and sedate.

An archivist approached them as soon as they entered. Juliet was a familiar presence there, but in addition the Home Secretary had apparently prepared the ground on their behalf while they were still in the air.

The archivist was Ms Plummer. If she had a first name, Juliet had never heard it used. Ms Plummer had a grey bun and a pair of gold-wired spectacles on a thin chain. She also boasted a photographic memory, though 'boasted' was probably the wrong word. Her perfect recall was an attribute she acted as though everyone shared. It was a discreetly used gift.

Ms Plummer invited Juliet and Paul into her office. This honour was a first for Juliet. The office was small and book-lined and its shelves smelled of Morocco leather. Lozenges of light flushed the wooden floor through a single latticed window.

The archivist cleared her throat and said, 'The Baron Fleury's papers have never been catalogued. You'll know why immediately when you see the chest in which they reside. There is a royal seal on the lock.'

Paul said, 'Did the chest originally arrive here accompanied by a key?'

'It did. But at the time it arrived, if you broke a royal seal, you took a one-way trip to the Tower, by boat, through the Traitors' Gate.'

'In what circumstances is it permissible to break a royal seal in the present day?'

'When it's life and death, Mr Beck. When it's a national emergency, which the Home Secretary insists this is.'

Juliet said, 'Where is this chest located?'

'In the most impregnable of our secure basement rooms. Some

of the material in this library is priceless. Some of our Bibles, some of our books dealing with cartography. And the whole world knows it. And there are some very unscrupulous collectors out there with extremely deep pockets.'

Paul said, 'Which monarch's seal is on the lock?'

'The one who married all those wives, Mr Beck. The one with no compunction about cutting off his subjects' heads. Some of them, at one time, his friends.'

The room wasn't absolute in its period detail. Ms Plummer's oak desk was ornately carved but equipped with an Apple laptop and a modern landline phone. And on the deep sill under her window, there was a very modern looking espresso machine. Now she nodded towards it.

'Would either or both of you like a coffee, before I take you through?'

Paul accepted. Juliet declined. She didn't need to have her heart jump-started; it was already thumping along merrily enough. She was nervous, not about what they might find, but about what they might not.

Politicians exaggerated all the time. It went with the territory, was part of the game. But she did not think that the Home Secretary had exaggerated in the slightest in getting them their access to something censored, or embargoed, or just kept secret for hundreds of years.

Juliet Harrington did not want to leave this library without a solid lead. She was desperate for some clue as to the Almanac's location. She was painfully aware that after today, there was nothing to examine and nowhere left to look. So she waited patiently for Paul Beck to drink his coffee and she pondered briefly on the saying of a prayer.

And doing that brought Father Thomas Gould again, momentarily, back into her mind. And she wondered whether the priest was alive or dead.

They left Ms Plummer's office, which she locked behind her. They walked along a wood-lined corridor and reached a descending spiral staircase. She led them down and then past several basement doors in a second corridor. Finally, she stopped at one. She produced a single key from a pocket and unlocked the door and ushered them into a small room.

The chest had been placed on a table at the centre of the room, probably that very morning during their flight. And the room had been furnished with two chairs. The box was about three feet long, two high and two wide. Henry's seal was a belligerent looking lump of red sealing wax with the Tudor rose and the monarch's single initial branded forcefully into its centre.

Ms Plummer produced the third key her pockets had contained that morning and she placed it on the table. 'I'll leave you to it,' she said.

Juliet turned to her, surprised. 'Aren't you curious?' she said.

Ms Plummer smiled slightly. She pushed her glasses more firmly on to her nose. She said, 'I was faxed your security clearances. I can tell you that they were approved at the highest possible level. It's not a distinction I share. Apparently this is a matter of national security. I'm simply not permitted to witness any of this.'

TWENTY-SEVEN

Dawn Jackson called Handy Andy Baxter using her dead brother Pete's mobile phone. She personally didn't own a mobile. She wasn't on the spectrum, a fact proven on a daily basis by the lively and ongoing interest she took in current affairs. But she had no interest in selfies, texting, Instagram, Facebook, Snapchat, WhatsApp or any of the other tedious trivia with which teens tended to complicate their lives.

Pete's mobile functioned for two reasons. The first was that Dawn had remembered to charge it overnight. The second was that Grandpa's current account paid the bill by standing order every month. And, usefully, Handy Andy's name and number came up when you scrolled through Pete's contacts.

Dawn called Andy just as Paul Beck and Juliet Harrington walked through the courtyard on their way into the Bodleian. She'd spent most of the morning watching the crisis escalate on the TV. Grandpa had returned with even less interest in the exterior world than he'd had before his death. He was currently in the garden, hoping to catch a cat in the way his grandson had, twice, before Dawn arranged his incarceration in the cellar.

When Dawn had looked out of the kitchen window to check on her grandfather half an hour before calling Andy, he'd been squatting on his haunches eating a wood pigeon. The grossest thing about this was that the bird was still wearing its feathers. And those big yellow teeth he'd come back with appeared overnight to have got bigger and more discoloured. And sharper, Dawn thought.

She didn't think he was a danger to her. He was reasonably friendly, when he wasn't complaining about being hungry. He was quite communicative, in a basic sort of way. But he tended to sort of zone out, standing staring out a window like someone waiting for a bus in his own house. When obviously the bus wasn't coming.

Handy Andy Baxter was coming. And she was going to lure Andy into the cellar for a reunion with her dead brother. Sneaky Pete, who really *was* sneaky in this current incarnation, was overdue a visitor. And Handy Andy was the perfect candidate.

She made the call.

'Pete!'

'It's Dawn, Andy.'

'Where's Pete?'

'He's here. He's finally home.'

'Why doesn't he call me himself?'

'He can't. He's got laryngitis.'

'I thought he had meningitis.'

'He did. But now he's got laryngitis. He's lost his voice. He can't talk. He wants you to come around.'

'What's the point if he can't talk?'

'He can do a kind of hoarse whispery thing. Doesn't carry over the phone. Works OK face to face because what you can't hear, you can lip-read.'

'Have you seen the news, Dawn? I mean, have you seen what's going on? I mean, blimey.'

'There are going to be diseases spread by all the dead people they can't easily recover from collapsed buildings, apparently. They hadn't even sorted out the bodies from the flood yet.'

'It's like the End Times. In the Gospel of St John?'

'I'd almost forgotten you were an altar boy.'

'Is laryngitis catching?'

'The word's "contagious", Andy. You need to learn that one. Going to be using it a lot.'

'Contagious,' Andy said.

'And the answer's no, by the way.'

'What time should I come around?'

'In an hour?'

'OK.'

'Another thing, Andy. So many people are leaving London that the food shortages are no longer a big problem.'

'What's that got to do with anything?'

'Pete's got laryngitis. Buy him some grapes.'

Dawn didn't think that the current iteration of her brother, which she'd admitted to herself would be his last, would have an appetite any longer for fruit. His tastes were a bit more basic and closer to home these days. It was a good thought, though, a nice detail. Fruit was what you brought sick people. Grapes, in particular.

She put the Pete channel on. She couldn't see her brother in the cellar and experienced an uneasy moment of panic before his face slid across the screen in extreme close-up, mouth leering and his one good eye vacuous. Then he suddenly scuttled backwards; tiny, rapid, insectile steps. And she got some perspective. She saw that he'd eaten his left arm all the way to the shoulder.

'Gross,' Dawn said, switching off the TV.

Andy Baxter was excited at the thought of seeing Pete again. It was perfectly possible that his hospital stay had reminded him of the personal hygiene routines he seemed to have forgotten living with his grandfather. He was still disappointed that Dawn hadn't had the decency to pass on his get-well card. He hoped they'd got rid of those bloody bastard little turtles. And he remembered the noises from below on his last, clandestine visit; Dawn had previously told him they were caused by remedial work next door. But with Pete there, everything would be different.

Andy got lucky on the route. His journey to Pete's grandfather's house took him past a grocery store and a convenience store. The grocery store was closed now and had an abandoned, almost

derelict look. When Andy peered into the window, all the vege-
tables in their wooden crates looked diseased. Peppers were
collapsing in on themselves, cabbages blackening, potatoes
growing white tendrils that groped out from their skins. It was a
proper horror story.

But the convenience store was open and even though they were
an outrageous price, they had bags of green grapes. Those grapes
people in the know called white grapes, which Andy knew they
definitely weren't. He wasn't colour blind.

He got to Pete's house holding the brown paper bag out on his
flat right hand so as not to crush any grapes. He was inside the front
garden gate, on the gravel path, when he happened to look up.

Pete's grandfather was standing at one of the upper windows
in striped pyjama bottoms with a generous yellow patch of dried
pee at the crotch and a vest daubed down the front with what
looked to Andy like blood and feathers. Andy stopped dead, though
the grapes he was holding didn't and their momentum made them
fall from his hand to the ground. They did so, to Andy's ears,
with a soft and fruity thud. This bit of unintended slapstick seemed
to snap Pete's grandfather out of some sort of daydream or trance.
His face split in a grin exposing a mouthful of joke-shop teeth.
They weren't funny, though. They were grotesque. He was
grotesque. Andy turned, and he fled.

Dawn observed the Andy part of this process through the
security spy hole in the front door. She had to stand on tiptoe
to reach that, which hurt her calves. She hadn't heard her grandfather ascend the stairs but could guess at what had freaked
Handy Andy out. He was a sight for sore eyes, was Granddad.
He was a fucking apparition. He'd have to go, basically. Frankly,
that was the least the wood pigeon population of Crouch End
deserved.

And Handy Andy? There was always the sleep spell, the sung
lullaby fatal for its subject. She'd need a photo, and he was bound
to be on Facebook. Child's play, really. Except Dawn thought that
dying in his sleep was altogether too easy a demise for so
troublesome a character. Andy Baxter needed to go out with more
of a bang than a whimper.

TWENTY-EIGHT

The box contained a rapier, laid diagonally to accommodate its length, the Toledo steel surprisingly untarnished by time. That sat atop everything else.

'His calling card,' Paul said.

'A warning, too. It's a graphic way of saying to anyone opening the chest, *Go no further than you already have*. And with his reputation it would have been a warning taken seriously.'

Juliet pried the rapier out of the box and examined it. The guard was filigreed, the blade engraved, the sword light, its balance perfect. It was more a forensic tool than a weapon of war, she thought. It spoke of poise and quick reflexes, feathery footwork, a masterful arm. And utter ruthlessness.

'So much for the loving husband and devoted father,' Paul said.

'I keep telling you, Paul. You can't judge people from five hundred years ago by the standards of our time. Thomas More wrote *Utopia*. He was still a zealous advocate of the death penalty.'

'And he paid the ultimate price.'

'You know quite a lot of history.'

'Paul Scofield, *A Man for All Seasons*. I like movies.'

'Robert Shaw was Henry in that.'

'And a very fine job he made of it. Though he was even better as Quint in *Jaws*.'

There were papers, under the sword. There were title deeds and land registry documents, all handwritten on sheets of parchment, some stamped with official seals. It was the detritus of someone wealthy and important, a man of status and significance, but it was of no relevance to their purpose.

The papers lay at the top and so concealed further artefacts. A steel helmet, such as a knight might have used for protection when jousting. A beret-like hat decorated with an ostrich feather, time-faded but probably once a rich purple colour. A pair of exquisitely stitched leather gauntlets. A locket that when unclasped proved to be a portrait of a blonde female child of about nine or ten. An engraved silver pocket watch. A purse filled with French gold coins.

Paul frowned. 'Weren't the English at war with the French during Henry's reign?'

'Not at the time when he met King Francis at the Field of the Cloth of Gold. Sporadically, after that. Regionally, and always expensively. The campaign of sieges and burning and looting in Picardy almost bankrupted England. That was why Henry eventually confiscated the property of the monasteries. He needed to raise cash.'

'And Fleury was of Norman extraction,' Paul said. 'He might very well have had French cousins.'

'His wife was French,' Juliet said.

'How would that have played with the king?'

'Anne Boleyn had spent some time at the French royal court as a girl.'

'And look what happened to her. Geneviève Bujold, *Anne of the Thousand Days*.'

'You need to get out more, Paul.'

'I'll be OK, now I've met you.'

'Netflix shares will probably never recover.'

'Ouch.'

There was a book at the very bottom of the chest. It looked like a prayer book, leather-bound, embossed with a design illustrating a Christian cross inside a circle of flame. Its pages were delicate when Paul riffled through them.

'Do you recognize that motif?'

'I've never seen it before,' Juliet said. 'I'd say it's the Tudor equivalent of a company logo.'

'Or a secret society,' Paul said, 'given that royal seal we broke to open this up.'

He opened the book and turned to the title page. 'Latin,' he said. 'Handwritten. Personal. He wrote this himself, unless he dictated it to a scribe. But I don't think he did that.'

Juliet took the book from him and looked at the ink on the page, which was black and tightly spaced. 'No scribe,' she said. 'The calligraphy is wrong. I hope I'm right in saying this is what that seal was protecting from prying eyes.'

Paul began to read, not aloud, but to himself. Then he nodded at the contents of the chest, at the helm and sword and ostrich-feathered hat and leather gloves; at the cloth bag of glittering gold coins and the stamped, stiff parchment documents. The Baron Fleury's wedding ring was there. His Order of the Garter insignia. Some pendant-style symbol of high office set with rubies on a heavy silver chain.

'These are his stage props,' Paul said. 'But this book, Juliet? This book is who he really was.'

December 17, 1527

And so I travelled to see his Royal Majesty the king, not at one of his own palaces, but at Hampton Court, where he resides during Cardinal Wolsey's absence in Rome. The king schemes at Hampton Court, guest of an absentee host. I believe it is a property he greatly covets. The deer are populous in the region and our monarch much loves the hunt. And there is no swifter or more comfortable mode of transportation than the royal barge gliding serenely along the river on a full tide. A hazardous state of affairs indeed, for the cardinal.

Secrecy being paramount, I was summoned to arrive at midnight, when witnesses are scant in the darkness and the bitter cold. Quartered at my London residence, I came by horse, the night ride not easy over the frost, my mount skittering on puddles turned to ice by the harshness of the season, my body warmed though by the bearskin cloak my beloved wife bought me on my birthday in September as the winter approached.

I discovered the king in ebullient mood. He is a man of mercurial temperament. His humour is not easy to predict, and his summons had given nothing away concerning the mission with which he sought to charge me. Those gimlet eyes of his gave nought further away as he poured brandy with his own hand into generous goblets for us both, to warm me and perhaps to steel him for what it was he had to say.

He has been plotting with the king of France. Henry and Francis are sometimes friends, sometimes enemies, always insistent rivals. Together they have been in correspondence, hatching a scheme. Their motive is the achievement of grace, the currying of favour with our stern and eternally judgemental God. That was my conclusion later, warmly wrapped in a strange bed, my head resting on a bolster. Henry wishes to be rewarded with a healthy and legitimate heir. But I get ahead of my story.

'What do you know of the practice of magic, Fleury?' the king asked me.

'That Mother Church abhors its practice,' I replied. 'Is it even a subject fit for upright men to discuss?'

'Its practice gives power to those with no right to possess it,' the king replied. 'They are able to influence events in a manner they should not. Fate can be perverted in their mischievous hands. They are pernicious and greedy, these occult practitioners.'

'So, you are not a sceptic, sire?'

The king was quiet for a moment. He sipped brandy – a gift, I believe, from the French court. An excellent vintage. Expertly distilled, half a century ago.

'I have seen a demonstration,' he said eventually. 'I have seen the impossible proven from a distance no greater than that between the two of us now. I know what can be accomplished by those in thrall to the Devil. Villages, towns, cities can be undermined. Empires could fall, if these magicians colluded to make that happen.'

'Do they collude?'

'Not generally. They work in a necessarily clandestine world. But they communicate, as a cabal would, in code and in secrecy.'

'And what is this to me, Majesty?'

The king outlined the scheme hatched with his French counterpart in their correspondence.

'You are rich, Fleury, which makes you plausible. The money to finance this will come from my coffers and those of the French exchequer. But the point is that you could afford to do it, should you ever so wish.

'You have achievements to your name that single you out as a man of ambition. Again, that makes you plausible, because who is to say where the limits of that ambition lie?

'You are possessed of courage and nerve, you are resourceful, and you are clever. But none of this would signify without one final, vital fact. Which is that I trust you. You have my faith. Now sleep on it and we'll talk again in the morning after you have tested me with a blade.'

'Rapiers, sire?'

'Broadswords,' said the king, laughing. 'A more even contest, Fleury. Sport is only sport when each man has a chance.'

Paul Beck stopped reading. There was a stunned expression on his face. He said, 'The commissioning of the *Almanac of Forbidden Wisdom* was nothing other than an elaborate sting operation.'

'The Almanac was never intended to be used,' Juliet said. 'Keller burned. Mary Nye was hanged. I don't know what happened to Hood or Cortez or van Vaunt, but I'll bet they didn't live long lives after their collaboration in England.'

'Why didn't Fleury destroy the Almanac?'

'It was designed to protect itself,' Juliet said. 'There would have been dire repercussions if he had.'

'So, he stored it somewhere safe.'

'Safe, until very recently.'

'Henry seems to have been a vigorous man, wanting to fence with a broadsword against someone as formidable as Fleury obviously was.'

'He was vigorous. He was a gifted athlete in his own right, well over six feet tall, slim and extremely physically strong. He led his knights into battle. He was also a talented musician, a thinker who spoke three languages fluently.'

'What went wrong?'

'He was knocked unconscious jousting nine years after the meeting described in these pages. That was the start of his physical decline. That was what triggered it.'

Her phone vibrated in her pocket. She took it out and saw that the caller had been the persistent priest, Father Thomas Gould. She was relieved the earthquake hadn't killed him. And she thought she owed him a return call, but the signal wasn't strong enough in the library basement.

She showed the number on her display to Paul and said, 'I'll be as quick as I can.'

TWENTY-NINE

'I'd still like to speak to you.'

'I'd have spoken to you last night, but for an act of God.'

'That wasn't God,' Father Gould said. 'Quite the opposite.' There'd been no rescue party. The capital had been overwhelmed. He'd performed the last rites three times and done what he could to comfort the dying in the carnage of the rubble-strewn train carriage until they passed, and then he'd crawled back along the track to the station they'd left a minute before the quake struck, led by the feeble glow of emergency lights on the platform.

Though its walls were stained to head height by the recent flood waters, the station itself was relatively undamaged except for the exit, which was partially blocked by fallen masonry. But he was a man of ascetic habits, spry for his age, and clambered over the obstacles, remembering how he'd climbed the cemetery wall a couple of days earlier. That had been prior to reading Professor Harrington's monograph. He might not have been so keen to do it afterwards.

He walked the five miles back to Crouch End through scenes of utter devastation. He thought that the foundations of many of the buildings now destroyed would have been undermined by the flood waters. But the quake had been powerful in its own right, something emphasized by the aftershocks. The earth would spasm and he'd clutch at any support just to try to stay upright on the route.

The very few people on the streets as dusk came were daubed in plaster dust and sometimes blood and walked with a zombie-like shuffle, uncoordinated, slow, seemingly aimless.

The devastation grew less the closer he got to home. Crouch End had not flooded much either, due to its elevation. It was strange, as though the locality enjoyed some sort of protection. Divine, perhaps? His own church, when he reached it, was missing only a few slates from its steeple. There was a devout roofer in his congregation who would repair that damage cheaply.

His home too was intact. He was exhausted, could not remember having felt in his life such bone-wearying fatigue. But before going to bed, he went into the church to pray for the victims of this most recent catastrophe. He lit a single candle, wondering how many more of these biblical afflictions he could endure before they began to cost him his faith.

Speculating on loss of faith might have been what provoked Father Thomas Gould's last conscious thoughts on that long night. It suddenly occurred to him that it was a long time since he'd seen one of his most faithful servers on the altar. Peter Jackson had stopped turning up to masses, benedictions and even requiems, which were profitable for the boys.

Peter's grandfather too had stopped attending mass on a Sunday, which he'd done for as long as Father Gould was able to remember. Perhaps he should pay his parishioners a visit, the old-fashioned way, without prior notice. Putting both on the spot might clarify their attitude. As well as solving a bit of a mystery.

Now, to Juliet Harrington, he said, 'Where are you today?'

'I'm in the courtyard outside the Bodleian Library in Oxford.'

'How on earth did you manage that? Friends in high places?'

'Not that high. I spent the night sleeping in a very muddy Hyde Park.'

'Turbulent times,' he said.

'Some people are saying the End Times, Father Gould. Do you believe that?'

'I believe they will come, but they're not here yet. Crouch End remains relatively unscathed. I slept in my own bed.'

'There's an exodus from the capital,' Juliet said. 'Fear is contagious. So is despair.'

'Agreed.'

'You read my monograph on the *Almanac of Forbidden Wisdom*. It was commissioned by a Tudor baron named Edmund Fleury. His agenda was to lure its compilers into the open so that they could be dealt with harshly in their homelands by the relevant authorities. It worked. Fleury never intended to use the Almanac personally. He believed magic a crime against both Man and God.'

'This isn't information in the public domain, is it?'

'I'm sure you're capable of priestly discretion.'

'I am, professor.'

'The problem is that the main architect of the Almanac also had an agenda. Gunter Keller wanted to accelerate the End Times. He wanted to see the triumph of Lucifer personally, for himself. Every time a spell from the Almanac is used, a price is exacted.'

'You believe it's being used now?'

'I do.'

'I still need to see you, to discuss what occurred at a burial service I performed.'

'I'll call you later today and arrange a day and time.'

'Thank you.'

Father Gould ended the call and a flare of brightness caused him to look up out of his sitting room window at the sky, where a double rainbow vaulted across the unsullied blue of the heavens.

'That's not possible,' he said aloud. 'You require clouds for rainbows. You require showers of rain. It's the reason they're called that.' What had Professor Harrington called this phenomenon in her monograph? *The Auguries*. The inexplicable events that sometimes signalled catastrophe when the Almanac was being used.

Earlier that morning, he'd reminded himself of old Henry Jackson's address. Henry had lost a son and daughter-in-law to a fatal motorway crash that had only served to deepen the pensioner's faith. He'd taken Peter and Peter's female twin in. Dawn Jackson was apparently extremely bright but not a believer, and Father Gould had never met her. But it was inexplicable that old Henry and his grandson had stopped attending church.

He'd called Professor Harrington just before setting off. As he did so, he was immediately aware that a brisk wind had arisen. It flapped at the jacket he wore and sent his hat careening across his lawn. As he went to retrieve it, the wind strengthened, a sustained blast making the exposed struts groan and whistle where his steeple had lost slates the night before.

A gust blew him backwards at a stagger as he reached the latched gate at the front of the church grounds, one hand holding on to his hat and the other held out for balance at the end of an extended arm.

An empty Sainsbury's bag, wind-filled, blew across the sky in front of him, a hundred feet in the air and gaining in altitude. He saw a helicopter wobbling above, clattering in the distance uneasily like a child's shaken toy.

The wind was a sustained roar gaining all the time in volume. Street trees in full leaf bowed in it like billowing sails. He heard a crash behind him and saw that a window in his home had exploded into a mess of blood and feathers caused by some avian creature propelled through the air like a puppet.

Another crash, this time from the street, where a roadside ash tree had snapped at its base and now lay atop two crumpled parked cars, their surviving windows frosted and spidery, an alarm from one adding a chorus to the banshee wail of the wind.

Father Gould realized he was going nowhere. He had been looking forward to his first missionary outing in as long as he could remember. But he could also remember the 1987 hurricane, of which this accelerating event was reminding him. The flooding had undermined many London buildings. The earthquake had inflicted structural damage on many more. This windstorm would be the coup de grâce for some of the oldest and most cherished structures in the capital. It didn't even resemble a capital any longer, except perhaps in a period of catastrophic war. The End Times? He struggled back to the shelter of his home without the will to try to answer his own question.

THIRTY

D awn had needed to use the displacement spell to put her grandfather down in the cellar with her brother. Bringing him back had been a terrible mistake, something brought home to her forcefully by Handy Andy's horrified reaction on seeing him. She just had to face the fact that they came back monsters. Maybe it was a process you could refine. Her grandpa had been slightly less of a monster than Pete, but only an incremental improvement on her brother.

Dawn didn't have the will, the patience or, in truth, the opportunity to polish that particular procedure. Their house was large and sited at the end of a substantial drive and their garden wasn't overlooked. But they were on a public road in a populous suburb of London and two neighbours had knocked on her door anxious

about their missing cats. Cats were no different from kebabs to
these versions of her grandpa and brother. People would become
suspicious, if they weren't already.

So she'd taken the book and studied its intricate rite and then
summoned the energy and concentration required to perform the
displacement spell and now her grandpa was down there with Pete
behind the magically secured obstacle of the impregnable cellar
door. And she wasn't missing him a bit.

Dawn had hoped to have a conversation with her grandfather
about what, if anything, lay on the other side. But that level of
communication had been too sophisticated for the creature he'd
returned as. Perhaps there was such a thing as the soul after all
and her grandpa had returned without one, just a husk, a kind of
human parasite. Maybe that particular spell was simply
self-defeating.

When she'd regained some of her post-spell strength, once the
pills kicked in and the headache became manageable, she'd put
the Pete channel on and seen them scuttling around one another
like a pair of cannibalistic fighting crabs. Grandpa was by far the
older of the two, but he'd returned with that disconcerting vigour
they brought back with them. And he'd grown a vicious set of
teeth. She thought too that her dead brother's missing arm made
it a more even match than it would otherwise have been.

She didn't bother to watch. Dawn wasn't at all a squeamish
person, but she didn't take much of an interest in sport and was
opposed on principle to blood sports such as hare coursing and
fox hunting and badger baiting. Foxes were enterprising creatures.
Badgers were cute looking. And hares were funny when they went
bonkers in the spring.

Something both serious and sombre had occurred to Dawn, and
it concerned cause and effect. She had finally begun to think the
odd goings on in the Greater London area were perhaps connected
to the spell book. She'd noticed that double rainbow immediately
after performing the displacement spell and had known from
physics that it was an impossible contradiction, meteorologically
absurd. And it had been followed by the wind now raging around
her four walls.

The wind was strong enough to be classified as a hurricane.
They'd said so excitedly on the radio. The house she considered

herself now to have inherited was extremely substantial in its build. But the hurricane had flattened their garden shed. Its roof had cartwheeled away over the garden wall. If she was extremely unlucky, it might have flattened a neighbouring cat. She just didn't know. But she knew she'd know all about it if it had. There'd be a querulous, complaining knock on her door.

She did know that the *Esmeralda* disaster had followed a weird and unpredicted solar eclipse. Statues had wept blood prior to the bubonic plague outbreak. There'd been that weird fog before the flooding. Something odd must have preceded the earthquake, but everyone was too preoccupied by the flood's death toll and the scale of general damage to notice it. A maelstrom in the English Channel? A unicorn turning up at London Zoo? Something odd and generally overlooked, and then the quake. And then the impossible rainbow auguring the storm.

Good word, 'auguring'. Dawn didn't think many people her age would know what the Auguries were. Her dimbo brother wouldn't have known. She was pretty confident Handy Andy Baxter wouldn't know either.

Magic exacted a price. That much was becoming clear to Dawn. And it made her think two things. The first was that even if the consequent hurricane really battered London, she hadn't actually had a choice over her grandfather. He'd come back with an ungovernable appetite and no discretion whatsoever. He pissed himself, for God's sake. He chomped his way through pigeons. She'd had to get rid of him.

The second thing that occurred to Dawn was that it might be possible to practise magic without it incurring these rather unfortunate repercussions. What was required was further study of the book.

Her brain felt a bit stale from all the Special Study Group revision, if she was honest with herself. She'd had to take two extra-strength paracetamol caplets after the effort required to cast the displacement spell successfully. And the elemental weather raging outside wasn't helping her head at all. But a girl had to do what a girl had to do, and Dawn knew, sighing, that she was in all truth a bit of a perfectionist.

She put on the TV. Not the Pete channel and the crab action, but the news channel for the latest on the crisis, because Dawn took the interest in current affairs which absolutely proved she wasn't on any kind of spectrum.

The lead item concerned the capital of England. That was no longer London, where the infrastructure was so badly damaged that no timeframe could be put on its repair and rejuvenation as any sort of business or domestic hub. Most Londoners were now living in a vast impromptu refugee camp established in the New Forest. Though some had dispersed to live with relatives elsewhere and many others had returned to their countries of origin. Since there were no civilian flights, they'd boarded ferries.

Birmingham was sulking about it, but Manchester was now the capital. It was the seat of government. It had excellent communication facilities. It had two first-rate football teams and a thriving gay community. On the downside, it was in the shadow of the Pennines, and it rained a lot there.

There'd been a chemical attack on the Moscow underground. The Kremlin were pointing the finger at MI6, who were saying it was Chechens, who in turn were blaming the Ukraine.

An Air France Airbus had exploded at 30,000 feet over the Alps. Too early to say whether it had been triggered by a suicidal passenger with a bomb, or by a heat-seeking missile from the ground.

In the US, an outspoken isolationist Republican senator had been shot dead at a political rally. The chief suspects were a Cuban American and a Mexican American, possibly working together. To Dawn, they both looked deranged, with their matching *Viva Zapata!* moustaches in old police mugshots.

'Maybe they're the same bloke,' Dawn said at the TV. Two passports, two identities, one assassin. Just a thought. She switched the TV off again, thinking that it might be a slow news day, but at least she didn't have to go out in the appalling weather. She'd stumbled upon her grandfather's cash stash, three grand in twenties in a thick roll bound by an elastic band in an ancient sports sock hidden in an equally ancient canvas cricket boot at the bottom of his bedroom wardrobe. The significance of this find was that she'd been able to stock up on supplies at the supermarket anonymously, without having to use a debit card that didn't belong to her. So she didn't have to risk attracting curiosity and unnecessary attention.

She'd been in that wardrobe before, when they'd first arrived here, groping for fir trees in the darkness, hoping with all her heart for Narnia. He'd told her off at the time and now she knew why. She'd been a lot younger in her mind then, had dreamed often of happy endings. The difference was that now, she knew there were none.

THIRTY-ONE

February 24, 1528

He claimed to be a mathematician only. But our spies found proof that he studied astrology and divination and dabbled also in alchemy. He was not a significant figure in the secret world of occult practitioners. What was done to him was done only on the understanding that he might reveal a significant name.

He was a defrocked priest with what he termed a workshop buried among the warren of such establishments used by the skilled and industrious clockmakers of Clerkenwell. In truth, when I went there after his incarceration to witness the actuality, I discovered it was more of a laboratory, with astral charts pinned to walls sooty with the residue of experimentation involving bellows and a forge. Equations on a slate testified to the partial truth of what he had claimed, but there was clearly mischief at work there. A mathematician would not need a pestle and mortar, or the herbs and minerals stored on shelves in labelled jars.

He became the subject of a severe interrogation. Pliers were used to pull a healthy tooth from a gum reluctant to part with it. But it was only after the second fingernail was pulled from his right hand that he surrendered a name and location. The name belonged to a German alchemist named Gunter Keller. The city where Keller could be located was given as Hanover.

I disapprove of torture, and have yet to have it proven to me personally that magic is capable of doing anything more than entertaining a gullible child or adult fool when practised by a skilled illusionist. But the man we questioned clearly lived in fear of Keller. The name was given up only with the utmost reluctance to practised purveyors of human pain in a cell deaf to his cries of agony deep in the bowels of the Tower.

For reasons which must be obvious, I did not confront this unfortunate man myself. If Keller is genuine and a significant figure in this murky occult underworld, he must believe my own motives to be innocent of conspiracy, fuelled entirely by worldly ambition, nothing to do with a general desire to eradicate evil. He cannot know that my intentions towards him are in any way hostile.

If he suspected that, he would go to ground when he must be teased out and must take on the lucrative project dreamed up for him. He must recruit fellows as misguided as he and thereby expose them. Though I confess I would have greater personal enthusiasm for the plot if I had seen proof first hand of what these people claim to be possible.

We dispatched spies straight away to Hanover. They discovered that Gunter Keller is not a wealthy man. Quite the opposite, in truth. His antics have proven costly because he lives like a fugitive, moving from address to address, only ever a step or so ahead of discovery and arrest and exposure. Thus he is sometimes obliged to abandon equipment and expensive texts. The authorities have yet to prove that any of this compromising evidence has ever been in his direct ownership. But they strongly suspect it and the man is generally unpopular wherever he has settled. He brings with him a bad odour, the stench of human corruption.

I have written to Keller, the letter coded, the content characterized by flattery, promising to dispatch my emissary with the lure of fifty gold sovereigns, should he agree to cooperate in my scheme. A down-payment only, I have made plain.

I have to hope that greed and desperation trump his innate habit of suspicion. My own name has been sullied, quite deliberately, in an effort to make my ambitions concerning Keller seem genuine to him. I am a womanizer. I have killed a host of unfortunate opponents in duels fought over trivial insults. I am a petulant loser at the card tables of London. I flogged a horse to death for refusing a jump in the hunt. I live in relentless defiance of the teachings of the Church and am a moral corruption to my daughter as well as my sons. And I am the richest man in England.

This last detail might be the only truth Keller is aware of concerning me. Certainly, I think, it will be the most significant to him. I await his reply with some trepidation. That is indeed if he bothers to reply. I think avarice and vanity will combine to compel him to do so. I wait, and I hope, and I pray. I pray to the God in whom by report I do not believe. There is much more than the loss of fifty sovereigns at stake. There is the heartfelt will of kings.

I have confided all to my wife. Catherine is my love, my ally and, I am unashamed to say, my best, most constant, most loyal friend. I know my wife, but she listened with an expression I confess I had not seen on her comely face before. It was as though she was preoccupied, remembering something. She did not speak at all until I had finished.

Then she said, 'Scepticism is dangerous in this enterprise of yours, husband. You would be wiser to believe until Keller's powers are disproven.'

'Is there a reason for your caution?'

'It is a story I have never spoken of before. I will tell it now, to you.'

Catherine grew up the daughter of a vicomte, at his castle above a village thirty miles north of Amiens. The story she related occurred when she was fourteen. An impressionable age for a girl, on the cusp of womanhood.

There was a string of deaths in the village, all children, all taken in the same way. They would develop an uncontrollable fever and eventually suffer a series of brain seizures their immature bodies could not endure to live through.

Catherine's father paid for physicians. They were summoned from Paris at considerable expense and they were learned men. They were also skilled at saying what this fatal condition was not. It was not cholera, or dropsy, or typhus. It was not some virulent strain of influenza. It was not plague and black humours were not responsible for it either.

The water supply was blamed. Someone was poisoning the village wells. Though no one could explain how this poisoning afflicted only the young. Catherine's father paid for water to be brought to the village in barrels bound to carts from a pure spring source five miles away. More expense; but the same result, the deaths simply continued.

It was inevitable that eventually witchcraft would be held responsible and accusatory fingers pointed.

They pointed at one village resident in particular. A crone, this woman. An elderly spinster with the requisite ugliness and deformities: facial warts and a hump where old age had buckled her back. And the usual reputation as a healer, someone skilled in the use of herbs for poultices and potions, dressings and cordials. A woman said to be able to heal wounds and stop bleeding and even restore sight in those stricken blind.

'A woman to whom I have personal cause to be grateful,' her father told Catherine. 'You came into the world enfeebled by an early birth. The physicians said you would surely die. Your mother had no milk. My heart was cleaved in two.

'And the crone came to the castle. She had with her a wet-nurse. And she begged an audience, which I granted only out of desperation. She said the wet-nurse was her niece and that her milk had an enchantment, a blessing that gave it special potency. She said this enchanted milk would make you grow strong and enable you to live. And it did.'

Catherine's father grew afraid, after the accusations, that the crone would be lynched. Fourteen years after his only daughter's birth, she still had his gratitude. He stationed an armed guard outside her cottage. This guard had been there for a month and had not seen the crone for a week when he smelled a scent he knew from the battlefield – the smell of decomposition. He went inside. And the crone was stretched out stale with death on her floor of beaten earth.

Then he noticed three wax effigies by her fireplace. They were the size of small dolls and they were clothed as children. The likenesses were so uncannily good that he recognized two of them as children he had seen playing in the village square on his occasional trips to the tavern. There was pooled wax in the fireplace. There were swatches of fabric burned to ash in the wax.

Thus ended Catherine's story. I confess I found it contradictory.

'She was a healer who murdered using magic,' I said. 'She killed those children, but when you were a dying baby, she saved your life. It is too paradoxical. Why would she do both?'

'Only because she could,' Catherine said. 'I think, Edmund, that such people become seduced by the potency of their powers.

There is no good or bad to them any more. There is only the reach of what they can accomplish.'

'I see.'

'And that sentry recognized also the face of the third little doll. Which, of course, he should have, since he saw me at the castle almost every day.'

There is one more detail worthy of note. And it is this. The sometime mathematician tortured in the Tower was found dead, hanged by the neck, in what he called his workshop, two days after his release. I do not think it was the prospect of re-arrest that led to the victim's hasty self-murder. I think instead it was the fate he feared would befall him were his betrayal of Gunter Keller ever to reach that man's ears.

THIRTY-TWO

Juliet and Paul walked to a pub on the banks of the Cherwell to get some lunch. The blissful summer weather held. There were wild swimmers and punts and canoes sharing the sparkling river waters. To Juliet, the scene that had greeted them on waking in the park only that morning seemed surreal and nightmarish. Something out of a disaster movie or a science fiction film. There was a post-apocalyptic look to London, and an atmosphere of bewilderment and defeat. The fleeing population was still unable to grasp the magnitude of the carnage. Juliet didn't really think that the city would ever come back from this. Not the heart of it, which was coming to resemble a modern version of Pompeii.

She studied Paul as he examined the bar menu. Their shared bed experience of two nights earlier had been neither innocent nor chaste, in the end. The lovemaking had seemed to her slow, deliberate and inevitable. There had been almost a therapeutic quality to it, as though they both craved human intimacy after the appalling flood footage they had seen on the screen in that German bar.

Well, I craved intimacy, Juliet thought, blind now to the words on her lunch menu despite her strong appetite. Quite what you wanted out of it, I can't be sure. Had there been an opportunistic element on his part? She didn't know. Neither did she feel she was familiar enough with him to know how to couch that question aloud, in words. It would have to remain a mystery.

He placed his menu back on the table in the pub's river garden and smiled at her and held her eyes with his, which were a pale blue she wanted to believe honest. They could be cold, eyes like that, and hypnotic, equally. Charm and callousness were qualities that could happily walk side by side, even hand in hand.

'I know what you're thinking about,' he said. 'You're thinking about the sex.'

'Was it only sex?' The sentence sounded limp and self-pitying to her own ears as soon as it was completed, but it was out of her mouth before her brain could control her voice. Or her thinking.

He said, 'That was badly phrased. I think that Germans tend to discuss this subject in blunter language than the English.'

'Everyone discusses this subject in blunter language than the English, Paul. But I suppose actions speak louder than words, and there was no shortage of action from either of us the night before last.'

'The truth is that I wanted you from the moment I laid eyes on you,' he said. 'But it's also true to say that I believe you only ever get what you give. That goes for all our human relationships. I very much want you, and not only in bed. I want you in my life.'

'You're on the rebound.'

'You insult yourself by saying that. And it isn't true.'

'It was true when you told me about the break-up.'

'It's a lie now, because of you.'

'Lousy time to start a romance.'

That made him smile. 'It's been my experience that one never chooses the time.'

And that made Juliet flash back briefly to her months of internet dating. She said, 'It's been my experience that it's disastrous when one tries to.'

He reached across their table for her hand and squeezed it. 'Let's just not overthink it, Juliet, and see where this takes us. The world could end tomorrow.'

As if on cue, her phone rang then, and she recognized the Home Secretary's number. *Godspeed*, he'd said to her.

'Any progress to report?'

Edmund Fleury's baronial pile had been destroyed by fire in the late Victorian period. His hunting lodge on the edge of Dartmoor was no more now than an ancient set of foundations. The house in London had been one of the spectacular early casualties of the London Blitz in the autumn of 1940. These facts had set Juliet thinking about where precious family items might have been stored after the Blitz.

She said, 'There's a location where the Almanac might have resided for at least some of its history. If so, it may have been stolen from there. If we can isolate the time of the theft, we can maybe identify the thief and we'll be getting somewhere.'

'Where is this place?'

'It's a castle in France, thirty miles north of Amiens. I google-earthed it and then looked up its history half an hour ago. It's intact and until late in World War Two it was still occupied by the descendants of our boy's wife.

'Fleury's journal suggests they were a cultured family, seigneurial, in the best sense. Probably why they survived the Revolution and the revolutionary Terror. They would have had an extensive library, and that library would have been scrupulously catalogued. You need to get someone with some smarts over there, sir. They need to go through that catalogue, fastidiously.'

At the other end of the line, sounding more stressed than he ever had to her before, he said, 'Anything else?'

'Send someone with linguistic and possibly code-breaking skills. The Almanac would have been clandestine library stock. Its presence would have been noted, rather than flaunted.'

'Romeo?'

'Not him. I need him here.'

The Home Secretary said, 'Heard about London?'

'I've been a bit preoccupied, sir.'

'Hurricane raging there as we speak. The coup de grâce for a great metropolis, I fear. And I'll get someone from Manchester to that chateau.'

'Castle. Why Manchester?'

'That's the capital now, Juliet. And my name is David Anderson.'

'I know that, sir.'

'It's just that "sir" seems absurdly formal, in the circumstances. Please call me David, in future. If any of us has a future.'

'Goodbye, David.'

'Good luck, Juliet. And say hello from me to Romeo.'

'I will.'

'And keep me up to speed.'

Godspeed.

'I will.' She ended the call, put her phone on the table.

Paul said, 'You really think that's a lead?'

Juliet shrugged. She said, 'Beggars and choosers. Fleury's last descendant perished in 1944. The castle became derelict until the end of the conflict. There's a window for looting and I'd imagine looting occurred. Could have been a soldier. I don't know enough about the specifics of the fighting in France to know whether German, American or French.'

'Could equally have been a light-fingered civilian.'

'Or a member of his household staff. Or a Resistance fighter. Or a similar scenario in the Great War, except that the vicomte was still living then. Or the Franco-Prussian War. Or the Almanac might never have been there at all. Slim pickings, but it's all I had to offer him.'

'There's plenty more to learn.'

'And we'll get back to it in a few minutes. But he wanted a progress report. That's what I gave him. A hurricane is raging in London, Paul, apparently.'

'London's like a boxer taking too many punches, except without a merciful referee to intervene and end the punishment.'

'It strikes me as a bit more biblical than that. It's like a contagion. It's spreading all over the world.'

Except that it wasn't, not quite. They had just eaten a delicious meal served them politely in idyllic surroundings. Oxford was effortlessly sustaining its movie-set perfection. It was comforting in a way that Juliet thought mythological. Like believing in a fairy tale.

The charming and well-educated man in front of her wasn't out of a fairy tale. He wasn't the handsome prince. The crisis condensed matters, she thought, forcing you into a kind of blunt honesty. It was more than just the cultural and semantic contrast between an English woman and a German man. In these circumstances, you talked about your emotions in a sort of shorthand.

She thought that they were responding to the crisis in the same way that people responded to war. And that was what the crisis really amounted to, wasn't it? Their world, its fabric, its values, its people were living – and dying – under a sustained assault. On a scale that was epic.

Her phone rang again after they'd left the pub and were walking back to the Bodleian, refreshed, if still subdued. The Home Secretary again.

'The storm in London is abating, thank God,' he said. 'It's weakening.'

'That's something, David,' Juliet said.

'It's raining, now.'

'Strongly enough for another flood?'

'Not strongly, Juliet. Oddly.'

'How so?'

'This rain is very fine. It's also saline. We've had it analysed. Thought it might be a chemical attack, so we quickly got samples to a laboratory.'

'Is it hazardous?'

'Benign. But still odd.'

'You're speaking in riddles, David.'

The Home Secretary cleared his throat. He said, 'In London, out of a clear blue sky, it's raining tears.'

She ended the call.

'Who was that?'

'David Anderson again. In London, the sky is weeping.'

Paul remained silent for a moment. Then he said, 'The city grieving for itself.' And Juliet knew that the words should have sounded absurd. But they didn't, to her, not remotely.

THIRTY-THREE

Dawn's intense new study of the spell book, as the wind outside her four walls weakened and then subsided completely, had brought no ready solution to the problem of the side effects or repercussions of using it. But a passage she hadn't come across before did give her great cause for excitement.

It contained the precise instructions for bringing a new life into the world. Not to give birth to your own progeny, but to fashion something corporeal from nothing. From the void, to use the words used in Latin in the book. It was a complex ritual requiring some recitation, a bit of physical choreography and even a few props. But Dawn was sure that with a bit of ingenuity and a few pounds of Grandpa's cash stash, she could gather those together. She wouldn't do it until she had either done her Special Study Group tests or received official confirmation that they had been postponed, which seemed even more likely after the latest disruptive weather event.

She'd phoned the school a couple of times but had got no answer other than a voice recording that seemed frustratingly vague. They weren't saying so outright, but teacher absenteeism seemed to have made reopening impractical. Dawn understood the reasons for this. Some of the teachers who commuted to Crouch End from Finsbury Park, or Camden Town or Islington, might now be without habitable homes. Whilst everyone wanted a good Ofsted report, no one wanted to sleep in the gutter.

Either way, whatever happened, Dawn knew she would do it eventually because, once she knew it was possible, it became in her determined mind an ambition that just had to be achieved.

In the meantime, some domestic anomalies were occurring entirely without her intervention. The first of these was that the terrapins, after being the empty shells of her grandpa's spontaneous snack, were now active again in the fetid green water of the fish tank, busy once more feasting off one another in that industrious Darwinian manner they had.

Dawn didn't mind this. She thought that they might nip if she went too close to the tank, but there was plenty of space in her roomy kitchen and she could easily avoid doing that. She thought there was actually a symbolic element to their return. She thought it meant that her grandpa had lost the crab-fight she'd seen only the start of downstairs. Given his age, he hadn't really been the favourite, even against a one-armed Pete. But it slightly worried her that feasting on Grandpa after, or even during the win might have made Pete even stronger.

Then there was the man on the lawn. Dawn looked out of the kitchen window at the back lawn, where rain that was somehow pale and whimsical was falling to the soundtrack of the roiling terrapins, and there he was again.

He came, and he went, this man. He was blurred or smudged, as though portrayed in the sepia tones of an early photograph. He had thick blond hair he wore to shoulder length in a blunt cut. He wore a garment that was black and ankle length, generously buttoned like a priest's cassock, except that he wore it cinched at the waist by a thick brown leather belt.

Because he didn't move, because he faded in and out of view, Dawn knew that he wasn't real. The man staring at her house from the lawn was what was termed an apparition.

Dawn wondered whether this apparition was the consequence of too much revision. Maybe she was working her brain too hard. But he wasn't Thomas Malthus, who'd been known to his chums as Robert. She'd seen a photograph of him. He'd worn the clothing of a later period and his hair had been styled in a far more conservative manner.

The other, far likelier possibility was that the apparition was from the time of the spell book's compilation. Use of the spell book had stirred the apparition into its weird half existence. Not even half, Dawn thought; fractional, actually. That theory neatly explained the period dress and frightful hairdo. And those heavy leather boots that had no laces.

Dawn didn't want the apparition to become any more solid than it was, thank you very much. The man didn't look like much fun. No one would confuse him with a party animal. He had a cruel face with a stern expression. A thin, twisted mouth, a permanent frown, intense eyes. And his fists were clenched in what looked to Dawn like an attitude of barely controlled fury.

Was he becoming more solid? If so, then only incrementally. If she concentrated hard, Dawn could still see the brickwork at the back of the garden through his torso. So he was still pretty insubstantial. And he did come and go. He wasn't there all the time.

The other weirdness in the house concerned the mirrors. Except for those fronting the bathroom cabinets, these were all old-fashioned. They dated from the time long before Grandma had died. That had happened so long ago that Dawn didn't even remember her. She'd probably bought them in the middle of the previous century.

There was a mirror in every room, all wall-hung, all depending from chains time had blackened.

The mirrors weren't really, strictly speaking, mirrors any more. They were still glass, insofar as Dawn could tell. But they were pictures now. They were paintings. They were all portraits.

There were two women. One was dowdy and sorrowful looking. The other was drop-dead gorgeous and wearing a lot of bling. There was a man with a white beard and white hair who looked to Dawn like someone attending a fancy dress as Gandalf. There was the garden apparition man with his terrible hair and a third man who looked cruel enough to be the apparition's brother.

The portraits were definitely to do with the spell book, Dawn knew. And if she lingered for any length of time in the rooms where they hung, she got the distinct feeling that their subjects were watching her.

This made her feel more self-conscious than uncomfortable because she sensed that the scrutiny was curious rather than hostile. Except possibly on the part of the apparition man. Both on the lawn and on the wall, the apparition man seemed permanently pissed off. Like someone had played a trick on him in life and he'd fallen for it, big time.

The mirror situation was tolerable because it hadn't occurred in either bathroom and there was no mirror in the kitchen, where Dawn mostly hung out. And she only had a hand-held one in her bedroom, which when used still did a proper job of reflecting her face.

Dawn sat at the kitchen table and mused on the creation of life. She didn't think Thomas Malthus would at all approve. It was deliberately increasing the population by unnatural means. But increasing it with precisely what?

Dawn went and fetched her sketch pad and pencils and began to draw a series of imaginary creatures. Some were hybrids of existing creatures. Some were arachnoid. A couple were dragon-like. She believed she had a good imagination, but she knew it had its limitations. The spell book, by contrast, seemed to know no limitations at all.

Eventually she got bored with sketching and turned the TV on and flicked through to the Pete channel using the remote. And what she saw made her gasp.

Her brother had grown rather substantially. The cellar had a high ceiling, but in its gloomy confinement he could barely stand upright. His head had further distorted, concave at the temples, his one eye shifted cyclops-like almost to the centre of his face, his mouth huge and bristling with those sharp, feral teeth. But the real surprise was that his missing left arm was no longer entirely missing. It was growing back in the manner seen in some species. Just not humans. Of her grandfather, nothing seemed to remain.

About an hour after the wind had died down, there was a knock at the door. Dawn briefly considered not answering it. But then she decided to take the bull by the horns, grasp the nettle, face the music, whatever.

She opened the door to a man in a black suit and a black fedora hat, wearing a clerical dog collar. She thought it was probably Father Gould, of whom her brother, before his death, had spoken both respectfully and fondly.

In the face of the priest, Dawn felt her first pang of guilt about her brother's murder. Her second surprise of the day after Pete's reptilian arm.

He shook hands with her, quite formally. He introduced himself. He said, 'Is Peter at home? Your grandfather?'

'They're in Ireland on a fishing trip,' Dawn said. 'You can get there by ferry, though there are no planes. Grandpa took Pete as a treat, because there's no school.'

The priest had taken off his hat. Now he put it back on. 'I'm sorry to have troubled you,' he said.

'No trouble, Father. Would you like to come in for some tea?'

She'd seat him in the study. No eccentric mirrors in there. None in the loo, if he needed to use it. Nothing odd for him to see on the lawn, as there might be out of the kitchen window. No orgy of terrapin cannibalism for him to witness. If Pete kicked off, she'd tell him what she'd told Handy Andy Baxter, that it was remedial work next door. You wouldn't place the noise accurately from the study.

'I know you're not a believer, Dawn.'

'But I'm curious,' she said. 'I'd like to have a theological discussion with you. I want to know something about your beliefs concerning the human soul.'

THIRTY-FOUR

October 10, 1528

His Royal Majesty the king thinks progress slow. Impatience is a regal characteristic, I think. The monarch is used to saying 'Make it so' to his privy councillors and having policy put into play, not at some far remove in time, but at once. He is headstrong anyway in temperament. He has the will to getting his own way which befits his status.

I believe that Gunter Keller has already assembled his collaborators in this dark enterprise. But he is secretive by instinct as well as of necessity. He is a naturally conspiratorial man. He is distrustful, and he is cautious. His meddling with the fabric of the world could, as its consequence, see him chained to a stake atop a lit pyre and he is understandably fearful of that fate. Therefore he is vague and ambiguous and non-committal in his correspondence with me. He resorts to opacity, and prevaricates where I seek straight answers and clarity.

But he is also a vain and arrogant man assured of his powers and he consequently has a boastful way about him. In his confidence he tells me that he has assembled the dubious talents required to deliver what I have already spent a king's ransom commissioning from him. He does not sound indebted. He sounds self-satisfied.

I know this because last week we had our first encounter face to face. Obliged by circumstance to meet him eventually, I would have liked to have met him at his laboratory, about which I confess to having a good deal of curiosity. But that would have been too dangerous. Englishmen of reputation are routinely followed by agents of the state when they travel abroad. These spies are immensely skilled at concealment. The safest course is simply to assume that you are being watched and to do nothing that might compromise.

Keller's calling has made of him a man who cannot settle at a single address for long. Inevitably, he begins after a while to evoke suspicion. He is of necessity an inveterate traveller, almost nomadic, shifting between cities and even between countries with a nonchalance bordering on indifference as to his own whereabouts. This suited me. I did not want the stigma of association with the man. And so I suggested we meet at sea, and he readily agreed to this proposal.

I chartered a ship and hired its crew and ordered the captain to sail across the English Sea and anchor a mile off Calais, where my signal to the waiting Keller that I had arrived for our rendezvous was three lanterns hoist into the rigging and lit one by one.

After darkness had fallen he rowed himself out to us across a choppy sea in an open boat which he tethered to our stern. And he climbed the rope ladder to our deck, a powerfully built man of around six foot in height, his face marked by a permanent sneer and small craters across his cheeks and brow carved there by the smallpox suffered, I supposed, either as a child or in his youth.

Even without knowledge of his dubious calling I would not readily have taken to the man.

Some men are entitled to a high opinion of themselves. King Henry is such an individual. There is no more formidable man-at-arms than the monarch either on foot in the practice pit or mounted on his saddle in the tiltyard. He is a skilled musician, adept at the keyboard and sweet-voiced. He is a gifted linguist and can hold forth eloquently on most subjects.

Is there a grubbier vocation than occult tinkering with the natural order? I think not. Yet Keller carried himself in the manner of someone high-born or eminent in some professorial capacity. And yet there was something so threatening about his presence that I found myself fingering the pommel of my sword as though to draw the weapon simply in self-protection.

I should add that I had ordered captain and crew ashore armed with funds ample even for thirsty sailors in order that they might get extravagantly drunk and afterwards find berths for the night on shore. I wanted no witnesses to this godless encounter of ours. I did not want to be there myself; it was only on the king's commission that I was submitting myself to a single moment of this unsavoury ordeal.

Despite all that, I made Keller a welcome guest aboard the vessel. I invited him into my absent captain's cabin and provided him with bread and cheese to eat and wine to drink with it. He ate and drank voraciously and with the table manners of a pig. I confess I was unsurprised by this, which made it easier to mask my disdain for my uncouth guest's miserable habits.

I had opened a second bottle of wine for him when I said, 'It seems to be taking rather a long time to compile this Almanac.'

'And Rome was not built in a day,' he said, chewing.

'What does that mean?'

'Some of the spells need refinement. Some of them need to be evolved, tailored. It is a long and complex process. It has inherent dangers. Some of it is a matter of trial and error. Risks are being taken on your behalf by people who do not wish to die before they can spend their share of the money you are paying them.'

'Much of what you are saying is simply incomprehensible.'

He drank and belched and fixed me with his baleful stare. He said, 'Most practitioners of magic, the serious practitioners, have some occult talent. Either they were born with it, or they have struck a hard bargain with fearful consequences.'

'A deal with the Devil?'

He grinned, showing me a mouthful of rotting teeth. 'Exactly that,' he said.

'I qualify on neither count,' I said.

'And yet you seek occult power. That is why the Almanac is such a challenge. And that is why the spells described on its pages require the refinement they do. They must work for an amateur. It is not impossible, but it will take time.'

'How much longer?'

He reached for a rind of cheese and tore a strip from it and put it into his mouth and chewed, thinking carefully. And I thought, this at least is impressive. He is taking the task set him and his acolytes very seriously indeed.

He said, 'All of next year. We have a timetable. We correspond and, when we can, we meet. By the spring or summer of 1530, we will be ready for the final distillation of what we have achieved. We will gather then to collaborate in person and you will have your Almanac, I swear it.'

'Is gathering in person not a risk?'

'Everything concerned with what we do is a risk. But we will unite in London. And only one of us is a native of England. Only one of our number is recognizable to the authorities. And you will find us an address at which we can work discreetly. Your wealth will safeguard and insulate us. We will enjoy privacy. Your gold will keep us all from harm.'

I must have looked dubious. Keller said, 'What?'

'I have yet to see a demonstration of these powers you speak of so assuredly. The man who sits before me pisses and farts. You could not save yourself from the smallpox.'

'I was six years old.'

'You cannot keep your own teeth in your skull. Or not for many years longer, I warrant.'

At this, he looked furious. Then petulant. And then his expression changed to one of resolution. 'Come with me, sir,' he said.

I followed him on to the deck. A light rain was falling. The chop of the sea, the hiss of lantern wicks, the emptiness of the night water surrounded us; the planks of the deck, slippery now, become treacherous beneath our feet. Once more the fingers of my sword hand caressed its silver pommel. I was as a little girl, seeking the reassurance of her painted wooden doll, hugging it to her chest.

Gunter Keller closed his eyes. He began to mutter in a language new and alien to my ears. He folded his hands in a series of complex gestures that seemed entirely meaningless. In that moment, I was certain he was nothing more than a glib charlatan, a mountebank and a thief.

Suddenly, a few feet away from the starboard side of the ship, the sea began to foam and bubble and hiss, as though tormented at the spot. Then something was spewed, writhing, from the depths and into sight, bursting, rising, flung on to the deck before us with a loud and fleshy thud. There it continued to twist and churn, its eight suckered tentacles finding no purchase, its one eye opaque and expressionless, its beaked maw opening and closing with an audible chitter as the creature drowned in air.

'Can you put it back?'

'You put it back,' Keller said, or rather whined, peevishly. 'I'm tired. You have dragged me all the way to the coast of France, only to insult me with your foolish scepticism. I am Gunter Keller. I am the greatest magician in Europe. It is within my power to return a man from the dead.'

'Yet you can do nothing about the carrion stink of your own poisonous breath.'

He stared at me. His eyes swelled in their sockets. Or they seemed to. He waved vaguely at what surrounded us. 'I could put you down there on the bed of the sea. I could do that with a thought.'

The insight occurred to me suddenly then that Keller's collaboration with his fellow compilers of the Almanac had increased his own powers greatly, as though magic was itself a contagion. He was boasting of a trick only recently acquired, I was sure.

But could he summon himself back from the dead? I very much doubted that. And never has the temptation to run a man through been stronger in me than at that moment. I could – and perhaps should – have unsheathed my sword and simply skewered him. Never have I stood before a man more deserving of that grisly finality. He had usurped nature, had undermined what was sane with this godless perversion I had just witnessed. But of course, I did not do the world the favour of killing him. Instead I pulled on my gauntlets and lifted the stinking creature by two of its boneless, suckered limbs and flung it over the side back into the sea.

I had my proof, I suppose. After his welcome departure a few minutes later, I wondered which of the two alternatives was true of Keller. Was he born with occult powers to refine and perfect, or had he struck a bargain with the demon who rules Hell?

Despite my colourful new reputation, I am in truth no betting man. But if I were, my money would be firmly on the latter proposition. I do not for a single moment believe I would lose it.

I recall a recent conversation with the king. I asked him whether it would not be better to leave these meddlers with human destinies to their earthly corruption and let them reap their inevitable fate of damnation when judged after their departure from life. He was adamant, stubborn, even defiant in the face of my tactful suggestion that it might be healthier to pursue this scheme no further.

'What do you seek to gain from it, sire?'

'An accord with King Francis,' he said. But there was something of the rote in that reply and so I pressed him further.

'Nothing more?'

'I want what you already possess, Fleury,' he said. 'I hope to

earn sufficient of God's grace to have him grant the one entreaty
that is the subject of my daily prayers.'

'And what is that, sire?' I asked him. But by then I knew the
answer.

He looked me in the eye. He said, 'I want a legitimate heir. I
want a healthy male boy to be born to me in wedlock. I want
nothing else so much in life as to father our future king.'

He seeks the routine miracle that delivered me my own beloved
sons. That is something I can appreciate entirely in commoner or
king, with all my heart and soul.

THIRTY-FIVE

The pounding on the cellar door began early in the afternoon.
Dawn thought it more determined than ever before. Her
dead brother, Peter, was growing stronger all the time.
He was hungry, probably ravenous. She felt her arm tingle at the
memory of pain where he had taken the chunk of flesh out of
her bicep with that lightning cobra strike with his teeth. She
remembered the exultant look on his contorted features as he'd
subsequently swallowed a piece of her.

The noise was thunderously rhythmic, as though some heavy
metal drummer sat demented at his kit, amp cranked all the way
up, hitting hard enough to break the skins, playing at some vast
venue in front of thousands. Except of course that the reality was
much more ominous and alarming than that.

She did not know how long the spell that had strengthened the
door would hold for. The magic seemed to wax and wane a bit in
a way that made it sometimes unpredictable, not wholly reliable.
She decided that she would put on the Pete channel and take stock
of exactly what it was she was now up against.

He was almost at the height of the cellar's ceiling. That was
about eight feet. His left arm had grown back but had not exactly
been restored. Proportionally, it was about the same length as the
original limb. But it was scaly and sort of crescent-shaped. He
was using it as a club to beat the door, the obstacle to his freedom.

Studying it, Dawn realized with a feeling somewhere between shock and dread that it was just like the fin of a terrapin, only swollen to giant dimensions.

How long did she have before he battered his way out and ascended the stairs to devour her?

She didn't think she had very long at all. Dawn tried to calm her juddering heart by breathing deeply and counting to ten, knowing that only the displacement spell could offer her anything close to permanent safety from the monster her dead brother had over the passing days become.

She had read about the Mariana Trench in geography. It was the deepest place on the planet at the section called the Challenger Deep at 11,000 metres. It was in the Pacific Ocean at a point equidistant between the Philippines and Japan. You could place Mount Everest in the trench and its peak would still be two kilometres below the surface. It was an unimaginable depth. The pressure down there would be colossal, many tons per square inch. Not even the thing her brother had evolved into could tolerate that. It would crush him completely.

But Dawn couldn't risk it. If she displaced something half way around the world, there would be consequences. Reverberations. Ramifications. Things might get very serious indeed as a result of invoking magic on that enormous scale. She might not survive it personally. The headaches had worsened; the fatigue was now set deep in her bones and, without stepping on the bathroom scales, she knew she'd lost weight. The clothing had grown loose on her diminished frame.

So where should she send him, when all her screaming senses told her there really wasn't very much time to ponder on the question?

She decided she would aim for something more modest. A crevasse at a remote spot in the high Alps would suit her purposes. If Peter ever got out – which he wouldn't, because he had no climbing gear or climbing experience – he would be a perfect candidate for the role of the Abominable Snowman. But he wouldn't get out, would he? And eventually he would freeze or starve to death. His second death. Slower and more predictable than his first.

Displacement that distance was a four-extra-strength-paracetamol spell, probably requiring two Naproxen and an exhausted sleep to follow. But Dawn didn't feel she had any choice whatsoever. The hammering at the cellar door, the fate it signified for her, was too much for her reasonably to bear. She felt cornered, forced to act. Just for a moment she saw a snapshot in her mind of the boy her twin had been: innocent, religiously devout, gentle, generous, a bit scruffy after the death of their mum and dad, loyal, loving.

She closed her eyes and emptied her mind. Then she visualized her dead brother's remote and inhospitable new home. She wasn't imagining this, she saw it, as an eagle might soaring above the mountains: a glittering abyss of snow and ice stretching down for hundreds, perhaps thousands of feet into pitch darkness.

She said the words. Recited them without pause in a clear, strong, unhesitating tone. The hammering beneath her all at once ceased. The sudden silence was blessedly complete. She was aware of a smell a bit like that when a fuse box blows, the air charged with energy, burned by it, atoms in flux, particles shifted in a manner that defied what was supposed to be possible.

Dawn smelled something else, something coppery; blood was pooling on her shirt from her nose, which was bleeding freely. Always a practical person, she went to get a towel from the bathroom to use as a cold compress. She didn't in the slightest mind the sight of blood, and nosebleeds – while messy – didn't hurt at all. Unlike her head, which was pounding as a consequence of the effort used to effect the spell successfully.

And it had been successful. She'd experienced a sort of afterimage, had felt the thing that used to be Pete groping around in the icy darkness, trying and failing to lever himself up with his one good arm and that grotesque fin thing in the profound cold at the bottom of his crevasse. His new home. His lair. His prison and, over time, his tomb.

Once the bleeding had stopped and she'd swallowed a few pills, Dawn went outside for some fresh air. She felt a bit guilty, not about what she'd done, but about what would now happen as the fallout from working so potent a spell. The garden was gloomy, devoid of light. Black clouds, Dawn thought absently, blinking and then tilting her head upward at the sky. But it wasn't cloud cover blocking the strength and brightness of the June sun. Instead, the sky was black with birds, filled with everything in the world capable of flight, it seemed, feathers spiralling down as their wings rubbed and collided in the dense, jostling air.

'An augury,' Dawn said out loud. 'Now we're for it.'

She spent an apprehensive hour before putting on the television. On the news channel several huge churches were shown on fire in London. Then the voiceover informed Dawn that the burning buildings were not churches but cathedrals. She recognized two of them as the bulletin progressed. They were St Paul's Cathedral and Westminster Cathedral, and they didn't look as if they were going to survive the ferocious blazes that had taken hold.

The cathedral fires had apparently started spontaneously with worshippers in their pews and tourists in their aisles. Not many people had managed to get out. Those who had said the fires all started the same way. The tabernacles on the high altars had burst open and tongues of fire had billowed out.

'Like a ferocious dragon exhaling,' said one soot-blackened boy survivor Dawn took to be a *Game of Thrones* fan.

The cathedrals had been full. They had survived the flood and the quake, and those people tenacious or just stubborn enough to remain in the erstwhile capital had taken this to be a sign. Prayer had become popular as the political crisis deepened. Natural disaster and the threat of war made people think about mortality and their own spiritual welfare.

Or so the commentator was saying.

Dawn now knew a bit about spiritual welfare, thanks to Father Gould. She'd liked the old priest. She'd have worked the lullaby spell on him so that he could be that little bit closer to his God than he was currently, but she didn't have a photo of him and doubted very much that he was on Facebook.

She wondered what kind of tourist would still come to London after its litany of recent catastrophes. Then she remembered that the passenger planes were still grounded. They were people who couldn't get home, making the best of things. And experiencing the worst.

She was sadder about the buildings than she was about the human victims. Compassion fatigue had set in for Dawn, where the human cost of these apocalyptic events was concerned. She'd just seen too many bodies in news footage floating in the river, battered by falling debris in the streets, bulldozed into those fetid piles on corners now being blamed for the typhus outbreak.

She felt saddest of all about St Paul's. She'd been there on a school trip. She wasn't personally a religious girl, but she knew the cathedral's long history, knew it had defied the bombs dropped by the Luftwaffe in the London Blitz. And she'd thought its giant organ pipes cool and the Whispering Gallery, with its strange dome-inspired acoustics, even cooler.

She watched now as that great dome collapsed in on itself with an audible whoosh that became an ominous rumble and had the firefighters all around the building fleeing for their lives on the screen like so many scurrying ants.

Dawn surprised herself by shedding a tear. For nearly eighty years, since the autumn of 1940, St Paul's Cathedral had been a proud symbol of British resistance. Now it had gone, was just ashes and rubble, its lovely white stone scorched black, its great pillared portico no more than a memory.

From what the pundits were saying on the TV, there was currently precious little resistance either. The mood in the former capital, they were saying, was now one of abject despair.

THIRTY-SIX

His name was Daniel Carter. He was thirty-six years old and had been attached to the British Embassy in Paris for four of the most recent of those years. He was Dan to his friends, one of whom was embassy colleague Paul Beck. They played one another at tennis. Parisian clay, which Dan joked put him at a handicap because he was a Brit and preferred the grass. They played on the same five-a-side football team in the overseas league.

Dan's background was military; he'd served in the SAS in Afghanistan and Iraq. His most recent military deployment had been in London when the domestic terror threat got cranked up so high that SAS soldiers were deployed as armed officers wearing Met Police uniforms and insignia. The press and public had begun to comment on how lithe and agile these armed response officers appeared, how comfortably they handled their serious assault weapons. Dan had thought this covert deployment probably as open a secret as secrets ever got.

But now he was a civilian with a fairly vague and ambiguous job description working in, though more often out of, the British Embassy in Paris. He did quite a bit of liaison work with the French security forces. Officially, he was a minor diplomat usefully fluent in the language of the country to which he had been posted. Unofficially, what earned him his salary was playing an important link role in a complex but generally effective counter-terror network.

The call he got that Thursday afternoon came on a secure line and was made personally by the British Home Secretary. He was trying to locate a library and, in it, a specific book. There was reason to believe that the family of Baroness Catherine Fleury, French wife of an English baron of the Tudor period, Edmund Fleury, had been at some time in possession of this book. The provenance was inexact and to Dan Carter unconvincing; he made a couple of lines of notes from the Home Secretary's words.

This very senior politician sounded to Dan extremely stressed. He thought that completely understandable. Things were unusually fraught in Paris, in the aftermath of the Airbus disaster in the French Alps. That was thought to have been sabotage and the finger was pointing at Turkey. Left-wing militants, frustrated at how slowly EU membership negotiations were going. Right-wing militants, intent on distancing themselves from Europe in the cause of extreme nationalism. Evidence-wise, so far, the flip of a coin.

But if things were bad in France, in England Dan knew that the situation was dire. Half an hour before taking this call he'd seen on television the destruction of St Paul's Cathedral in an inferno of flame. The embassy staff had clustered around the wall-mounted flatscreen in the bomb-proof basement canteen observing this event in a silence more stunned and complete, he thought, than any since that September afternoon when two hijacked passenger planes had hit the Twin Towers in New York.

Dan had watched that too on a wall-mounted TV, surrounded by his fellow officer recruits at Sandhurst. A lot had happened in his eventful life since then. But he would never forget the experience, and the St Paul's footage he had witnessed that afternoon would be equally indelible.

Forty-eight firefighters had died when the cathedral dome collapsed, a figure that was only going to rise in the aftermath of the blaze. But it was the symbolic significance, more than the immediate death toll, which would stay with him, despite the valour of the men and women of the fire crews who had been wiped out. To all intents and purposes, London had fallen. And Dan Carter figured that the reeling shock he had heard in the Home Secretary's voice was the consequence of that realization.

He made his first call to the tourist office at Amiens. They were immediately helpful, giving him the name and contact details of a local archivist and historian who was an authority on Catherine's family. Her maiden name had been du Lac.

'Her father was a vicomte, Fernand du Lac,' the archivist told him, when he called to explain his mission. 'A very patrician man, the perfect aristocrat, if there could be said to be such a thing. Civilized, benevolent, cultured. And at that time the Fleury and du Lac connection already went back three centuries. Their ancestors fought shoulder to shoulder in the crusades. Both a du Lac and a Fleury fought at the Siege of Jerusalem.'

'What about the library?'

'There isn't one. Never has been, at the castle. Not to my knowledge, which is comprehensive. There may have been a Bible and a book of hours. But nothing so substantial as a library.'

'You're absolutely sure?'

'Of course I'm sure.'

'That's bad news.'

'As far as I know, the du Lac library is at the family chateau, much nearer to where I'm guessing you're calling from. It's sited about ten miles to the north of Paris. It's not theirs any more, though. The last of the bloodline died out in 1944. I've heard rumours about looting there, in the last year of the war, but I can't confirm them. My specialism is the Somme region, and Amiens in particular.'

'Anything you know about those rumours would be helpful,' Dan Carter said.

'It's unconfirmed, unsubstantiated. But the story I've heard is that a British special forces unit assembled to eliminate Vichy collaborators had a member who was what you British call "light-fingered".'

Dan thanked the man and ended the call. He didn't want to think one of his SAS predecessors in the pioneering days of the regiment a thief. But the spoils of war were a temptation to some and human nature was what it was.

The archivist had told him that after a few months of post-war dereliction, the du Lac chateau had been extensively restored. The family of an industrialist, Philippe Troyer, had bought and refurbished and still inhabited the place.

The book he'd been charged to locate might have been looted by a serving British soldier. If that rumour wasn't true, it could have been pilfered during the period of the chateau's dereliction. A war had been fought in France and a chateau was a big target. The roof could have been damaged by a bomb, or by artillery fire, or just by neglectful upkeep, which meant that the book could have been badly affected or destroyed altogether by water or just rendered unreadable by damp, splotched with mildew and broken-spined, its pages swollen, its ink run to illegibility.

It had been called the *Almanac of Forbidden Wisdom*. But the English academic advising the Home Secretary didn't think that would be written on its cover, or spine, or frontispiece. Its main author had been a man from Lower Saxony named Gunter Keller, but he didn't think that detail would be included either.

Clandestinely compiled, it was probably handwritten rather than printed. It might be written in English or Latin or a combination of both and some of it was mathematical formulae and some of it almost certainly written in code.

What Dan Carter didn't appreciate was the significance of the book. The Home Secretary hadn't told him that. But he was used to clandestine work, to the gospel of need-to-know. There'd been urgency in the voice of the man who'd charged him with this mission, and he liked a challenge. This one wasn't run of the mill, it was unusual, and that made the task both challenging and enjoyable.

He decided he'd gather his embassy credentials and just turn up at the chateau. Knock on the door. He didn't want to be put off on the phone by some snooty retainer if the Troyer family weren't in residence. If they were there, he was capable of being exceptionally courteous. If they weren't he'd bring his steely persistence into play. Not taking no for an answer was one of his less diplomatic skills, something learned the hard way in his former life, lethally armed and clad in combat gear.

He'd hail a taxi, he decided. Paris streets were always busy, but north was the easiest way out of the city and the only practical way to reach his destination was by car.

It was hot, on the street. He was immaculately attired in a grey Savile Row summer-weight wool suit and black polished Grensons and a Hermès necktie. And all he could think about really were those vast, billowing infernos of flame the cathedrals of London had become earlier that day; the hundreds of tourists and worshippers who had met their horrific end trapped inside. It had looked apocalyptic, biblical. It had looked to Dan Carter like he imagined the end of the world would. He glanced at his wristwatch, got into his cab and settled on to the rear seat. It was just after five p.m. on a sunny June Thursday. A day already rendered unforgettable.

THIRTY-SEVEN

October 15, 1528

We have become a family in the midst of bereavement and tragedy. We are sundered suddenly, for ever now incomplete. Our beloved daughter did not appear for breakfast two mornings ago. I went to rouse her. She seemed asleep, when I entered her room, but was cold and pale and quite dead. She appeared entirely serene, which was of course no comfort. Matilda was ten years old. Children die. Wealth and rank guard no parent against this too common eventuality. But she slipped from life without warning, without illness or disease or even any sign of visible discomfiture.

Already I have been delivered a letter of condolence from the king. He is at present visiting the nearby monastery in Shaftesbury, where he must have heard the news. He writes generously and sympathetically, and his words seem heartfelt enough. But they offer not a shred of consolation. My emissary has been dispatched to deliver the melancholy tidings to my brother at his friary in the hills outside Florence in Italy. I expect Gerald will return home for a vigil of prayer for his niece that will not in the slightest alleviate the suffering in grief we are all undergoing. Catherine and my sons Jacques and Sebastian are utterly heartbroken. Our household is in the grip of the most painful lamentation imaginable.

Grief makes men mad. I have on occasion witnessed this. But I do not think it madness to believe that Matilda's death is wholly unnatural in cause. There are two alternatives. Perhaps this is a painful reverberation, just the price exacted for the lurid and revolting magic Gunter Keller performed off the coast of France before my return to England.

There is, though, a second possibility. And it is this. I insulted Keller personally. I slighted his appearance and demeanour and called into question the authenticity of the powers of which he boasts. And he was angered and offended. Perhaps our daughter's death is his revenge for those supposed affronts to his miserable character and dubious capabilities. His brittle, fractious pride.

I am inclined to believe this latter possibility to be the more likely. It is not probable that I will ever be able to prove it. This loss has not, though, deterred me from the course of my commission, as it might in truth have done. It has had the opposite effect, in making me all the more determined. My daughter's death will earn its rightful retribution. I will see Gunter Keller burn. I will hear his anguished dying cries and smell his flesh as it roasts, and he will see me there, laughing into his flame-blackened face at his extinction. This I swear, in God's grace, by all that I hold holy. This I most solemnly swear.

Paul Beck stopped reading. Quietly, he said, 'This mission of the king's is killing Edmund Fleury.'

'Corrupting him,' Juliet said. 'Eating him up, polluting him with hatred.'

Paul nodded at the chest on the table between the two of them. 'The locket in there. That miniature?'

'Matilda,' Juliet said. 'Do you think he ever recovered from his grief?'

'Infant mortality was a great deal higher then,' Paul said. 'You know that.'

'Around fifty per cent.'

'And we know he pressed on with this business. But my intuition is to say no, that his heart never recovered from the loss of his daughter. He was too loving a father and husband for that ever to be possible.'

Juliet looked at her wristwatch. The museum was about to close. Paul read her thoughts and stood and lifted the lid and put the book back into the chest and closed it again.

'We could probably take that away with us.'

'I doubt it qualifies as loan stock,' he said.

Juliet sighed. She said, 'I think we can do as we like, to be honest, with our bright shiny new security clearances.'

Paul shrugged and looked at her. 'I don't think it's going to tell us where the Almanac is now.'

'I don't either, but we've got this far, Paul. I'd still like to get to the end of it.'

'Agreed. And who knows? They might be making headway with the search for the Almanac in France.'

'Long shot.'

'Beggars and choosers, Juliet.'

He lifted the chest lid again and rummaged carefully until his fingers found the locket miniature. He opened it and came around the table to Juliet's side of it and squatted on his haunches beside her. He undid the locket's delicate clasp. A tiny portrait of a little girl was revealed. Flaxen hair, vivid green eyes, a bright bud of a mouth, pink against a pale complexion.

'Pretty little thing,' Juliet said.

'Looks like the style of Holbein,' Paul said.

'Holbein didn't do miniatures – not at that stage anyway.'

'He might have for Edmund Fleury.'

She shook her head. 'It was a specialist skill. And Holbein didn't settle in England until after this was written.'

'I'm surprised he wasn't buried wearing it. The same goes for his wedding ring. He was devoted to Catherine.'

'Who outlived him. Edmund Fleury died quite young, though not before Keller.'

'So perhaps he kept that promise?'

'We'll find out. But the point is that before he died, Edmund left Catherine all his most precious possessions.'

'Until they were confiscated by the king.'

Juliet thought about this. 'I don't think it happened like that,' she said. 'I think Catherine willed the contents of this chest to the Crown. The story they tell about their father was not one she wanted her sons to have to hear.'

'You're strong on human nature, Juliet. You're very intuitive.'

'Strong theoretically,' she said. 'When it comes to the practical side of things, I'm crap.'

That made Paul smile.

But Juliet meant it. She was thirty-five. Her one really meaningful romantic relationship had ended in sordid betrayal. She would be classified as elderly on a maternity ward. Her life had passed her by in a tedious blur in recent years as she busied herself with spinning classes and a bit of yoga and Sunday supplement recipes for one. Preparing lectures, marking papers, trying to stay as far off Martin Doyle's radar as was possible. Matters had degenerated to the point where sipping a flat white in a branch of Costa was something looked forward to as a treat.

Edmund Fleury five hundred years ago had had his strong and valiant heart broken by the sudden death of his daughter. But he had experienced the intense joy of a parent's love for their children and Juliet hadn't, and she was gloomily sure she now never would, even if the world recovered from its current calamitous state of chaos. That possibility was lost to her. And she felt pretty wretched about it, even though now wasn't really the time for any sort of self-indulgence.

'What are you thinking?'

'Where are you thinking of staying tonight?'

He said, 'I suppose I'll book into a Novotel.'

'You must know I live in Oxford?'

'I do, but I wouldn't presume,' Paul said.

'Cold feet already?'

But he didn't look amused by that. He said, 'Not taking anything for granted. That's all.'

'Kiss me.'

He kissed her. Given the odds of Ms Plummer bursting in to tell them it was closing time, she thought the kiss a commendably long one.

'Now what?'

'Now we go back to that charming pub on the Cherwell for some dinner. And after that, Paul, I'm taking you home.'

They were watching footage of the cathedral fires on the TV news in the pub when Paul Beck's mobile showed a number he recognized. A fortnight earlier they'd both watched these epic conflagrations in a shared mood of stunned disbelief. But calamitous was getting to be the new normal and all either of them felt was the sort of helpless sadness everyone viewing the screen seemed to share.

He went outside to take the call. It was Dan Carter, against whom he played tennis. Dan, with whom he played five-a-side, a mate from the embassy. Both a nice bloke and a bit of a mystery man. Someone perennially affable who never said anything at all about his own personal history.

'Got a story for you, Paul, about the Almanac.'

'This is an open line, Dan.'

'Doesn't matter, mate. Bit late in the day for cloak and dagger, with everything that's going on. Where are you?'

'Oxford.'

'But you've seen the cathedrals?'

'I've been busy. Only just now. Is this about them?'

'It's about the missing book, mate. The chief said to brief you. Where are you specifically?'

'A pub on the Cherwell.'

'Well, take your beer goggles off, Paul, and put your brain into gear. In fact, put your brain into overdrive.'

THIRTY-EIGHT

Philippe Troyer had bought the du Lac chateau in 1946, after it had been semi-derelict a couple of years. Dan Carter thought the man who opened the door to him was probably Philippe's grandson, Albert. He was a spare, sinewy man casually attired in black jeans and a pale sweater that looked soft and fine enough to be cashmere worn over a soft-collared shirt. His dark hair was shoulder length and he looked friendly and inquisitive and about fifty years of age.

Dan introduced himself. He showed his embassy credentials. Albert Troyer (for it proved Dan was correct about his identity) raised an eyebrow, smiled slightly and invited him in. They stood for a moment in a rather grand, marble-floored vestibule. There were tapestries hanging on the walls and an enormous crystal chandelier was suspended from the ceiling high above them.

Dan looked around. He said, 'You open your own door, Monsieur Troyer. No faithful retainer?'

'My family are socialists. Wealthy socialists, but espousing the values, nevertheless. I have a team of people come to clean once a week. It suffices. We'll communicate in English, because I enjoy the practice of speaking the language. And in the informal English manner, I will answer to Albert and will call you Daniel, if I may.'

'Just Dan.'

'Pleased to meet you, Dan.'

'Likewise, Albert.'

The two men shook hands.

Albert guided Dan down a long corridor to a large and brightly lit and incongruously modern kitchen. The work surfaces were granite. The knives, Sabatier, were on a magnetic strip. The refrigerator was enormous and constructed from some shiny alloy. A TV on a wall bracket showed images of the London cathedral carnage with the sound turned down. Albert picked up a remote and switched it off.

'A bad day for London.'

'Lately they've all been bad.'

'My parish priest is whispering about the End Times.'

Dan thought about this. He said, 'How long before the one priest becomes a chorus and the whisper becomes a shout?'

Albert smiled again. He was a man, Dan thought, who smiled easily. But then life had given him plenty to smile about.

'Would you like a beer, Dan? I don't think it's too early.'

'In the circumstances, I could murder a beer,' Dan said.

They sat on stools at opposite sides of the counter and sipped from the bottles. Albert said, 'I'm guessing Royal Marines or the Parachute Regiment. Who knows? Maybe SAS.'

'You're an astute man.'

'Did three years in the Legion after graduating from the
Sorbonne. My dad's idea of a post-grad in life. Shared exercises
in Belize and other places. There are characteristics you come to
recognize.'

'Shared characteristics.'

'Quite so.' The smile again. 'What can I do for you?'

'I've reason to believe the library here housed a book until
sometime in 1944. A very rare and valuable book. I'm trying to
locate it.'

Albert nodded. 'I've heard rumours,' he said. 'An occult almanac.
A spell book from the sixteenth century, no?'

'Yes.'

'The library was more or less intact when my grandfather
bought the place, except that most of the books were damp. If
they hadn't been, when the place was deserted, villagers from
hereabouts would have taken them to fuel their fires. There's a
glass display case. Something was once displayed in it. I can't
confirm it for certain, but it might have been your spell book.'

'Why do you think that?'

'There's a warning on a brass plaque screwed into the wooden
table on which the case rests. Translated roughly from Latin it
reads, "Open this only at your peril and the peril too of humanity.
These pages have the power to unleash the Auguries."'

'A legionnaire who can read Latin,' Dan said. 'Who knew?'

'Italian comrades,' Albert said. 'It's a short hop.'

'Did you ever hear any rumours about the theft?'

Albert shook his head.

'Do you know anyone who might?'

Albert sipped beer thoughtfully. He said, 'The last du Lac to
live here was Olivier du Lac, who died late in 1944. My only
living link with him is one of my cleaning team who told me
her grandmother worked for the family as a scullery maid as a
twelve- or fourteen-year-old. That means that she's in her late
eighties now. Quite a character in her own right. Still lives in
the village, still drinks a ritual cognac every evening at her
neighbourhood café.'

'Near here?'

'In the village, half a mile away.'

'Do you know which café? Do you know this woman's name?'

Albert took an iPhone from his hip pocket. 'I can find out from my cleaning people.'

'You're being enormously helpful.'

Albert narrowed his eyes, awaiting a reply to his call. He said, 'Which outfit?'

'SAS.'

'Ha! I knew it.' He got a connection, asked his questions, gave his thanks. Then he took a pad and pen from a kitchen drawer and wrote down a name and a location. 'She'll be there at seven p.m. That gives you an hour and I'll give you a lift down there, if you need one.'

'Thanks.'

'I expect you'd like to see the library before we leave.'

'You're a mind-reader.'

'I'm a man starting to put two and two together, Dan. The Auguries?'

More corridors. The chateau was vast. Dan wondered whether Albert lived there alone. He'd given plenty away, just not very much about himself.

The repair work to the vaulted ceiling of the library was immaculate. There was a substantial number of books and no hint of a scent of damp. Original oils hung on the wood-panelled walls. One Dan would have bet money was a Manet. A Sisley country scene. A much older painting he thought might be a Delacroix.

Albert guided Dan across the library to the wooden table with its mounted glass case and burnished brass plaque. Dan thought the wood of the table black enough to be ebony. The writing etched into the plaque was italic. The glass of the case was flawed by a single diagonal crack old enough for dust to have seeped into it in microscopic quantities, incrementally, so now it resembled a long grey scar.

Albert slapped Dan lightly on the back and said, 'I'm going to fetch my car keys. I'll see you at the library door in five minutes?'

'Perfect.'

The feeling of despondency arrived subtly, after Albert's departure from the room. It crept through Dan Carter's mind like a poisonous fog. He felt his buoyant spirit ebb away from him as though it bled from some existential wound. A mortal wound, he thought, confused, dismayed, almost unable to think.

While he still had the mental strength to do so – and he didn't
have long, and he didn't have much – Dan reeled away from the
table and lurched drunkenly in the direction of the door. Recovery
was as rapid as contagion. By the time he got to the door he felt
OK, relatively. Albert Troyer was already there, a concerned look
across his lean, tough, friendly features.

'Is it always like that?'

'It's getting worse,' Albert said. 'I think it's to do with the
Auguries. You need to find that book, my friend. The cathedrals?
Someone's using it.'

The café itself was like something from an earlier time. A zinc
counter, an enamel Pernod sign, elderly metal chairs and zinc-
topped tables, some crooner warbling his way through a French
ballad on an ancient, perforated leather-covered transistor radio
on a shelf behind the bar, the liquorice tang of French tobacco.

Dan Carter got there at five minutes to seven and ordered a
beer. The woman he wanted to speak to walked in at exactly seven
o'clock. It had to be her – white-haired, immaculately attired in
a summer coat and hat, lipstick neatly applied and precisely
punctual.

She looked around. Her eyes alighted on him and she smiled.
She had been forewarned, of course, by her granddaughter. She
had consented to meeting him and answering his questions, if she
could. Though impromptu and hastily arranged, it was an appoint-
ment rather than an ambush.

They shook hands, Dan doing so with a slight, courteous bow
that earned another smile. Yvonne Dupont had lavender-coloured
eyes that even after eighty-odd years retained their intelligent
sparkle. Dan bought her a cognac and pulled out her chair and
waited until she was properly settled before sitting himself. She
cleared her throat without a prompt from him and began to speak.
A confidential voice, one that wouldn't carry to a neighbouring
table. Maybe a skill learned in her Resistance years? The French
Resistance had used children a lot.

'After my master died, I made it my task to check every day
on the book. It was the master's belief that if the book fell into
the wrong hands, the whole world would suffer great harm. He
thought this his secret, but there are no secrets servants do not
know. Of course, the war meant that the world was suffering great

harm anyway, and many of its people real anguish. But wars are won and lost. The master thought the book could bring the End Times.

'I hadn't given back my keys. There was no one left to give them back to. So, every day, I checked on the book. Right up until the afternoon of October twenty-eighth, 1944, when I went to check on it and it simply wasn't there any more. Someone had taken it.'

Yvonne Dupont raised her glass and emptied it at a single gulp. She put the glass down and said, 'They call it Dutch courage. I find it works equally well for the French. Forgive me, these reminiscences are difficult.'

'Nothing to forgive, madame,' Dan Carter said, getting to his feet and fishing for his wallet to go to the bar and buy her another.

He sat back down with fresh drinks for both of them.

She said, 'This was only a couple of months after the liberation of Paris. It was a turbulent time. There was much settling of old scores, especially in the countryside. Summary executions. Hangings, shootings. Sometimes there would be a trial, more often not.'

'Have you any idea who might have taken the book?'

Her lavender eyes looked at him incredulously. 'I know who took it,' she said. 'It was the British. There were twelve of them,' she laughed, 'like the Apostles. Only they were here to kill rather than to preach. They drove around in jeeps with machine guns bolted on to their rear. They were long-haired, scruffy, bearded, most of them. Not as you imagine a soldier to be, even in a time of fierce combat. Thinner than men are today. And they laughed a lot.'

'Did you suspect anyone in particular?'

'The one I saw twice in the chateau grounds, poking around. He was quite sly, this one, skilled at concealment. But I knew every inch of those grounds. What's the English word for when a pattern isn't quite right?'

'An anomaly.'

'Just so. I knew every path, plant, tree, bush, flower and patch of gravel. I spotted the anomalies there and then I spotted him, twice.'

'Did you ever learn his name?'

'No.'

'His rank?'

'I didn't know anything about insignia on uniforms. I was fourteen.'

'Could you describe him?'

'To what end? He was about thirty and will certainly be dead.'

'To the end of finding and retrieving the book, Madame Dupont.'

She sipped cognac and appraised him and said, 'And so preventing the onset of the End Times?'

THIRTY-NINE

Juliet Harrington and Paul Beck breakfasted on Friday morning listening to the radio. It seemed a bit surreal to Juliet that the device still functioned, just as it seemed a bit surreal that the gas cooker functioned as she scrambled their breakfast eggs. They listened to Radio 4, to a variety of experts and officials and pundits discussing the cathedral blazes of the previous day, all of them tactful, diplomatic, skirting around the evidential implausibility of what had occurred. They brought to Juliet's mind skaters on ice they well knew was very thin. The more of them who took to it, the greater the weight, and the more alarming the consequent risk they all ignored.

The BBC was no longer broadcasting from central London. Everything was in Manchester now, so the guests still on the spot in the old capital were being patched through to the new in any way audio trickery made possible. The flooding and the quake had combined to write off most of the city's landlines. A lot of mobile masts had also become casualties. Communication with London, directly or indirectly, was becoming more and more difficult. And the disruption seemed to be spreading outward, like a contagion, Juliet thought.

Only one of the radio experts was really prepared in Juliet's view to call a spade a spade. He was a veteran fire-fighter who'd retired to make a lucrative living assessing fire risk in listed buildings. He said that the water saturation from the recent flooding made the fires that had consumed the cathedrals physically impossible. He said that even with accelerants, it was implausible that the waterlogged pews and still soggy carpeting would have burned with the ferocity they had.

'But it still happened,' the presenter kept saying, sounding to Juliet's ears like a truculent child.

'I know it bloody happened,' his exasperated expert eventually said. 'It happened, yet it was impossible. I'm just having a bit of a struggle mentally with that obvious contradiction.'

Juliet switched the radio off, thinking that the insane world she now inhabited didn't really suit the medium. It didn't work in print, either. It worked best in televised pictures with the sound turned down, when you didn't have to struggle with a commentator's inane efforts to describe calmly the fundamentally indescribable.

Seated at the table, Paul swallowed a piece of egg-smeared toast and said, 'At least last night was fun. The horizontal part of it, I mean. Before we fell asleep.'

'And dinner wasn't bad. And you can read my mind.'

'Only some of the time. But opacity can be an attractive quality in a woman.'

'Can be? When isn't it?'

'When she's trying to hide something.'

'Come on, Paul. I'm as transparent as a pane of glass.'

He mused on this. Then he smiled. 'Frosted glass, maybe,' he said. He looked around her kitchen. He said, 'This is a nice place. Your flat, I mean.'

'Easy to keep things pristine when you live alone.'

'You make that sound like a sort of rebuke.'

'In another life I'd have liked a family, is all. A faithful partner, a couple of little ones. Instead, I've got an orderly home and letters after my name. I ought to be satisfied.'

'But you're not.'

'No. I'm not.'

'It isn't too late, Juliet. You're still young enough. Assuming the madness ends.'

She didn't comment directly on that. Instead she said, 'What do you intend to do about what Desperate Dan Carter told you last night?'

Which made Paul laugh. He said, 'You wouldn't call him that if you'd met him. He's a very cool customer, is our Daniel. Enigmatic. I suspect as hard as nails.'

'And on to something,' Juliet said.

'Divide and conquer,' Paul said.

'What does that mean?'

'I think you should follow the du Lac chateau trail. I'll stay here and read the rest of Edmund Fleury's story. There might be something significant there.'

'Where does the du Lac chateau trail lead to?'

'I hope to the Almanac, eventually. But in the first instance to the Imperial War Museum. It's going to be closed, I expect. All the ground-floor exhibits are going to be flood-damaged. But the Home Secretary will get you in and their papers are filed above the ground floor. If there's anything on that SAS unit running riot in northern France in October of 1944, that's where you'll find it.'

'A needle in a haystack,' Juliet said.

'But you're experienced at finding those. And not necessarily, if the material has been catalogued. You might get there and find something straight away with a preliminary computer search.'

'You think Yvonne Dupont a reliable source?'

Paul was quiet, still chewing his breakfast egg on toast, still sipping his English breakfast tea. Then he said, 'I think Madame Dupont got virtually everything spot on.'

Paul was about to add the detail that Dan Carter suspected Yvonne Dupont had played a role in the wartime French Resistance, something he thought added weight to the woman's credibility as a witness to events. But he didn't get the opportunity because, at that moment, their doorbell rang.

'I'll get it,' Paul said.

Their visitor was a tall, rather gaunt man in a black gabardine suit and a black fedora hat and a white clerical collar. He took off the hat, revealing a full head of white hair. There were white whiskers on his cheeks and his eyes were slightly bloodshot. He said, 'I'm looking for Professor Harrington. That's plainly not you. I hope I haven't got the wrong address.'

'How did you get this address at all?'

'Martin Doyle gave it to me. Dr Martin Doyle. He's the professor's head of department at the university.'

'Indiscreet of him.'

'These are not normal times, sir. My name is Thomas Gould. Father Thomas Gould.' He peered around Paul, examining the hallway. 'Would you kindly tell the professor I'm here, if she's in?'

He'd driven all night to get there. He'd begged a jerrycan of petrol apiece from two of his more faithful parishioners to fuel the journey at the wheel of his twenty-year-old Rover. There'd been the roadblocks to navigate, and the fields of rubble and quake debris which formed makeshift roadblocks of their own. He'd had to skirt the gangs of looters and divert around the roads that had subsided after the flood. He'd driven for ten hours straight to cover a distance of just over sixty miles.

Now, he said, 'Forgive the imposition, but I could murder a cup of tea.'

'I must apologize, Father,' Juliet said somewhat later, after they'd got through their introductions and preliminaries. 'I promised to call you yesterday afternoon but got distracted.'

'These are not normal times, professor,' Father Gould said, making that observation for the second time in only twenty minutes. 'I'm just glad finally to be able to get to see you face to face.'

Juliet frowned. She said, 'I still don't know what you hope to achieve by speaking to me.'

'Clarification,' Father Gould said.

'Please explain.'

They were seated by now, all three of them, around Juliet Harrington's kitchen table. It was just after eight a.m. Father Gould described the funeral of the unfortunate flat fire victim, starting with the requiem mass at which the atmosphere had seemed unnerving and the incense in its ceremonial burner had smelled somehow rank.

Then, without naming Andrew Baxter or describing the circumstances in which he came by the story, he told them about what Andy believed he had heard coming from inside the coffin at the graveside.

'The man we were interring was emphatically dead. The fire which killed him had deprived him of three of his limbs. But the boy was adamant about what he heard. He was shaken by the experience and remained understandably troubled recalling it.

'Subsequent to his telling me the tale, the phrase "the unrestful dead" recurred to me. I couldn't remember where I'd heard it, but my bishop did, reminding me of a seminar we attended as novitiates over forty years ago; the speaker had speculated on the existence of the *Almanac of Forbidden Wisdom*. I believe the name of Gunter Keller came up, and there was some further discussion on the book's author. And then I read your monograph, professor. And now I'm here.'

'How honest is this boy?' The question came from Paul Beck.

'Totally. Almost painfully. He's not the most imaginative soul. And though he's only fourteen, he's very experienced at participating in those sorts of services. He'd have seen it as routine right up to the moment when, for him, it became anything but.'

Juliet was thinking. She said, 'If this really was the phenomenon of the unrestful dead, it means someone at that service had come into recent contact with the Almanac. I'm guessing close and prolonged contact. And it certainly wasn't you.'

'It only happened at the graveside,' Father Gould said. 'It certainly didn't happen prior to that, in the church.'

'Though there was an atmosphere you thought strange there,' Paul said. 'So maybe not prolonged contact. Maybe contact that was second hand, once removed.'

Juliet said, 'Can we exclude gravediggers?'

'They weren't present until after the service.'

'So, one of the mourners,' Juliet said.

'Or one of your altar boys,' Paul said.

'I've brought the book of condolence with me,' Father Gould said. 'It's in the boot of my car. That will furnish the names of the mourners, though not their addresses. There were six boys serving on the altar that day. One of them was aboard the *Esmeralda*. One of them is fishing with his grandfather in Ireland. I'd be very surprised if any of the remaining four is still in London. My parish is in Crouch End, which is pretty much unscathed. But the locale is deserted. I'll be performing the sacrament of mass on Sunday. If the congregation is in double figures, I'll be amazed.'

Paul said, 'People have lost their faith?'

'After the cathedral fires? What do you think?'

'Things are happening where they are because the Almanac is there,' Juliet said. 'There'll be an epicentre, I suppose, but the area

affected spreads across Greater London. Give me the contact details
of the altar boys who served that day. I've had a meeting already
with the Met Police Commissioner. She's a woman more than
capable of diplomacy. It'll be handled tactfully, I promise.'

'No dawn raids?'

'There's been enough drama, Father,' Paul said. 'We just need
to find the Almanac.'

Juliet said, 'Going back to London when you leave here, Father?'

'Why is that important?'

'I'd appreciate a lift. I need to get to Kennington and the War
Museum.'

The priest smiled. He said, 'It used to be the lunatic asylum,
you know. Bedlam. Except that all of London is bedlam now.'

FORTY

At midday on Friday, standing on tiptoe and straining her
calf muscles to reach the front door spy hole, Dawn Jackson
saw that the person who had rung their bell was a uniformed
police officer. He looked to her a bit like a medieval knight,
prepared to mount his charger and gallop into battle. He wore
articulated armour to protect his limbs. He had on a stab vest.
When he stood back to look in an upstairs window she saw there
was a utility belt around his waist, equipped with a Taser and
handcuffs and a baton and pepper spray. A radio-phone crackled
in a Velcro sheath on the left side of his chest and he carried a
helmet with a Perspex visor under his right arm.

They all looked like this, now. And Dawn knew why. They were
on high alert because of the looting and rioters, what the TV
commentators called the 'feral gangs' from the teen underworld
taking advantage of current circumstances to exact fatal revenge
in long-running feuds, mostly on sink council estates in the inner
city. They were a disproportionately large section of London's
remaining population because the affluent inner-city dwellers had
fled the former capital.

Dawn wasn't in the inner city. She was in a rather grand house

on a sedate street full of such houses in a genteel suburb. That
was why the police officer was alone. That was why he wasn't
with half a dozen colleagues and a van at the kerb, with his baton
drawn or his Taser out, or struggling to contain a slavering German
Shepherd dog on a heavy chain lead.

At that moment, before opening the door, Dawn was very
glad that she had got rid of her clumsily animate dead brother.
She was relieved the police officer couldn't see her dead grandfather waiting for the bus that never came in his piss-stained
pyjama pants and soiled singlet by one of the upstairs windows.
She was thankful that she had flushed away the last two survivors
of the Great Terrapin Cannibal War down the loo and sneaked
the foul-smelling fish tank into a skip outside an address several
doors down from hers where presumably remedial work really
was being done. The spell book was safely buried again in the
back garden.

Thursday evening had been industrious for Dawn. All mundane
enough, nothing fancy or downright miraculous, but therapeutic
after the upsetting images of St Paul's Cathedral flattened to a
field of smouldering rubble.

There was other stuff she could do nothing about. There was
the killjoy in the garden who came and went. But he tended to
manifest mostly just before dusk, as though the effort of mani-
festing had taken him all day. There were the disconcerting mirrors,
but Dawn could do nothing about the mirrors, except maybe try
to pass them off as antiques, or an unusual hobby, if the police
officer asked. And she was going to let him in, just as she had
invited in the priest. She wasn't going to ignore the knock. Dawn
thought of herself as a grasp-the-nettle sort of girl. As well as
being one who absolutely wasn't on the spectrum.

She opened the door.

'Afternoon, young lady.'

'Only just.'

That made him frown and look at his wristwatch. An encour-
aging start, even if the watch itself was one of those cheap digital
jobs.

'Come in, officer,' she said.

He showed her his ID. He told her he was Police Constable
Richard Jones. That matched what it said on the laminated card

he'd shown her. He shook hands with her, but she didn't return the compliment by telling him her own name.

She tried to lead him straight to the study, but he paused in the hallway. He said, 'I'm looking for Peter Jackson?'

And Dawn thought, You'll be lucky.

'Is he at home?'

'He's my brother. My granddad's taken him on a fishing trip until the schools reopen. They're in Ireland.'

'So you're Dawn Jackson. And you're home alone.'

'But like the boy in the film, I'm more than capable. Also, I'm fourteen, so no laws are being broken.'

'Mind if I have a look around?'

Dawn didn't like that question much. But she just smiled sweetly and said, 'Be my guest.'

He headed for the drawing room and Dawn felt her heart flutter. That was where the mirror hung with the pale, beautiful lady wearing all the bling. It was positioned over a rather grand marble fireplace, stone veined in purple and green, which her granddad had told her had been quarried just outside Florence, in Italy.

The police officer walked around the room. Then he turned to the mirror and the bling beauty portrayed there. And he raised a hand and finger-combed a hair that must have been ruffled out of place when he'd taken off his helmet after ringing the bell. And Dawn realized that all he could see in the mirror was his reflection. The portraits were solely for her. Her next, slightly hysterical, thought was, *Cash in the Attic*. Along with a recently discharged Luger pistol.

But Constable Jones only looked around the ground floor. He didn't have a search warrant, after all. It wasn't as though Dawn had committed a crime. Well, not one anyone living or sentient knew about.

'Is your brother contactable? Does he have a mobile?'

'He does, but he left it behind.'

'Isn't that a bit unusual? Most youngsters are glued to their phones.'

'That's true, but it's also true that adolescents are extremely forgetful. And Grandpa might have encouraged Pete to forget his phone. Might have incentivized Pete's forgetfulness with a bribe.

He likes solitude, my grandpa. That's why he chose Ireland, where solitude is not in short supply.'

'Do you know where they're staying? Is there a booking confirmation with a landline contact number?'

Having felt neutral when she opened the door, Dawn was liking this police officer less and less. 'Grandpa hired a camper van,' she said. 'They're moving from fishing spot to fishing spot. A bit of sea fishing from a boat. A bit of freshwater from a river bank. All over, basically.'

'And Grandpa doesn't have a mobile?'

'Doesn't believe in them.'

'I see.'

'No fixed schedule. They'll just book with Ryanair on the day when school announces it's reopening or they get fed up.'

He was watching her now with an expression she didn't much like. She rather wished she hadn't put the attic Luger back. Despite its age, that pistol worked a treat. But there'd be a rota at the station. People would know Constable Jones was here. Someone higher up had told him to come. He'd been ordered to do this. If she shot him, the trail would lead straight to her.

'What's this about, officer? What's my brother done?'

He didn't answer her. He took out a small spiral-bound notebook and wrote something in it and ripped off the page. He said, 'As soon as you hear from your brother, or your grandfather, get them to ring this number without delay.'

'I will.'

She was showing him to the front door, trying not to skip along the carpet with sheer relief, when he paused and looked her directly in the eye and said, 'Has your brother recently come into possession of a book?'

'Pete isn't much of a reader. Not even comics. What kind of book?'

'An old-fashioned book. An antique book, really. Probably bound in leather or vellum. Do you know what vellum is, Dawn?'

'What they used to bind books with in the olden days?'

'Exactly. This book is probably handwritten rather than printed using a press. Heavy, stiff paper pages. Probably coarsely textured by modern standards. Maybe scripted in Latin. Can Pete read Latin?'

'My brother can barely read his name. He'd struggle with the text on a box of breakfast cereal.'

This wasn't all that far off the truth. The latest iteration of Pete had shown zero interest in literature. Anyway, where she'd put him there were neither books nor the light to read them by.

'That description ring any bells, Dawn? You strike me as a reader, with your very grown-up vocabulary. You're a bright girl. Have you seen a book like that?'

'I can say for certain that I haven't. A book like you've described, even though I couldn't read it, I'd hardly forget it. It sounds unique.'

The police officer said goodbye.

Dawn watched from one of the upstairs windows as he walked away. There'd be a colleague in a patrol car a discreet distance down the road. They travelled in pairs these days. It just wasn't safe to do otherwise. The country faced two crises, one international and the other domestic, and Dawn knew that the reverberations, the Auguries from her use of the spell book, had created both of those.

She didn't think Constable Jones had really been suspicious of her. He'd asked probing questions and they'd been inconvenient to have to bat away. But he'd only really been following a protocol. The questions had seemed aggressive and intrusive, but that was only because she had so much to hide. They'd been thorough questions, but they'd been routine.

The bigger inconvenience was that someone knew the spell book was being used. And they were actively trying to find it. Someone had believed bloody Andy Baxter's graveside story about the unrestful dead. Peter hadn't believed it, not at first – which was ironic, because moments after she'd killed him he'd personally treated her to a pretty good demonstration of the phenomenon.

They were going after the altar boys from that graveside episode. They might go after the priest. They'd go after the mourners. And when everyone except for her brother had proven their innocence, they'd be back asking for Pete again.

Was she worried? Yes and no, Dawn thought. It was entirely plausible for two inexperienced sailors to get into trouble in the volatile Atlantic waters off the west coast of Ireland.

When they came back, she'd remember that her grandpa had planned to fish with his grandson off the coast of County Clare, near the Cliffs of Moher. That was a hazardous spot, even in June. This cover story left the loose end of the camper van, but you could always infer that some of Ireland's travelling community were responsible for its disappearance. Dawn didn't much like pandering to prejudice, but sometimes you just had to do what you had to do.

FORTY-ONE

April 10, 1530

They are here, finally assembled. They are Lorenz Hood from the Austrian Tyrol, Tiberius van Vaunt from the Netherlands, Cordelia Cortez from Spain, Mary Nye from England and of course their infernal recruiter and leader, Gunter Keller from Lower Saxony in the Germanic lands.

Mary Nye is unprepossessing in appearance for all her apparent talents. Hood could be Keller's brother, even his twin, given the commonality of their sour and arrogant expressions. But van Vaunt has the venerable air of a distinguished scholar and the Spanish countess Cortez carries herself regally and is a porcelain-skinned, swan-necked, raven-haired beauty. It is a cold beauty, though, in truth. A glance from her is a shard of ice through the heart.

I have put them in my own hunting lodge on the edge of Dartmoor, so they have spacious berths and all home comforts in an isolated spot behind a high wall. The gate is secured by a dozen pike-men hand-picked by the king from his personal bodyguard. Their loyalty is intense, their warrior spirit forged in battle and their silence on the matter of this singular duty guaranteed.

Henry is in Paris as a guest of King Francis. Matters have not always been so pacific between these two men or between our sometimes fractious countries. Today they are not only allies but victors; they are celebrating the success of their scheme to smoke out and expose the most powerful occultists of our time. And, over time, to end their mischievous lives in just punishment.

Emissaries have been dispatched in secret to each of their

homelands to alert the authorities to their identities and their guilt. The finished Almanac will be the proof of this that condemns them. I am to take it personally on a progress to their homelands in a demonstration that will damn them.

These are powerful and dangerous people with an array of lethal skills. They will be weakened before they are seized and tried, probably, I am told, with doses of poison. This poison, skilfully measured and secretly administered, will debilitate each of them to the point that makes arrest possible without their gaolers or their judges being harmed by enchantment as they carry out their rightful duties.

Before the king departed Dover, I asked him why not simply administer a fatal dose of this deadly draft to each of them now?

'Justice needs to be seen to be done,' he said. 'Their hangings or burnings when they have been judged and condemned are required as a public lesson to others not to dabble in the squalid mischief that so insults our Creator.'

I did not know our monarch, an enthusiast for matters theological, was also such an ardent student of justice. It seems to me he bends the law often to his own will. But that is a private thought and though this enterprise has made us close, his rule has taught me it would be most unwise to share this opinion with so capricious a ruler.

Even as I write, on the edge of the wilderness that horrid litter of magicians pool their arcane knowledge and formulate their spells. That they do so under my roof pains me greatly. They pollute the very place from which I have forayed on the hunt, run down my most prized trophies.

Hunting is one of the few pursuits that permit me some freedom from my melancholy meditations on the daughter we lost. Time has not healed the pain and nor have the passing months lessened my conviction that Keller is guilty of her murder. I now know with certainty that I will have my retribution, but that conviction brings no comfort either. I have paid an unpayable price in my service to the Crown. It is all I can sanely tolerate, and I only tolerate it at all for the sake of my lovely wife and noble sons.

They will be here, they say, for six weeks or so. Six seems a number close to their frozen hearts. They demand luxuries as well as the gold they are being paid. The finest wines. The choicest cuts of meat. Patiently matured cheeses. Fruit fresh and fully ripened. Bread baked daily.

Servants from my own household wait on them for a generous bounty from my own purse. These are people loyal to me and it seemed the most practical and safest way to proceed. They are instructed to close their eyes and ears to what they see and hear. This only for their own security and safety.

There is a strange affliction of weather in the region for which I believe this ghastly coven responsible. There are sudden deluges of rain from a cloudless sky. There are noxious fogs that yellow the air and choke the breath and make travel on foot or horseback all but impossible. The nights are bright with lightning the colour of the coals in a blacksmith's forge when the bellows blast at full strength. These jagged bolts paint the land crimson. It looks blood-bathed.

The animals too are behaving strangely. Deer stampede in panicked hordes. Birds fly in a black frenzy of feathers in flocks the size of which I have never in my life before witnessed. Their feathers fall as lazily and thickly as black snowflakes in these episodes and all light is eclipsed.

My dreams have been disturbed. I see a vast metropolis from some godless future flood and fall to ruin. I visit a house with outlandish furnishings were lives alone a little girl attired in strange garments. Last night I dreamed she stared out of a window at Gunter Keller, standing in her garden. The alchemist was not solid, as he is in the flesh. He had the faint fabric of an illusion. It was almost as though he was composed of nothing more solid than smoke.

The girl looks a little like my lost daughter. She has the same green eyes as Matilda. But there is a troubling callousness to her expression which I never saw on my daughter's face. Nor would I ever have wished to.

It is as though this girl, though prettily featured enough, is unengaged with her world. It is not scorn, or disillusionment, or boredom. It is easier to describe as an absence of something. It is as though something has been abstracted from her. I cannot put it more honestly or plainly than that. And the resemblance to Matilda is not strong enough for the dream to have symbolic significance. I do not believe it to be a portent of anything. The irony is that were it not for my own experiences of the last couple of years, I would not be a superstitious man at all. I am by nature sceptical.

My hunting lodge is very fine. It is constructed, walls and roof, from heavy timbers of English oak. They are a foot through and a foot across and massively strong. I gathered the craftsmen who worked the wood and completed the building from among those whose regular toil involves more substantial dimensions. Some I recruited from the naval shipyard at Portsmouth, where they build our fleet of battleships. Others were men who had worked on the strengthening beams in the interiors of our great churches and cathedrals.

Such grand and ambitious projects as the construction of my lodge cannot be scrimped over. They are only ever successfully achieved at considerable financial cost. And, as I earlier wrote, it is a place which has fostered the most blissfully thoughtless moments of a life otherwise subsumed by grief.

But the next few weeks are the last few weeks of the existence of this refuge of mine. For truthfully, it is no longer that at all. I cannot abide the thought of ever sleeping there again. It will be a place tainted and despoiled by its current inhabitants and what they are gathered to achieve there. Its rooms will be malign, its very timbers corrupted by the evil quintet they currently provide with shelter.

When the magicians have presented me with that Almanac and taken up their things and departed, I will first find a safe place in which to secure the book. Then I will return to put my lodge to the torch. I will do this personally, having daubed pitch into its exterior nooks and crannies to encourage and nourish the flames. I will scorch the place off the earth, leave nothing to remind me or anyone else of the dark mischief that has so corrupted the building's soul.

October 2, 1534

It is finally done. Gunter Keller, the last living of the blighted crew he led, is gone. Gaunt from the poison and lame from the torture when they led him in chains to the stake, he was not the arrogant man who once threatened to put me on the bottom of the sea with a single thought.

Nor did he die easily. It is the custom in this country to strangle the person sentenced to death before the pyre is lit, so they feel no pain; their burning is symbolic, just the denial of a death dignified by an intact corpse and a burial rite.

That was not done in Keller's case and so his death was as prolonged and agonized as he so fully deserved. It was a good hour between the first flames fluttering at his feet and his last breath. For him, it must have seemed an eternity. A small sample only of the fate awaiting him in Hell.

His death closes the final chapter of a story that began on a bitterly cold night when I rode from London to Hampton Court wrapped in a cloak given me by Catherine, my wife, in the autumn which had just passed. The king was a guest at Hampton Court back then, though I rightly considered it a palace he coveted. Now he resides there in splendour as its owner. Had I known then what the enterprise he outlined was going to cost me, I would have risked his notorious kingly wrath by refusing to play any part in it.

This is because my heart tells me some years on that my part in that enterprise was responsible for the death of Matilda; she was robbed of the life she should have enjoyed into adulthood. And I lost everything.

I have a loving wife and two loyal and obedient sons. I have lands and entitlement. I might be the wealthiest man in the kingdom. I know none with greater worldly riches than mine. I enjoy the gratitude of the monarch, who calls me friend and who has honoured me with the highest offices. Yet I know in my heart I have nothing.

The bitter lesson harshly learned since that long-ago December night is that magic always exacts a price. The cost of it is inescapable. There is always a reckoning to pay. And it is one I know I will go on paying for as long as I continue to breathe.

This I say in God's eternal truth,

Edmund Joseph Fleury

In a basement room in the bowels of the Bodleian library, Paul Beck looked at his wristwatch. It was midday. He'd read the last entry in the sad story of how a noble man's life was blighted by kingly hubris. It was a singular tale. But as to the current location of the *Almanac of Forbidden Wisdom*, in the creation of which its author was so instrumental, it gave no clue at all.

Would Juliet have reached London? It was only sixty miles, but once the priest's car reached London's outer suburbs it would become hazardous. Paul thought it a mistake not to have accompanied her, and not only because his last hour or so of research had produced nothing concrete. He was concerned for her safety. The wasteland of England's former capital was an increasingly wild, desolate, dangerous place.

Paul had told Juliet honestly what he wasn't. He hadn't played football in the German Bundesliga. He'd been straightforward about what he hadn't done, but rather more opaque about those things he had. They called them sins of omission, didn't they, in the circles Father Gould was used to moving in?

He'd been part of the same recruitment intake at the embassy as Dan Carter four years earlier. He strongly suspected that their applications had been successful for reasons that were very similar.

FORTY-TWO

There were twenty-four men in the elite combat unit and it was led by a major named John Creed. They were experienced men, having been blooded in the Middle East prior to the European theatre and their disruptive sorties behind the German front line, usually parachuted in with their vehicles tumbling through the air on night parachutes after them. Yvonne Dupont had said the ones she saw had numbered a dozen, but Juliet found no details enabling her to whittle the twenty-four down by half, which was a pity.

They had seen a lot of combat, most of it hand to hand. They had done a good deal of sabotage work and were expert at setting lethal traps for advancing enemy troops. Their snipers had assassinated some very senior enemy commanders. Their mission in France was to harry retreating German forces and to eliminate spies and some of the more vindictive collaborators. This was execution, plain and simple, but it wasn't ever called that. And the

British weren't the only ones doing it. The Americans were doing it too, with some enthusiasm.

The War Museum archive had photographs of most of the men in the unit, their names handwritten on the reverse side. But there was no mention of what had happened to any of them after the end of hostilities, and twenty-four was too big a number anyway for Juliet to be able to follow up. She needed some lead or clue that would thin them out and leave her eventually with a single, culpable individual. She didn't feel at all confident of getting that.

The museum itself felt very strange to her. Some Home Office phone calls made on her behalf as she travelled to London had gained her access and cooperation, once she'd briefed the Home Secretary and advised him of her plans. There was a skeleton staff and only emergency power; wall-mounted lights with an industrial look and a feeble, greenish glow.

The quake had left the building largely intact. But the effect of the flood had been to leave the ground floor with a layer of stinking mud nobody had yet attempted to clear up. The place was gloomy, smelly, all but deserted. Looters had smashed a couple of the ground-floor display cases, either to get at pistols in the hope they hadn't been decommissioned, or to access valuable antique swords. Or possibly both. Shards of glass glinted amid the mud and murk down there.

Juliet was at an upper-floor carrel equipped with a computer. She had access codes to open files that might be relevant to what she was doing. The physical documents concerning Major Creed's SAS unit were faded and time-worn and fragile with age. They gave little hint of the violence which would have characterized the military lives of the men to whom they pertained.

Some material had been computerized. Juliet switched the machine on and accessed the software package she needed and did a search for Major John Creed. Both sides of a handwritten letter came up. The letter heading told her that it had been sent from Aldershot's Cambridge Military Hospital. The caption underneath told her the letter had been written when the major was a patient at the hospital after an infected shrapnel wound in his foot gave him septicaemia, from which he fully recovered. According to the caption, Creed lived on until his death from heart failure at the age of fifty-nine in 1978.

The letter was dated 'May 1, 1945', just a week before the German surrender and V-E Day. Juliet enlarged the size. Major Creed had possessed the small, neat hand of a punctilious man. He'd probably been very thorough in the organization of those executions carried out in a recently liberated area of northern France.

Dear Mabel,

Everything's absolutely fine at this end. Sawbones no longer talking about the possibility of amputation. I'll keep the foot, apparently, and therefore the day job. And when this show is over and done with, no golf course will be safe. And we'll even be able to have a crack again at playing on that tennis court at your father's place. Not that my fragile ego needs another beating.

TJ came to visit on his leave, which was damned nice of him, even if he is a rum sort of cove. I've suspected for a while that there's something underhand going on under the veneer of schoolboy charm he affects. He's awfully fond of what he calls his 'souvenirs'. But there's a very thin line between taking battlefield trophies and looting. It wouldn't be one I'd be comfortable treading and I've told him more than once that it could end up getting him shot.

This isn't rhetoric either. Military discipline is much more severe in wartime for reasons that are bloody obvious (please excuse my French). A Beretta pistol is a very nice thing to own and I'm told some very fine wristwatches are manufactured in eastern Germany, but neither artefact is worth the price of standing in front of a firing squad. TJ has put paid to enough men personally to know that no one comes back from the dead. That's very much a one-way street.

There was some sort of commotion after TJ left. An orderly got the jitters rather badly in the mortuary. Started spouting nonsense, had to be sedated in the end, which was ironic in his own hospital. Or it would have been when he came around afterwards on a ward.

What else can I tell you? The food here's improving, unless I'm just getting used to it. The staff are as cheerful and friendly as ever. A chap could get used to being waited on,

*and on a serious note, I'm getting stronger and feeling more
my old self every day.*

*Wishing our Edinburgh home wasn't quite so far away,
because what with the requisitioning of train tickets and the
petrol ration, it makes travel so ruddy difficult generally, and
I know visiting me here is impossible.*

*For that reason, missing you terribly, Mabs, and can't wait
to get out of here and hold you in my arms again.*

Much love,

Johnnie

Juliet switched off the computer. She went through her list of
names. There were five possible men from his unit the major could
have been writing about. They were Trevor John Gordon, Tommy
Jackson, Tim Jessup, Tony Jones and Terry James Fisher.

She got up from her chair and phoned Father Gould. He
answered on the first ring.

'Home safe?'

'Everything is relative these days, Professor Harrington.'

'As I told you in the car, please call me Juliet.'

There was silence on the line. Then he said, 'Please call me
Tom, Juliet.'

'Do you believe in coincidence, Tom?'

'It's not mathematically impossible. But not generally.'

'When your unimaginative altar boy heard the unrestful dead
that day, wasn't one of the others named Jackson?'

'You know that. His name was on the list we compiled just this
morning for the Met Police Commissioner.'

'Tell me about him.'

'Peter Jackson. Normal boy with a tragic recent history. Parents
both killed in their car at the end of last year in a motorway
collision. Has rather a neglected look about him. Devout boy,
sweet-natured.'

'The police will talk to him today, if they haven't already.'

'His sister told me he was on a fishing trip to Ireland with his
grandfather.'

Juliet was quiet, thinking. Then she said, 'Do you believe that?'

'I was disinclined to believe her there on the doorstep; she
sounded a bit glib. But then she invited me in. Would she have

done that if Peter had been skulking up the stairs with the *Almanac of Forbidden Wisdom*? I didn't think so. She was far too cool a customer.'

Juliet was quiet again, remembering the verbal profile the Home Secretary had sketched of the Almanac's likely user on that day less than a week earlier in her office at the university. Someone with an adolescent's sullenness and anger, he'd said. Someone spiteful and uncaring.

'What's her name, Father?'

'Dawn.'

'How did she strike you?'

'Extremely bright, and I use that adjective intentionally. Almost certainly on the autism spectrum, though at the less severe end. An Asperger syndrome sufferer.'

Juliet ended the call and her phone immediately registered another.

'Juliet Harrington.'

'Dan Carter.'

'Desperate Dan.'

'What?'

'Sorry, a joke. I know who you are, what you do. How can I help you?' Juliet asked.

'It's more a case of how I can help you,' Carter said. 'Are you anywhere near a fax machine? Or if you give me your email address, probably best to send you a scan.'

'A scan of what?'

'A drawing, Professor. You know about our material witness to a wartime theft?'

'Yvonne Dupont,' Juliet said.

'She called me this morning and I drove out and met her for lunch. Transpires she's an excellent draughtswoman. Attended art school a few years after the end of the war. She gave me a detailed likeness of her jeep-driving thief. If you can cross-reference it with a photo of the chaps in that unit, I think we'll possibly have our man.'

Juliet gave Dan Carter her email address. A minute later she switched the computer back on and opened what he'd sent. It was done in charcoal and depicted a handsome man whose dark, side-parted hair was rather long for that of a serving soldier. He

had a moustache and was good looking in a rakish, Errol Flynn
sort of way. It was a period face, that of a man probably in his
late twenties.

She sorted through the photos in front of her. Like the charcoal
sketch, they were black and white. She found a photo of Tommy
Jackson among them, a snapshot really, slightly blurred. But the
resemblance was striking. Unless he had a twin in the unit, he
was Yvonne Dupont's chateau thief.

Her phone rang again. Paul Beck.

'I think I know who's got the Almanac. I think I know where
it is,' Juliet said.

'Who has it?'

'An adolescent girl named Dawn Jackson. Her great-grandfather
stole it. She must have found it quite recently among the things
he left behind.'

There was a silence. Then Paul said, 'She's dangerous, isn't
she?'

'She's powerful with that book. And she's completely reckless,'
Juliet said.

'Sit tight until I get there. I hired a car just after midday. I'll
be with you in less than an hour.'

'We should call the police.'

'And they turn up with dogs and a loud-hailer and a battering
ram. And how does Dawn react to that?'

'OK,' Juliet said.

But she didn't do nothing. She called back Father Thomas Gould
to get Dawn Jackson's address.

Paul arrived, as he'd said he would, within the hour. Juliet was
delighted to see him. It was close to six o'clock by then and the
museum's official closing time. But they had a pass key to one of
the rear entrances as part of their access-all-areas security clearances. She ran to him and hugged him hard and he hugged her
back and they kissed.

'If we ever get out of this I'm going to ask you to marry me,'
he said.

'Like I said before, you're on the rebound, Paul.'

'Like I said before, it's because of you I'm not.'

'Desperate Dan for best man?'

'Dan Carter can be godfather to our child. He's a good bloke.'

'It's a pretty dream,' Juliet said.

Paul shook his head. He said, 'We'll go into it wide awake.'

'Only if we survive this nightmare we're living in.'

He looked at her seriously. He said, 'There's something you don't know about me. I wasn't always a translator. Not for a living, I mean. I spent five years as a special forces soldier in the German Army. I was an officer in the Kommando Spezialkräfte, or the KSK.'

Juliet said, 'That sounds a lot more impressive than playing in the Bundesliga.'

'We were seriously underpaid.'

'I'll bet there was plenty of job satisfaction. And I'm sure the work was varied.'

'My point is that there are things I'm trained to do. I can get us through a locked door. I'm good at evasion. We need a plan for Dawn Jackson. I think that involves you distracting her while I find the book.'

'If it isn't sitting on her lap. My understanding is that no military plan survives the first few seconds of action.'

He smiled. 'That's true. But I'm good at improvisation.'

'How good?'

'Five years at the sharp end. And I'm still alive.'

'How does the plan start?'

'Under cover of darkness. We wait for nightfall, Juliet. Then we move.'

FORTY-THREE

Dawn Jackson was currently what she'd often heard described as 'on the horns of a dilemma'. She was still irritated by the thought of Handy Andy Baxter using Pete's key and stealing through the house to have a nosy while she studied in the library for tests she was pretty sure now she wouldn't sit this term. If ever, frankly.

She wanted to get even with Andy and she'd thought of several ways in which she could do it. For a start, she could single out

Andy's dad for the blindness spell, so he'd lose his job; maybe then, as a consequence of that, Handy Andy would become homeless. Or she could blind Andy's mum. You weren't in all fairness much good as a librarian if you were blind, unless all the books were written in braille.

Or she could kill one or both of Andy's parents with the lullaby spell that put people to sleep for ever. If Andy's mum and dad died, Andy was the prim sort who would respond by immediately dialling nine-nine-nine. It wouldn't occur to him to do the sensible thing and bury their bodies in the garden at night and just keep quiet. Although that might unravel a bit when the mortgage payments stopped going through. Andy's parents probably didn't own their property outright as her grandfather had. And they probably didn't have a couple of grand hidden in a rolled-up sock in their bedroom wardrobe either.

She didn't have a photo of Handy Andy's parents, but Dawn thought she could probably take their picture without them seeing her do so if she stalked the library on one of those evenings Andy's dad gave his mum a lift home from her volunteer job there. She could do it using the phone for which her brother no longer had any practical use. Then Dawn could make Andy an orphan and he'd have to go into a home just because he hadn't had the sheer resourcefulness she possessed in such abundance.

There were other spells she could inflict on Andy. If she made a sketch of a spinning top and posted it to him, then recited the quite simple liturgy, he would have a permanent problem with his equilibrium. He would lose his balance for the rest of his unbalanced life to the point where he literally wouldn't be able to stand up without immediately falling down. He'd careen around like a delinquent dodgem at a funfair, and that would be genuinely funny. Probably a single Nurofen spell.

Or there was the hunger spell, which was a bit more serious. She'd have to send him some vomit for that, probably most practically in one of those bubble-wrap-lined envelopes they sold at WH Smith. Then every time he ate he'd throw up, until the moment he perished, having starved to death. Death by starvation was notoriously agonizing so that was obviously quite a tempting one to inflict. Except that Dawn could only acquire puke by puking

personally, which she really didn't fancy at all. And it would probably take Diazepam to deal with the fallout.

There were some very simple spells that would seriously inconvenience Andy on a permanent basis. There was one which caused
in its subject's mind, whenever or wherever they were walking,
the delusion that they were barefoot on a bed of nails. Almost as
medieval as the lopping-off spell, but effective nevertheless. Two
aspirin? One paracetamol? Very tempting.

Speculating on getting her revenge on Andy Baxter got Dawn
quite excited. And that made her think there might be another
way altogether of doing it that didn't have to involve any magic.
She'd heard that adolescent boys thought about sex, on average,
about every five seconds. They were completely obsessed by the
subject. She'd seen the way he'd looked at her the day he'd
knocked on the door asking for the hospital address when Pete
had suffered the imaginary bout of meningitis Dawn had given
him. He'd looked at her in that pervy way grown men sometimes
looked at grown women.

She could call him and lure him around with some seductive
half promises. Dawn had not personally felt the stirring of any
sexual impulses, but she could pretend to convincingly, she knew.

Except that Pete had told her ages ago that Handy Andy regularly confessed his sins to that nice Father Gould. That was a
sobering disincentive to any sort of hanky-panky, wasn't it? Maybe
not, if the hanky-panky was just a bullet in the temple from the
attic Luger before using the disappearing spell to make Andy's
incriminating corpse vanish completely. No Andy, no confession
to Father Gould. And no body, no murder conviction. Dawn knew
that from the Netflix crime dramas she sometimes watched on TV.

But Dawn truthfully felt rather torn. And that was where the
dilemma occurred. Much as she wanted to get even with Handy
Andy Baxter, she also very much wanted to see if she could pull
off the spell that created a new life out of nothing. It was the most
complex and ambitious ritual in the book. It required great concentration, total focus. Offing Andy would be satisfying, even fun;
but it wouldn't give her the same sense of accomplishment that
creating life would.

She'd read Mary Shelley's *Frankenstein* in her Special Studies
Group. She'd had her own recent experiences with her grandpa

and her brother. She knew that restoring someone, reanimating them, was a process that could go seriously pear-shaped. But creating a life? It was a clean slate, wasn't it? What could possibly go wrong with that?

'So much magic, so little time,' Dawn said out loud.

She'd had that feeling for a few days. It was a sort of inkling, or instinct, that some kind of conclusion was coming to all this. On the television, Russia had declared war on two neighbouring countries. Israel had invaded Jordan, which was fighting back furiously. Only eleventh-hour peace brokering had stopped the Chinese navy taking on the American Pacific Fleet. And that treaty looked unlikely to hold. There was anarchy in the sub-Saharan African states, where dozens of seriously pissed-off tribal groups were all armed with Kalashnikovs. Sweden was in the process of building internment camps for its militant Muslim population. Norway was threatening to follow suit. Nobody was calling it that, but a race war was being waged in South Africa. Turmoil, Dawn thought, all over the world. People were openly talking about the End Times.

London was practically a ghost town. Well, ghost city, because of its size. But its size on the TV made it look terribly empty. Distinctly short on population, apart from the high piles of decaying corpses no one was clearing up because of the exponential risk of disease.

Would one more spell, even a complex and ambitious spell, really do that much damage? Dawn was familiar with the saying that there was no point crying over spilled milk. She was familiar too with the one suggesting that you might as well be hanged for a sheep as for a lamb. She agreed with both sentiments. She thought in the end it might come down to the toss of a coin. Getting even with Handy Andy, or creating a life out of thin air.

She was in the kitchen, musing on all this. She was watching images on the TV with the sound turned down. She knew that there were swathes of what had once been the capital which had been without power since before the flood. Water and electricity apparently didn't mix. But her area was mostly OK. There'd been a couple of outages, but their supply had been quite quickly restored. It was evidence to Dawn that some people were still trying to convince themselves that things would eventually return to normal. She'd come privately to the conclusion that they were wrong. It was the reason she had stopped revising and dug the spell book back up.

The images on the TV screen were apocalyptic. There was no other word, really. People were dying on a Malthusian scale and had been ever since that weird eclipse and then the sinking on the Thames with all hands of the *Esmeralda*. That had been the beginning of it, Dawn thought, looking back. And the *Esmeralda* sinking had been such a small-time event, in retrospect, that you could almost feel nostalgic about it.

The book was on the table at which she sat. Its vellum cover was plain, wordless, benign. The book gave off the slight musty smell of centuries of age. It didn't honestly look much, closed, in repose. It almost looked innocent.

Movement through the kitchen window caught her eye. He was there again, the angry looking man with the terrible haircut who wore a garment like a belted cassock and was shod in boots without laces. He was from the past, she knew. He was from history, though his part in history might well have gone unrecorded. Was he a ghost? He looked more solid than before, more substantial. She could no longer see the bricks of the back garden wall through his body. He looked almost real, to Dawn. And then he raised his bowed head and beckoned to her.

Curious, she opened the back door and went outside. The garden smelled of summer; of sun-warmed grass and scent-sweet flowers. But there was something else. It was an odour sweet and bitter at the same time, and Dawn knew what it was. It was the scent of the smoke drifting from the fires deliberately lit by the looters and rioters who were all that was left of London's population in the inner-city lowlands to the south of where she stood.

She knew that he would speak to her, this time. But it was still a shock when he did. His voice was a rusty echo, more like something remembered than something happening now. And he spoke to her in Latin.

'You must desist,' he said.

'Who are you? Who were you?'

'It matters not. I beg you to desist.'

'Why are you here?'

'Recompense. Remorse. Repentance. Attempting, after all this time, only to save my soul.'

The figure before her shimmered then, roiling a bit like smoke from a fire rising and twisting in the flue. And Dawn knew that the effort involved in this was enormous, for this man. And that soon he would be gone and would be unable to return. What he was doing, his being here, was unsustainable.

'How did you die?'

'Badly. Deservedly. It matters not. Desist.'

'Spoilsport.'

He raised his eyes to her. They were pale and sightless. His skin was cratered with scars. When he opened his mouth she saw that his teeth were black with decay. He said, 'You sport with your world.'

He faded then; he struggled not to, but slowly disappeared from sight despite himself, and was gone. Dawn guessed he'd been something to do with the spell book, possibly even its author. In life he'd been someone capable of powerful magic, but in death, after all this time, the magic had dissipated. It was still a pretty good trick, coming back centuries after your death and then eventually being capable of communicating with someone living. But Dawn didn't think she'd take his advice. She didn't think for a moment that she would desist. She wasn't at all the desisting type. And she was not in the habit, either, of taking advice from ghosts.

FORTY-FOUR

The trawler put out of Fleetwood Harbour quite close to dusk. Its skipper was a twenty-three-year-old man named Alan Turner. Alan was fourth or fifth generation, fishing was what he'd grown up with, the job less of an occupation than a family custom carried out with an air of contented inevitability. It could be hard in the winter, and was tough on social life for a man of his age because the fish were less elusive prey at night. But he was not apt to complain. Complaining was what farmers did. He had his own boat and was his own boss and the fishing suited his temperament.

Conditions were calm. The night was mild and the forecast

unthreatening. Weather could change very quickly at sea and often worsened severely and without warning over a short space of time. Alan didn't expect it to do that tonight. But he was prepared if it did. The craft he was aboard was properly seaworthy, a resilient little vessel, a former tugboat converted for its current role by the fitting of a hoist for the nets and some imaginative welding. The *Marnie* chugged into open water with a throaty purr Alan thought would be music to any nautical mechanic's ears.

His crew numbered two men. They were Phil Halsall and Joe Palmer. They were older than he was, in their thirties, but he wasn't so authoritarian a boss that they rankled at his style of captaincy. He didn't need to order them to do anything, really. They were sufficiently experienced to know what to do without being told. Crewing a fishing vessel was all they'd ever done and the only living either man had ever sought to earn.

The *Marnie* travelled at about eight knots. They were in no hurry. The best fishing to be had was about twelve miles offshore. But there was no point burning fuel unnecessarily in a rush to get to where they'd lower and tow their nets. Their progress was leisurely, the wake gentle at their stern, and the setting sun turned the water a pink that would deepen to crimson before the orb disappeared and left them in moonlit darkness.

Summer wavelets hit the side of their boat with a somnambulant slap. The craft pitched and rolled with the sort of gentle motion that had non-seafarers retching green-complexioned over the gunwale and into the water. These men were almost unaware of the movement. They were veteran sailors, afloat regularly since their teens. They respected the sea. It was a capricious element and could be deadly too. They'd each of them lost friends and shipmates to maritime tragedy. But they were relaxed enough on a serene and lovely evening.

Alan felt glad to get off the land. It was easier a few miles out to sea to pretend that matters were still normal. The London rioting, before the city emptied into the New Forest refugee camp, had proven to be contagious. It had spread to Southampton and Plymouth and Reading. Then it had spread to Birmingham and Leeds. And then to Liverpool and Manchester.

There was talk of the government resigning en masse. It was Alan's personal point of view that the Home Secretary, David

Anderson, was the only senior politician with the brains and backbone for the job. The only member of the Cabinet with the right combination of calmness and leadership quality. Though he hadn't shared that thought with either Phil or Joe. Discussion of politics was a great way for a boat crew to fall out with one another spectacularly.

He'd had a conversation about the wider situation with his new wife, Valerie, only that morning over breakfast. They'd been married for just over six months and Valerie was keen on starting a family. Valerie was a lecturer at the Open University and worked via computer from home. She could work through her pregnancy and return to work quickly if she wished to after the child was born.

Recent years had been good to Alan. The catches had been profitable enough and he worked hard and had quite a bit put by. They could afford to start a family. But money wasn't the point.

'We can't bring a child into this world, Val.'

'We're talking a minimum of nine months, Alan. Things will surely have calmed down.'

'Or they'll have got worse.'

'If they get much worse it'll all be over. Does anyone really want that?'

'I suppose not. Except for the real fanatics. But no one seems to know how to stop it, Val.'

'It's bloody depressing.'

'And scary.'

Alan had stopped then. He'd seen the tears in his wife's eyes. Escalation didn't only apply to the international crisis. Escalation could happen at his own kitchen table. He'd got the new wife he still couldn't believe he'd successfully wooed off the subject of a baby and on to something else less fraught.

They talked about the degree results her mature students were currently getting, how well some of them had done. Alan thought, following their unspoken coda, that this was not the time really to think about a fresh start or launching a second career. Normality would have to return to make a university degree a thing of relevance again.

Now, surrounded by the serenity of a calm sea, the situation on land seemed surreal, like a nightmare or a hallucinatory experience.

Post-traumatic stress or a batch of bad acid. An experience endur-
able only because it was temporary and not real. Except that the
world was their only reality and it was swiftly falling apart.

Alan was in the wheelhouse, piloting the craft almost by rote.
He could navigate easily just by noting the position of the prow
in relation to the setting sun. There was a binnacle-mount compass
next to where he stood. Or he could navigate on the return leg in
darkness, on a clear night, from the position of the stars.

At first, Alan thought the slight misting he'd begun to be aware
of was just smearing on the glass pane through which he watched
the sea, steering their course. A job for a bottle of Mr Muscle and
a clean rag. Then Phil came up from where he'd been repairing a
torn net below and said that a mist was coming up.

'Coming up?'

'It's rising from the surface of the sea, skipper. It's bloody
unusual. And it's got very warm, suddenly. Almost unbearable
down below, that heat.'

Alan engaged the auto-steer and stepped out on to the deck and
was immediately aware of how warm the air felt. He'd experienced
British heatwaves, but this was close to dusk and like stepping off
the plane on to a broiling runway somewhere like Antigua or
Barbados. Out at sea was always, always cooler than on land. That
was a fixed law, an article of nature. The combination of water
and wind made it so. This was more than strange. It was bizarre.

And Phil was right. That mist was rising from the sea. Except
that Alan didn't think it was mist in reality at all.

Just then something plopped to the surface and rolled lazily in
water starting to bubble. It was a large flounder and it looked
cooked, *poached*, and other fish were rising all around it to the
surface; bloated, also cooked, dead. The smell of them was rich
and overpowering and profoundly wrong.

'What the fuck, skipper,' Phil said to Alan, almost under his
breath, wide-eyed with astonishment and fear. 'The sea is boiling.'

Alan Turner bolted back into the wheelhouse and switched on
the radio. The airwaves were thick with the clamour of panicked
voices. They came from men aboard vessels off Padstow and
Ventnor and Barmouth and Hull. Off Brixham and Lowestoft
and Whitby. All around the coast, the sea simmered under a rising
blanket of steam.

FORTY-FIVE

'Clarify something for me,' Paul said. His eyes were on the computer monitor mounted in the carrel Juliet had used researching Major Creed's SAS unit. 'Are the Auguries the phenomena that occur prior to the disasters, or are they the disasters themselves?' He was listening to a BBC news bulletin, looking at footage of vessels returning to seething harbours through clouds of vapour, appearing out of it first in outline and then etched in detail like ghost ships crewed by sweat-lathered sailors mostly stripped to their underwear.

'They're the precursors,' Juliet said.

'Then I'd say we've a major disaster coming,' he said. '"Looming" might be a better word.'

'Unless we nullify the Almanac. That might prevent it from happening.'

'How?'

'They're not natural events. They're apocalyptic. It was Gunter Keller's intention to trigger the End Times. I think if we sow the book with salt, as he said to, it will lose its potency. The disasters will stop.'

Paul was quiet. 'Some of the ships have broken up and sunk,' he said. 'Some have drifted back with dead crews who've just succumbed to the heat. I think your salt theory might only be wishful thinking.'

'Don't we have to try?'

'Of course we do. But we don't arrive until after dark when concealment's easier.'

'We should set off now. We'll probably have to walk there. It'll take a couple of hours.'

Paul shook his head. 'I came here in a hire car, remember? It's parked outside. Illegally parked, but I highly doubt I've been given a ticket.'

They left at seven p.m. It wasn't a journey that would ordinarily take two hours plus, but these weren't ordinary times. Some of the roads had subsided in the flood. Sections of some had been

badly damaged in the quake. Others had been deliberately block-
aded. Before they left, Paul took a bayonet from one of the
smashed-in display cases on the ground floor of the museum. To
Juliet, it looked almost as lethal in length as a sword.

'Planning to skewer her?'

'This is for the journey. The streets are hazardous,' he said. 'It
will be a deterrent if anyone tries to stop our car. Big enough to
see through our windscreen. Big enough to discourage an opportunistic thief. Call it our insurance policy.'

'Would you use it?'

'It's anarchy out there. The car could get stopped by a gang
with ideas about raping you.'

'So your answer is yes.'

'Like I told you, Juliet, I wasn't always a translator. I'm not
squeamish about using necessary force.'

'I'm glad you're with me, Paul.'

'You'd do this alone?'

'With no alternative, yes. She has to be stopped.'

'She's pulled off something unthinkable,' Paul said, 'to make
the sea respond like that. She's reversed nature.'

'She's been reversing nature for a fortnight. We're living with
the consequences. Some of us are dying because of them.'

'Any idea what she's done now?'

'I'm guessing Keller's party piece,' Juliet said. 'The creation
of life from nothing.'

'He said that his attempt all but destroyed him. He had to use
all his power to reverse it. Dawn Jackson's an amateur. Whatever
she's done, she probably couldn't undo.'

They were in the car, Paul driving, dipped headlights, the streets
weirdly empty of traffic, human or otherwise. Juliet said, 'It strikes
me there are two ways you could bring a life into being. You could
start from scratch. You could create a separate entity. Or it could
inhabit you, possess you, kind of exile you from yourself. I'm
inclined to believe from the Keller account of the spell that that's
what happened with him.'

'So we might be denied the pleasure of meeting Dawn?'

'We'll meet what Dawn's become,' Juliet said. 'If my theory is
right – and I think it is, Paul. What Keller described sounded like
a very personal struggle.'

'And how dangerous is that?'

'All of this is dangerous. Safety belongs to the world we've left behind. Unless we're successful.'

'Hopeful?'

'Not really,' she said. 'Desperate. Which is nothing to do any more with your friend Dan.'

They pulled up and parked a few streets away from Dawn Jackson's address.

'Why have we stopped here?'

Paul nodded through his side window at a Victorian rectory in the grounds of a large Gothic Revival church. There were slates missing from the church steeple. 'I've done some research of my own,' he said. 'That's where Father Gould lives. He's expecting you.'

'For what? This isn't an exorcism.'

'I'm going to scope out Dawn's address. It isn't safe for you just to sit in the car alone on the street while I do it. He'll make you a nice cup of tea. Or you might hit the jackpot and score a glass of whisky.'

'I don't think so. We need to be sober for this. Paul?'

'Yes?'

'Be careful and come back safe?'

He grinned. He said, 'I'm always careful.'

He left the car at the kerb outside the church grounds and walked to Dawn's address. He walked past it on the other side of the road and glanced over with only the slightest turn of his head. The windows were dark, their curtains undrawn, the house entirely unlit.

It was a large and handsome period house, not just detached but isolated from its neighbours by its generous drive. Access to its rear was blocked by two high-flanking walls. The obvious route to the back garden was through, rather than around. And though its dimensions were opulent, to Paul the place had a neglected look. Even at dusk he could see that the windows were filmed with dirt. The front door was large, wooden and a lustreless shade of red. It hadn't been wiped clean or had its brass doorknob polished for a long time. Patches of moss were green scabs on the gravel of the drive.

Paul knew with sudden certainty that Dawn, whatever had

become of Dawn or whatever Dawn had now become, was entirely alone there. And her grandfather and brother weren't on a fishing trip in rural Ireland. Nothing so idyllic as that. Dawn had disposed of them. They'd inconvenienced or inhibited her occult cabaret. Three had been a crowd, and even two had been too much for Dawn. Dawn was a loner.

FORTY-SIX

Paul Beck got back from his scouting mission forty minutes after his departure. He knocked on Father Gould's rectory door with raw hands and the knees of his jeans stained with brick dust. He was invited inside. Juliet Harrington had said she wasn't drinking, but the priest certainly was. Judging by the pungent scent from his glass, Paul thought, probably the single malt, Oban.

He said, 'I thought whisky priests existed only in stories written by Graham Greene.'

'There's a time and there's a place,' Father Gould said, 'and it's now, here.'

'The boiling sea got to you, Father?'

'If you two don't find a way to stop her, we're living through the End Times.'

'Could you sketch me a plan of the ground floor of the house?'

The priest shook his head. 'She guided me straight from the front hall to what I assumed to be her grandfather's study. In retrospect, I know there were things there she didn't want me to see. Inviting me in was a double bluff. Clever, because it worked. I doubt her poor brother's still alive.'

Paul turned to Juliet. He said, 'I scaled the back garden wall. Sort of in the gloaming, not quite full dark. It isn't overlooked by a neighbour, which makes it a good hiding place. There's the remains of a shed I guess was totalled by the hurricane. There's an overgrown lawn with a shallow depression where the turf has been cut and relaid. The work's been done quite skilfully.'

'But not quite skilfully enough,' Father Gould said.

'She's buried something there. She's done it more than once.'

Juliet said, 'Obvious question, but why didn't you dig it up?'

'No time,' Paul said. 'The kitchen light came on. Or the light in what I assumed was the kitchen.'

'Did she see you?'

'There's a shrubbery a few feet from where she dug. Overgrown, neglected. I dived for that, hid there until the light went off again. Concealment was part of my training, back in the day. I'm able to remain quite still. I'm almost a hundred per cent certain she didn't see me.'

'Adolescents don't do that,' Juliet said.

'Don't do what?'

'Bother to switch off lights.'

'This one would,' Father Gould said. 'I've met her, remember.'

Paul looked at Juliet. 'We need to get this done,' he said.

Father Gould said, 'Is there any way in which I can help?'

Paul said, 'You can lend me a trowel if you have one, Father.'

'What about salt, Paul?' Juliet said.

'In the glove compartment of the hire car. Maldon sea salt.'

'As recommended by Delia Smith,' Juliet said.

'Never heard of her,' Paul said. 'Culinary tip from Desperate Dan Carter. I've never looked back, frankly.'

Juliet smiled. The levity seemed at once strange and completely normal. She knew that they were about to do something that could bring their lives to an abrupt and possibly grotesque conclusion. But she knew also that if the Almanac continued to be used, they would perish anyway. Their world had become bleakly, rudely impossible. It was their responsibility to try to do something about it. She believed it was also their fate.

Before they left, the priest insisted on blessing each of them. He'd had a drink or two but Juliet, only an intermittent believer, thought that was probably OK. Endowing a blessing wasn't driving a car.

Then they set off, a short and wordless walk through uncannily empty streets in the one area of London left largely unscathed by the once great city's catalogue of calamities. The people had gone from here despite that. Nowhere in the metropolis had been left immune to the mood of despair prevalent in choked gutters, along cracked pavements, housed in those deserted dwellings which were still intact, coursing like a poisonous current through air rank with death and despoilment.

Suddenly, they were there. The façade of the house was pale and blandly handsome. But the windows, lightless and black in the night, hinted at the dark secrecy within. With a last swift kiss, a final tender expression of mortal feeling, they parted from one another.

Alone now, Juliet took a deep breath. Trepidation made it shudder through her. She unlatched the gate and strode across the crunching gravel of the drive, a sound loud in the prevailing, brooding silence. She climbed the three stone steps to the substantial front door and, with a shaking finger, rang the bell. But that provoked no response. So she hammered at the heavily tarnished brass knocker and then waited, her heart a delinquent thudding in her chest and her mouth parched, wishing she had drunk something potent after all to prepare her for the impossibility of the moment she now faced.

The thing that had until quite recently been Dawn Jackson opened the door. And Juliet knew, even before it grinned at her. It had retained most of Dawn as it settled into its new life. It would walk and talk as Dawn, would retain Dawn's knowledge about matters, her idiom and even her mannerisms. They were the basics of its survival during its induction period in the ways of the world it now inhabited.

But it wasn't Dawn any longer, not truthfully. Children didn't have black eyes or skin with that sickly porcelain pallor. Human hair didn't possess that sandpapery texture. The nails were really talons on hands that now more closely resembled claws. Dawn had been a monster of sorts, of course. But she'd only been the precursor to this sly abomination.

'What can I do for you?'

The voice had the echoey resonance of a sound emerging outward from deep inside a cave.

'It's what I can do for you, Dawn. I can tell you interesting stories about that book you recently discovered.'

The Dawn-thing seemed to muse for a moment on this. Then it nodded its head slowly and turned and led the way into the house. There was something light and insectile about its gait that made Juliet think two things. The first was that four limbs were insufficient for this creature. The second was that she was blundering without hope into the sticky intricacy of a spider's web.

The Dawn-thing led her into what she assumed had been Mr Jackson's study. There was a Victorian fold-out desk and there were shelves full of books and framed lithographs on its walls. The once white-painted ceiling was nicotine-stained a sickly yellow. They sat in opposing straight back chairs and the Dawn-thing studied her with those obsidian eyes. They were as lustreless as her hair. It was as though this creature was completely animate without remotely possessing the spark of life. The feeling that she was prey had not left Juliet but only deepened in her. Her skin crawled with foreboding. She had to will herself not to let it turn into a sort of hopeless dread.

It treated her again to that dead-eyed grin. It said, 'You know, don't you?'

'There was an Augury. You might have missed it.'

'I didn't miss it. It was on TV. The sea boiled.'

'You've come into the world prepared.'

'I've everything of hers. It's insufficient.'

'It's Gunter Keller's most powerful spell.'

'Flatterer.'

'I speak only the truth,' Juliet said. 'Where's the book now?'

'In a safe place. There was a policeman here today. My predecessor dealt with him quite well for someone so immature in age. But she suspected a possible return.'

Juliet studied the thing facing her that until very recently had been a clever and capricious child. She said, 'How old are you?'

The immediate response was a throaty chuckle, not a young sound at all. The black eyes seemed to gleam for a moment in consideration of the question.

'Recently born,' it said. 'Older than you can imagine. Older than time.'

'You've been here before, haven't you? Summoned by Gunter Keller?'

That brought forth a smile of reminiscence. 'What a paradox he proved to be. Both a powerful adversary and the perfect host. It was close, that struggle, but the great alchemist of the age prevailed. No matter. I was younger and less mature and perhaps without the guile I now possess.'

'Dawn was weaker.'

'The girl had weakened herself. Her resilience had diminished.'

Despite herself, despite all the damage done, Juliet felt a stab of grief then for the lost child who would never now be redeemed. She said, 'Is there nothing inside you left of Dawn?'

The creature licked its upper lip with a tongue that seemed long, sinewy, serpentine. 'She had some qualities I've chosen to retain. But the frailness was a serious flaw. At present, it remains so.'

'Do you intend to use the book?'

'Oh, yes. I've ambitious plans.'

The Dawn-thing studied its clawed hands. The nails really were talons, thick and curved and horny and sharp. It let them clack and chitter together, apparently in thought. Juliet had become aware of a smell emanating from the creature; perhaps it secreted the odour. It was oily and rank with a hint of decay. Juliet had the giddy thought that this last ingredient in the cocktail of smells might be Dawn Jackson's parting gift to the world.

Juliet realized then that the thing in front of her was as much parasite as predator. What life it possessed was stolen. This gleefully malicious entity squatted in the body it had distorted already into something hideous.

She could hear it breathe. The exhalations had an ancient character, wind scoured off sand in a desert storm occurring thousands of years ago. Waves lapping in darkness at the edge of a land still emptily young.

'Do you want to know about the book you found?'

'I am Dawn. The new Dawn. The risen Dawn. I know all about the book I found. Some of it I know by heart. The rest I'll learn.' Another smile, this one splitting into a shark-toothed grin. 'I'm a quick study.'

'Using the book has consequences,' Juliet said.

'They're no concern of mine.'

'They're unforeseen, dangerous.'

'Not dangerous to me.'

'Where did you come from?'

'There's an obvious answer to that. The warnings were there. They've gone unheeded.'

That remark was followed by a silence between them, to Juliet a chasm of noiselessness she thought might swallow her. She was playing for time, of course, not just frightened but consumed by fear – and something else, something wretched she knew was dismay provoked by the abomination with which she was trapped in a small suburban room.

She said, 'You should fear them.'

'Fear what?'

'The Auguries.'

But the creature ignored this. It said, 'A child is inadequate. I need a more fitting host. One stronger, physically.' It gave a high-pitched giggle, with a loudness that made Juliet jump. 'But beggars can't be choosers,' it said. And abruptly, it stood and moved forward.

Paul had unearthed the book in the garden and taken it to the left-hand corner of the rear of the house where he couldn't be seen through the kitchen window. He decided to risk using the torch-light on his phone for illumination. Seated on the ground with his back to the house to shield the torch beam from being seen from within, he began to put the salt crystals between each page of the book.

He was horribly concerned for Juliet's welfare, deeply anxious about the jeopardy her decoy role would be placing her in. He was unsurprised at the depth of feeling he had for her after so short a period of time together. She was brilliant, she was beautiful, and she was demonstrating at that very moment how brave she was too.

There had been an intensity about their shared experience. As events brought their world to the brink of extinction, an intimate bond had been formed. He wanted to spend the rest of his life with her, certain they would be happy if they could just live through this latest, perhaps last ordeal. He knew, though, that this was far from guaranteed. Dawn Jackson had not been fastidious about death. She'd apparently treated the collateral damage inflicted by her occult antics with complete indifference. Why should the thing inhabiting her now come into the world with any kind of morality after a birth so profoundly corrupt?

Made clumsy by his hurry to join Juliet, he had a few false starts where sweat from the pads of his fingers caused the salt crystal he was handling to dissolve into uselessness. So the job took longer than he wanted it to, with Juliet all the while risking the deadly job of distracting the creature in the house.

He did it listening to his own breathing, thinking how scholarly the text looked that had triggered so much chaos and tragedy. The characters looked antique and entirely harmless, and when he completed the task and closed the book it just looked elderly, the cover untitled, the vellum blandly innocent.

When he tried the kitchen door he found it locked. Picking it with a hairpin he'd borrowed from Juliet earlier for the purpose was the work of only a minute. But the minute was stretched out almost infinitely for Paul by the dread of what he might find in the house.

He found Juliet almost immediately, on the ground floor. She was in the study, and she was quite alone there.

'Where's Dawn?'

'She wasn't Dawn any more.'

Paul nodded his head. 'So your theory was right. A host is needed. Where is she?'

'She just disappeared, a few minutes ago. She went like sand emptying out of an hourglass.'

'Did she say anything to you?'

'She called me a flatterer. Said a child was an inadequate host.'

Paul was silent, studying her. Then he said, 'Oh, Jesus. Oh, Christ.'

'Why are you staring at me like that?'

'Who are you? Who am I speaking to? Who are you really?'

'That's a deep one,' she said. 'Who are any of us?'

'I want the truth,' he said. There was desperation in his voice. 'I have to know.'

She got to her feet with a suddenness that made him rear back, and closed the distance between them in one long stride. She took his head between both raised hands and he was aware of the length of her fingernails as they dug into his scalp. She pulled his head forward and down to hers and kissed him, passionately, on the mouth.

Juliet said, 'That's who I am, Paul. That's who I'll always be.'

He searched her eyes and inhaled the scent of her. He stroked her hair and held her in his arms. He said, 'I'll go and get that book from the garden. We need to get out of this place.'

'It feels contaminated.'

'Yes, it does. Who was the creature, Juliet? Did you ask it that?'

'In a manner of speaking, yes.'

'And?'

'An emissary from Hell, Paul. A creature come to provoke the final act in the End Times. To witness it. And then to gloat.'

'But you beat it.'

'You beat it.'

He smiled at that. 'We beat it,' he said.

'Do you think the world is safe, Paul?'

'Safer, anyway,' he said. 'All we can do now is wait and see.' But Juliet looked unconvinced. 'What's the matter? The Dawn-thing said something else, didn't it?'

Juliet nodded. 'As it ebbed away. It said the door had opened a chink, now.'

'A chink of light?'

'Of darkness, it said. It said this is the beginning, not the end.'

'Hubris,' Paul said.

He went back then to retrieve the Almanac and heard a sound in the garden he couldn't recall having heard at all on his visit to London. Oxford, maybe, with its picture-perfect vistas and scrolled and filigreed architecture and the glittering charm of its pretty river. But it was a sound totally absent in his experience of a city he now realized he had come to think of as cursed.

It seemed to Paul a small miracle of which he ought to make Juliet aware. And so he went to fetch her so that she could witness it too. And they stood in the darkness together and held hands and listened to the infinitely sweet music of a blackbird singing on a summer night.

'It sounds so beautiful,' Juliet said. 'I'd almost forgotten. Do you think it's a sign?'

'Auguries can be omens of good as well as bad,' Paul said. 'If the songbirds can come back, maybe in time the people will return. Hope is either a human failing or a measure of our resilience. Right now, I think we have to embrace it.'

'Come on,' she said, after the bird had flown away, tugging at the shirt Paul Beck had torn climbing over Dawn Jackson's garden wall 'There's an old priest of our recent acquaintance who can treat us both to a drink.'